Origin
The Dreamcatch
Book 1

Copyright © 2023
All rights reserved
The characters and events portrayed in this book are fictitious. Any similarity to real persons, living or dead, is coincidental and not intended by the author.

No part of this book may be reproduced, or stored in a retrieval system, or transmitted in any form or by any means, electronic, mechanical, photocopying, recording, or otherwise, without express written permission of the author.
Author: D.L. Golden
Editor: C. Britt
Cover Art: PerkyVisuals

Dedication

To Emily and Kai, thank you for always believing in me.

Table of Contents

Chapter 1: Where There's Smoke
Chapter 2: Doctor
Chapter 3: Savior
Chapter 4: Michelle
Chapter 5: The Citadel
Chapter 6: Accusations and Interference
Chapter 7: Eons
Chapter 8: No Harm
Chapter 9: Oswald
Chapter 10: Inconsistency
Chapter 11: Untimely Revelation
Chapter 12: Zaman
Chapter 13: You Idiot…
Chapter 14: Training
Chapter 15: Roark
Chapter 16: Scalpel
Chapter 17: Parting
Chapter 18: Eclipsed
Chapter 19: Victims
Chapter 20: Vampirism
Chapter 21: Love and Loss
Chapter 22: Reunion
Chapter 23: Kai
Chapter 24: Reality
Chapter 25: Hero

Chapter 26: Escape
Epilogue
Tome Reference Guide

"It is not the strongest of the species that survives, not the most intelligent that survives. It is the one that is most adaptable to change." -Charles Darwin

Galaxias Kyklos

Origins

Chapter 1: Where There's Smoke

"Encoding 85% complete... Encoding 90% complete... Encoding error DC678 memory fragmentation may have occurred." A beautifully melodic voice echoed in Sai's mind.

As he opened his eyes, light streamed in and brought with it the image of the brilliant sky above him, dark blue and dotted with fluffy white clouds which drifted lazily past his line of sight. Sai placed his hands on the ground and pushed himself into a sitting position. All around him was a vast field with nothing in sight except a virtually unending sea of colorful flowers and unkempt, wild grass. The deep aromatic floral scent of the area infiltrated his senses as he inhaled and exhaled steadily. The air felt cold against his cheeks as it swept across the open field. As he took in the unfamiliar sight, a slightly painful twinge rang through his head, then faded almost as quickly as it had come.

"What is this place?" He murmured to himself as he took in the unfamiliar surroundings. He rolled over and pushed himself to his feet with a small groan.

As he stood, a small off-white note fell from the pocket of his dark calf-length pants and into the tall grass. The slight, crackling noise the slip made as it hit grabbed his attention. Reaching down, he grasped the slip of paper and turned it over in his hand a couple of times, examining it. Unfolding it revealed a scrawled message *Error code DC678...*

Those words again? What's that even supposed to mean? And more importantly, where on earth am I? Sai questioned.

Again the cold floral air swept across the field, prompting Sai to fold the note and return it to his pocket. This time stuffing it more deeply down to prevent it from falling again. Looking up at the sky again, he could see the sun hanging almost motionless in the west. With the

1

Origins

already chilly air, he knew he couldn't stay the night out in the open like this. He would need to find shelter, and before long, water and food would become issues all their own. With these thoughts pushing him, he began to walk. At first, his legs felt wobbly like a newborn fawn walking for the first time, but before long, he was gaining more control. Taking wider, more powerful steps as he went. After walking for what he felt could have only been a few minutes, he could feel his stamina fading. Every step took a steeper toll as he marched onward. His breathing became more labored as he tried to steal what little bits of air he could. However, no matter how much he took into his lungs, it never seemed to be enough.

What is this? He thought. *How am I already out of breath?* He gripped his chest and stopped suddenly. Quickly he realized the answers to these questions as he took in the spectacular view before him. A vast snow-capped mountain range extended as far as the eye could see. In between these mountains sat an endless sea of deep green spruce trees. Suddenly it clicked. He knew now that this was the reason for his exhaustion.

It's the altitude. The air must be extremely thin up here. He thought to himself. Then something else seemed to click into place. *This mountain top, it's different.* He looked back. *All the others are covered in snow, but this one is flat and adorned in these wildflowers.* This struck him as odd. How could this mountain, the highest peak, be covered in greenery while the lower ones were all snow-capped? *Something strange is going on here.* Slowly he scanned the area contemplating this. His concentration was broken as the wind howled behind him as if some invisible force were pushing him forward.

"Either way, I can't stay here…." He spoke to himself as he looked around at the mountain range below and spotted what appeared to be light stacks of smoke rising from between two of the lower mountains. *A fire? Maybe a camp or settlement? That could be my best shot. I need to find a way down.* Scanning the mountainside, Sai spotted what seemed to be a small stone path leading down the mountain.

Origins

I suppose that's my only way down. Sai trudged down the steep slope, heading for the small pillars of smoke that rose in the distance. As he got lower and lower, the temperature began to rise steadily. Sai's breathing eased, and the cold air of the mountaintop subsided, making way for the warmth of the spring evening to fill the area. With less than an hour of sunlight left, Sai finally made it to the bottom and headed into the thick forest below. Ahead of him, Sai could see and smell the smoke that had drawn him down from the summit. From here, the smoke seemed darker and more prominent than he had initially expected. He figured it would take at least another hour to reach the source, and with that thought, Sai strode into the woods.

As the sun sank behind the mountains, the woods grew darker. With the darkness, the smoke became less and less visible. However, it had revealed something else, the glow of a flame. It began to appear in the direction from which the smoke had initially come. As Sai approached the light, the acrid smell of smoke grew more intense, filling his lungs and burning his eyes. His eagerness for shelter quickly vanished, giving way to a newfound horror.

"What the hell?" Sai gasped. This was no life-saving campfire. Instead, he found death and destruction, an entire village set ablaze in a massive inferno.

"Someone, help me!" The words slashed through the poisonous air like a razor blade. Before he could think, Sai's muscles contracted, and he shot forward. As he headed toward the scream, he coughed and choked on the thick black smoke that filled the area. Pulling his shirt up over his mouth and nose, he pushed on. He flew down the burning streets past buildings that were nothing but ashes and rubble. Another scream rang out from a thatched roof stone building directly ahead of him. Bursting through the wooden doorway, Sai scanned the building listening for any signs of life. From above him, he could hear someone speaking.

Origins

"Do not fear, for you will soon know the truth. In the middle of the journey of our life, I found myself...." The voice from above spoke calmly.

Sai wheeled around and found a rough staircase that looked to lead to an attic area. In an instant, he was ascending the stairs as the voice droned on.

"...within a dark woods where the straight way was lost. Now awaken..."

Sai had just made his way up the steps when he saw it. Against the wall just before him sat a girl not much younger than himself. She was curled and cowering in the fetal position on the floor. This was where the scream had come from. About two feet from the girl stood a robed figure wearing a mask like a plague doctor. The long beak protruded from under his dark hood." ..Inferno." as the sentence ended, the hilt of a sword in the figure's hand sparked to life.

Again his body moved. Without a thought, Sai was diving for the girl, tackling her out of the way just as a pillar of flame exploded from the hilt. The dry vegetation of the roof and part of the stone wall exploded instantly, leaving a massive gaping hole just inches from where they lay. This blast alone set this entire section of the structure aflame.

Sai's mind raced as he glared at the man and covered the girl. *This monster, he did this. All these buildings burning, all this death. He's the one who caused this destruction.* The flames reflected off the masked man's goggles, and Sai choked again on the ever-thickening smoke. *How is he so calm, and how is he breathing in here?* Then it dawned on him. *That mask must be how he's handling all this smoke. It must be filtering it out somehow.* Sai shook his head furiously in a feeble bid to halt the dulling of his senses. *None of that matters now; I can't fight him. I need to find a way to get this girl and myself out of here.* He struggled to keep the thoughts coming and the world from caving in.

Quickly, he glanced back at the once-cowering girl only to find her unconscious. Her head nodding limply to her left side.

Origins

The masked man cocked his head to the side as if to question the legitimacy of what he was seeing. "And where did you come from?" The elegant voice took Sai by surprise. This creature, this demon, its voice was almost charming. "I thought she was the last one left? But here you are."

"The last one?" Sai questioned, glancing back again. "Who are you? Why are you doing this?" Sai yelled as his hands groped behind him, searching the floor for any item he could use to defend himself.

"Yes, the last one. The figure responded coldly.

As the figure spoke, Sai's hand found a fair-sized stone jutting out from the wall close to the floorboards. It was clear it had been jarred loose when the shadowy figure had attacked. With a slight tug, he freed the stone and concealed it behind his back.

The figure continued. "Who am I?" He contemplated this for a moment. "You may call me Roark. I am a liberator."

Sai tried to focus and take in his words, but his eyes felt like hot coals. They burned fiercely from the dense smoke; worse still, he could feel his mind getting cloudier by the second. It was apparent that oxygen deprivation had begun to take its toll.

It's now or never. The thought surged through Sai's mind. Sai mustered all his strength, and from his seat on the hardwood planks, he quickly thrust the stone forward, shifting sideways for only a moment as he released.

The stone soared from his hand with a tremendous amount of force. It flew out at a slightly off-kilter angle. Sai had aimed for the mask's beak, but the last-minute stumble had caused the stone to release early. Just barely, it impacted with the goggle on the right side of the mask, causing it to shatter into hundreds of tiny jagged shards. The shrouded figure grabbed at the lens as it exploded.

Sai had missed his target, but this action was enough; in that fleeting moment, Sai grabbed the girl, slung her onto his back, and forced both of them to tumble out of the burning hole in the side of the building. The resulting twelve-foot fall was more than he had anticipated, however. Sai landed hard on his feet with a thud and an excruciating crack. Pain surged up from his left ankle and knocked him to the ground, where his face met the damp earth. The girl still lay slung across his back motionless. He forced himself back to his feet, knowing full well that the figure wouldn't be delayed long. Practically dragging the girl along, he limped down the street and toward the city gate. The very same gate he himself had come through moments ago. Years ago? Lifetimes even? He didn't know anymore. All that mattered was escaping; all that mattered was crossing the village's boundary. He choked and gasped as the world blurred more with every breath. Dreadfully he looked back over his shoulder, but to his surprise, the shadowy figure didn't follow him.

Was that strike enough? Did the man ever exist at all? His thoughts, his very grip on reality, began to disintegrate. Still, he drunkenly staggered forward toward the town gate. His mind seemed to float aimlessly from one thought to another, but one thought remained, safety was within reach. His fear, however, returned in force as the shadowy figure appeared from the other side of the gate, blocking his path. The shattered eye socket revealed the figure's eye, blue as the ocean but swollen and bloodied from the attack.

The figure spoke calmly yet again. "That really hurt, you know. Regardless this is over." Slowly Roark reached into his long dark sleeve and pulled a light red book from deep inside. Slowly, decisively he began to repeat the same line from before. The red sword hilt emerged from within the pages of the book. "...awaken Inferno!" as the hilt sparked to life once again.

Struggling with all his might, Sai tried to remain conscious as the glow of the flame grew larger. Hopelessness poured over him like a waterfall, and with it, he collapsed to his knees. The smoke, heat, and pain in his leg all culminated, pulling his head to the dust.

"Be strong, saith my heart; I am a soldier; I have seen worse sights than this. Awaken Odysseia." The words rippled across the fog in Sai's mind. He was sure he was hallucinating as he lifted his head with the last of his strength, and a girl with hair as red as poppies in spring appeared before him.

      A beautifully ornate shield materialized in her hand and appeared to stop the column of flame in its tracks. As Sai tried to comprehend this turn of events, he could feel a darkness closing in on him. This was it. He had inhaled too much of the poisonous smoke. The world seemed to collapse in on itself as Sai drifted into the void.

Chapter 2: Doctor

The cool mountain top, the sprawling sea of flowers, the wild grass, the descent, the smoke, and the flames. As these images flashed in Sai's mind, a small delicate voice rang out across the scenes. "What are you doing? You're back already? No, no, not yet! Go back." The last word echoed, eventually giving way to fuzzy static, then nothingness.

Sai sat up with a start. He found himself lying in a somewhat uncomfortable bed with a soft brown blanket draped over the lower half of his body. Cool sweat covered his forehead, and he breathed heavily. This sudden movement was enough to make his fresh injuries painfully obvious. His shirt had been removed, and his chest and right arm were wrapped in thick white bandages. The smell of aloe seemed to emanate from every inch of him as he shifted. He sat in only his dark blue pants, which reeked of stale smoke. He could feel the various burns that dotted his upper body under the white linen wraps.

He looked to his left as something peculiar entered his peripherals. A large mirror hung on the wall above a small side table. In its shining reflective surface, a dark-haired figure stared back at him. This mirror image seemed familiar, yet somehow not. Then it dawned on him; this had been the first time he had seen his own face. Touching his cheek, he confirmed that this person was indeed himself. He had short raven hair streaked with vast grey lines of ash, which gave him the appearance of a much older man. Whatever age his ash-strewn hair portrayed was in stark contrast to the youngness of his face. His cheeks were slightly rounded and lacked any sign of facial hair. His pale blue eyes stood out from beneath his equally dark eyebrows. If he'd had to guess, he figured he couldn't have been more than seventeen years old, but with no memory, who could tell for sure?

Looking down at the side table, Sai noticed a glistening pitcher of ice water sweating in the open air. An empty glass and his white elbow-length tunic from the night before sat beside it. It was clear that his shirt had been folded neatly and placed there by whoever put him into bed.

"Where am I?" He murmured to himself. The raspiness of his voice surprised him. Although, it did make sense. It was a side effect of the massive amount of smoke he had inhaled. He held his head as it throbbed slightly, his lungs still burning from the caustic gas.

As he looked around, he noticed the eggshell white walls and dark parquet-style floor of the room, which bore unmistakable signs of regular maintenance. Off to his right, about mid-way up the wall, he noticed a small window. It was slightly ajar, letting in the cool breeze that brought with it the damp smell of morning dew. Beyond it was a brilliant view of what looked to be a small pond and a thickly wooded area. The water in the pond shimmered as the first rays of sunlight hit it.

Wanting to get a better look at his surroundings, Sai twisted in his bed and sat his feet on the hard floor. As soon as he went to stand, however, he felt it. A sharp, searing pain shot up from his left ankle. The shock of it knocked him onto the floor instantly, and catching himself with his hands didn't help at all. A burn on his palm that he could only assume occurred from clutching the hot stone of the crumbled wall the previous night caused contact with the floor to be unbearably painful. His face met the floor with a thud as the pain surged through his right arm. Using his left, he struggled to prop himself up.

Just then, the door at the front of the room creaked open. Rolling slightly, Sai finally righted himself and leaned back into a sitting position against the bed. An older balding man with a short salt-and-pepper beard, a dingy grey suit, and a lab coat entered the room.

"What are you doing out of bed?" The man chastised as he knelt beside him. He offered Sai his hand and prompted him to stand. "You had quite the traumatic night. You need your rest."

Sai put his right foot under himself, noting that he may never want to use the left again after that little debacle, and used it to stand. He could see now that his left foot was wrapped in a rough splint to keep it from moving around. It wasn't enough to keep it in place when his full weight was on it, that was for sure.

"Is it broken?" Sai asked uneasily as the man helped him to sit back on the bed.

"Unfortunately, yes, you caused serious damage to your ankle and tibia. These things tend to happen when you jump off of roofs." The man explained. "Not to mention the burns and smoke inhalation. Honestly, you're lucky to be alive."

"I didn't jump off a.." Sai stopped abruptly, realizing where he had rolled out of. It was the attic of that building. He had indeed jumped off the roof. These thoughts drew him back to the events of the previous night. The fire, the smoke, the demon… The girl.

"Did she make it? Did the girl survive!?" Sai's rough voice had raised to nearly a shout.

"Take it easy. You mean the one who was brought in with you?" The man stroked his beard as he spoke. "Yes, and apparently, that's because of you. She's fortunate that you came along when you did." He explained. "She's actually in the room next door. Her injuries were far less serious than your own. However, she isn't quite ready to wake up, so perhaps we should keep our voices down."

"S-sorry. So, you know about what happened last night?" Sai responded.

"Only what I was told when you were brought in. They said you fell from the roof and were found hauling that girl out of the inferno on your back," He replied.

Sai gave a quick nod. " And you're the one who wrapped my leg and bandaged me up, then?" He asked as the man took a seat beside him.

"Yeah, the name's Holland. I'm the closest thing this village has to a doctor." The man extended his hand in greeting.

Origins

Sai extended his good hand and gave it a quick shake. "Thank you. I'm Sai. Say, would you mind telling me where I am?"

"Of course, my dear boy. You're in the village of Iapetus. It's about ten miles from Dione, the village where you and the girl were found." The doctor explained. "That girl and yourself were the only two to be rescued after the attack last night. As for Dione, it was almost entirely destroyed." As the man explained, there was a knock at the door. A woman in faded jeans, a red short sleeve shirt, and tan boots entered the room. Her platinum blonde hair was pulled into a messy bun atop her head, and she carried a clipboard in her arms.

"Holl, you're needed in room four." She spoke sternly before turning on her heels and exiting again.

Holland stood quickly and caught the door before it could close. "Thank you, Mel." He half shouted after her. Turning back to Sai, he spoke again. "Get some rest. You did good, now take your time and recover." The door tapped the frame loudly as he took his leave.

Alone again, Sai felt the cool breeze enter through the window once more. He turned to the side table and reached over to grab his shirt. Slipping it on, he realized just how much damage it had actually received. Black scorch marks and large holes littered the fabric across the very places Sai's bandages were applied. It reeked of stale smoke, which made him slightly nauseous. With a low sigh, he removed the shirt and tossed it to the floor.

As he laid back on the bed, he ran through the events of the night before and tried to comprehend all that had happened. How much of that was real? Clearly, the fire, the fall, and the girl. What about the monster who called himself Roark or the girl who saved them? How many of those events were hallucinations brought on by lack of oxygen? And above all else, how had he gotten here in the first place? People don't just wake up on a mountain one day without any recollection of how they got there. None of it made any sense. Maybe it was all a dream, even this moment right now. Perhaps none of it was real. Before long, the soreness, exhaustion, and existentialism of it all became too much to handle, and he was dragged down by it back into that Morpheus realm of sleep.

Chapter 3: Savior

A quick, loud knock on the door pulled Sai back to reality. As for how much time had passed since he had spoken with Holland, he had no idea. Before he could give much thought to this, the door creaked open once again. This time, however, it wasn't Holland or even Mel. Instead, in the doorway stood a familiar-looking girl. He knew her. How could he ever forget that red hair which had seared itself into his memory? This was the girl from before, the one who had rescued him as he lay helpless in the dirt. In the mid-morning light, Sai managed to get a better look at her than he had previously been allowed. She was a tall, fit girl who he figured had to be close to his age, around seventeen or eighteen perhaps. Her red hair hung down to her shoulders and was held back by a simple silver clip near her left ear. Her emerald green eyes seemed to pierce straight through him like daggers, which caused him to stare for longer than he would have liked. Finally, he looked away out of a slight embarrassment as the girl spoke.

"It's good to see you're awake." Her voice was gentle and harmonious. "I brought you some new clothes." She took a few steps into the room. She carried a few dark-colored, folded garments in her arms, which she sat neatly on the nightstand where the old tattered shirt had once lay.

"Thank you? I was beginning to think I was hallucinating. You're… "

She cut across him. "The person who saved you? Yep, that would be me." She smiled as she grabbed the water pitcher from the nightstand, which now sat next to a bowl of freshly cut assorted fruit. She tipped the glass slightly and poured its sparkling contents into the nearby glass without any inclination of asking. "To the boy who took on a full-fledged tome wielder with nothing but a stone!" She proclaimed with a slight air of sarcasm as she raised the glass in a sort of toasting motion. She laughed slightly, lowered the cup to her lips, and took a quick sip. "Answer my questions first, then I'll answer yours. deal?"

Not really knowing how to take this, Sai simply nodded. "Deal."

She placed the glass on the side table once again, grabbed a piece of diced melon from the fruit bowl, again without asking, and took a seat on the bed beside him. Quickly popping the melon into her mouth, she spoke as she chewed." All right, first things first, what's your name?"

"It's Sai," He replied matter-of-factly. He was starting to become slightly annoyed by the brazenness of the girl. *Who just comes into someone's hospital room and starts eating their food?*

"Good; tell me, Sai, are you from Dione?" She asked as she took another cube of melon.

"Dione? You mean the town from last night?" Sai questioned.

"Yep, that was Dione. Guess town's kind of a generous term. At this point, it'd be more appropriate to call it an ash heap."

The callousness of this line surprised Sai. "Oh! No." He replied, "At least, I don't think so. I just woke up on a mountain a few hours from there and ended up there looking for shelter." Even before the words escaped his lips, Sai realized how stupid this must've sounded.

She looked at him with a sort of puzzled expression, but still, she pushed on."Hmmm, okay, were you there when the attack began?" She asked inquisitively.

"No, by the time I had reached the town, it was already mostly destroyed." Sai looked down with a bit of shame in his eyes.

"So you rushed headlong into that inferno on purpose? Why would you do something like that?" She looked dumbfounded as she popped another melon piece into her mouth.

"I'm not sure. I heard that other girl scream, and my body just moved on its own. I had no idea when I charged in that some psychopath with an exploding sword

14

had purposely caused all that destruction." Sai replied defensively.

She laughed at the inelegant description." All right, so fast forwarding here, you come across exploding sword guy, and your first instinct was to hit him in the face with a rock?" Still laughing, she continued," Well, you, Sai are either very brave or really, really stupid." She grinned slyly.

"Hey!" He shot back." I was doing all I could to protect that girl! Also, how do you even know about that?"

"I'm joking, I swear!" She replied while waving her hand in front of her face with a smile. "Brave it is. And captain explodey sword might have mentioned it after I goaded him about the shattered lens on his mask. You really pissed him off, actually. So much so, in fact, that he was determined to kill you for that little transgression."

"Think he decided on that before I hit him, but okay." The annoyance was apparent in his tone.

"Again, I'm kidding!" She waved her hand in front of her face trying to ease the tension. Suddenly her demeanor softened."What you did no doubt saved that girl's life, Sai. You really should be proud of that." She raised another piece of fruit to her lips.

Sai nodded as he relaxed slightly. "All right, all right. It's time you answered some of my questions." With his uninjured hand, he grabbed the melon piece in hers and sat it back in the bowel.

Amy smiled softly as she wiped the melon juice from her hands onto her pants." Fair enough; what would you like to know?"

"Well, maybe your name?" Sai questioned.

"My name's Amelia, but most people call me Amy."

"Okay, can you tell me about what happened the other night? And on top of that, how did you save us?" Sai continued.

"Hmmm, I suppose I could explain a bit. What exactly do you want to know?" She replied.

Origins

"That guy, Roark, I think he called himself. Did he actually cause all of that destruction alone? And if so, how?"

"Roark? You got his name? Why wouldn't you start with that?" She questioned.

"You didn't ask," Sai replied incredulously. "But, yeah, he told me just before we tumbled out of the hole in the attic wall. Which is what you all keep referring to as jumping off the roof."

"My mistake," Amy Added. "Well, from our understanding, he used his tome to incinerate Dione and all the villagers along with it." She replied solemnly.

Sai couldn't wrap his head around how she could make jokes one minute and then be as stoic as a sage the next. Instead of dwelling on this, he decided to move on. "You used that word again? A tome? Is that the name of the sword he was using?" Sai questioned.

"No?" Amy shook her head. "The tome is the book he drew the sword from. I'm sorry, Sai, but I have a hard time believing you've never heard of a tome. I'll admit you don't see wielders every day, but you had to have seen one at some point growing up."

Sai looked down, ashamed of his own ignorance." Even if I had, I wouldn't know. I have no memory of anything before waking up on the mountain."

"Hmmm, well, tomes aren't exactly easy to explain. They're kind of like magic books, for lack of a better explanation." She trailed off in a bid to find the words she needed. "Yeah, that's the simplest way to describe it. Although, I guess having zero memory would explain what you meant when you said you didn't think you were from Dione, huh? You have no memories at all?" She tilted her head slightly, puzzled.

He shook his head. "I woke up with nothing but the clothes on my back and this note." Reaching into the pocket of his pants, Sai's stomach dropped." Oh no! It's gone! Where is it!?" This was the only clue he had, and now it was gone. Panic fell on him like so many stones.

16

"Is this what you're after?" Amy held up the folded-in-half slip of paper that Sai had once clung to so tightly.

Sai looked shocked." How did you get that?" He grabbed at the note quickly, but Amy pulled it out of his reach. "Ugh!" Sai groaned in pain from the sudden movement.

"Hey, slow down there! I found this fair and square." She teased playfully. "What is it exactly?"

Sai rolled his eyes and replied with an exasperated sigh. "Again, I'm not sure. I just woke up with it. I was hoping when I headed toward that smoke that, someone there could answer that for me. As you may have noticed, that didn't happen."

"Oh, come on, stop sulking!" She pushed on his shoulder with her fist. "Again, I was only teasing! Here it's yours. I need to go anyhow. I'll be back at some point to check on you. Don't miss me too much!" She winked as she turned away from him and headed for the door.

Sai could feel his face get hot with embarrassment. His expression softened as she walked out the door. "Oh hey!" He piped up quickly before the door closed. "I almost forgot! Thanks for saving us."

"No problem Sai, anytime." She waved without a backward glance as the door clicked closed behind her.

Days passed, and each one brought with it visits from Holland or Mel. They'd arrive in Sai's room three times a day with food, a milky medicine, which could only be described as acrid, and ointment for his burns. Despite the medicine's horrendous flavor, Sai felt better for taking it each day. The soreness in his lungs and the pain of his burns faded slowly as the days turned into weeks, and before long, Sai had nearly made a complete recovery. The final piece of which was a hard cast that had been placed over his injured leg and would remain there for the duration of his stay.

*****

The cool air came in through the half-open window of the room like it did every morning. And again, the breeze caused Sai to stir slightly. The subtle knock that followed wholly woke him from his slumber.

"Come in." He said, sitting up and rubbing his eyes.

The door creaked open, and in walked both Holland and Mel. "Good morning; today's the day, Sai!" Holland announced as Mel stepped around him and sat a deep bucket full of soapy water near the bed. "It's time we get that cast off and see where we stand, no pun intended." Holland explained with a slight chuckle.

"Please submerge your foot in this," Mel asked as she stood back up from the side of the bed and indicated the bucket.

Sai nodded as he uncovered his legs and rolled up his long loose fitting pant leg. He gently sat his wrapped foot into the soapy water and waited. Mel knelt back down and began to work her fingers around the hard exterior of the submerged cast. After a while, Sai could feel the hard shell around his foot getting more and more pliable as Mel picked away at it. Layer after layer fell away, and Mel carefully removed it from the bucket. Before long, his foot had come free, and Mel was lifting his leg to pull it from the water. Holland stepped forward and gestured for Sai to lie back so he could examine the area where the cast had sat.

"This looks good. You'll need to take it easy for the time being, but I think it's healed far better than I had originally expected." Holland explained as he rolled Sai's foot over, examining it. "Let's get you a crutch and get you up and around."

Holland offered Sai his hand and helped him from the bed. Mel handed him a single crutch which Sai then placed under his left arm, using it to help himself stand. He placed his newly healed foot down gently on the floor. Even this tiny amount of pressure caused his ankle to feel stiff and sore.

"Today will be your last day here. That is, if you're able to walk with a crutch on your own. Why don't you get dressed, and we'll wait outside." Holland instructed.

With a nod, Holland helped Mel grab the water bucket, and they headed out of the room to give Sai some privacy.

Looking over to the side table, Sai grabbed the clothes that Amy had brought. He slipped into the dark pants, which he noticed fit more snuggly than the hospital pair. He grabbed the white undershirt and slipped it over his head and shoulders. As he reached for the blue and grey long-sleeve shirt that remained on the nightstand, he heard a familiar voice come from the hall. His room's door creaked open, and the familiar voice rang out again.

"Look who's up and about!" For the first time in weeks, Amy stood in his doorway, her red hair again pinned behind her ear. She wore a white, loose-fitting blouse which she paired with a red and yellow thigh-length skirt that swayed as she entered the room. Underneath this was a pair of obsidian leggings that ran down to her lower calf. Something was different this time, however. As she entered, Sai noticed what seemed to be a light leather holster hanging on her waist. An almost opal-colored book could be seen sticking out of the rectangular pouch that fell near her right thigh.

"What? Not happy to see me?" She said, walking over and plopping down on the bed. Without asking, she reached over yet again, grabbed the small glass bowl of grapes off the side table, and began eating them. Truthfully, this bowl was nothing special. Every morning Mel would bring some sort of fruit in the same wooden bowl for breakfast. And after weeks of recovery Sai had grown tired of fruit for breakfast. Yet still, every day, a new bowl of assorted melon, grapes, or on the rare occasion, orange slices would arrive.

"No, by all means, help yourself to whatever you like. I didn't want breakfast or anything." Sai said with a slight smirk as he slipped the over shirt on.

Setting the bowl down, she swallowed hard and spoke again. "You didn't answer my question."

"Eh, last time you were here, you were a bit abrasive…." He trailed off for a moment before continuing. "Also, my meals seem to last longer when it's just me eating them." He retorted.

"Abrasive? Is that so? Well, in that case, I'll leave you to it. Good to see you too, Sai." She said sharply as she stood up from the bed. Sai could hear the irritation in her voice as she walked toward the door. "And to think I came all the way here to see you."

"No, no, Amy, wait. I was just kidding." Sai pleaded apologetically. "I am happy to see you."

Turning on her heels, she stepped in close to Sai and looked straight into his eyes." Yeah, you are! And for your information, if there's one thing I can't stand, it's being called abrasive!" Getting in his face, she poked him in the chest for emphasis.

This flustered Sai. He could feel his cheeks getting slightly red with her face so close to his. "I'm sorry, abrasive was the wrong word; I simply misspoke, that's all." Sai rubbed the back of his head, closed his eyes, and smiled.

"Hmmph! Well, fine, but it's gonna take more than a simple apology to earn my forgiveness." She said, pulling back from him.

Sai cleared his throat. Turning to the side table, he picked up the bowl. "Grapes?" He held the bowl out to her. "A proverbial olive branch, if you will?"

"Why, aren't you such a gentleman!" Amy proclaimed as she grabbed the bowl again.

Sai scratched his head and smiled. "Now, what did you want to talk to me about?"

With a mouthful of grapes, she spoke again. "Think we could speak somewhere more private?" She looked over to both Mel and Holland, who were reentering the room.

Holland spoke up." I was actually wanting Sai to get outside for some fresh air and to get some use out of that foot. Would you mind escorting him around the premises while we clean this room up?"

Amy finished off the bowl, nodded, and grabbed Sai by the hand, pulling him toward the door. "Sounds good, come on then. Let's go for a walk."

Origins

Sai stumbled for a moment as she pulled on him, and they headed out the door. His crutch dragged clumsily across the floor as she pulled.

"Hey, slow down just a bit! I'm not used to the crutch yet." He exclaimed as she pulled him into the hall.

Releasing his hand, Amy nodded, and the two slowly walked down the hall together. As they passed the next room down, Sai couldn't help but notice the door was open. Peering in as they passed, he saw her. The girl from the night of the attack was sitting up in her bed, eating from the same bowl of fruit that Sai knew all too well.

As Sai passed, the girl popped a slice of melon into her mouth and glanced up. Their eyes met, and time seemed to slow for only a moment. She had ocean-blue eyes and jet-black hair. A look of shock appeared on her face as her stomach jumped, and she choked on the melon before swallowing hard.

Sai stopped for a moment and tried to speak, but Amy grabbed his hand again. "Let's go! I need to talk to you about something important." Dragging him down the hall, the two finally reached the front door and stepped out into the cool, foggy morning air.

Sai took in this new view as he stepped across the hospital's threshold. The hospital, if you could even call it that, sat on the southern outskirts of Iapetus. Sai looked back at the building, which seemed smaller than he had expected. It was a simple one-story building that, by the looks of it, had been recently whitewashed. If he hadn't just left Holland's care, Sai thought he could've easily mistaken it for a private residence.

Turning back to the north, he could see the village of Iapetus. The entire village was made up of dozens of buildings. Most were made of red brick with roofs that were covered in simple wooden shingles. He noted that these buildings differed from the ones he had seen Dione. They were nicer, made of more sturdy materials, and this place was quite a bit larger than Dione as well. Due to the positioning of the hospital, when Sai looked out his window each morning, he had only seen the woods and the pond that sat behind it. So as he stepped

Origins

out, it surprised him to see Iapetus, a village teeming with people, sitting just a few hundred yards away. He had never even heard the townspeople through his open window.

"Hey, come on, you're falling behind." Amy's voice snapped him back to reality. Sai nodded, and with the crutch under his arm, he followed her around the outside of the building. After a few steps, he felt himself becoming more accustomed to the crutch and could keep up much more easily. As the two reached the back of the building, they could see the pond that was Sai's only view of the outside world over these many weeks.

"Let's go over there. There's a bench near the water's edge where we can talk." Amy pointed off in the pond's direction and continued on.

With another nod, Sai hobbled on. As they reached the bank, a bench came into view just behind a large weeping willow. Sai followed Amy down the hill and took a seat. It felt good to be off of his sore foot for a moment. It had atrophied slightly, and it was apparent to Sai that it was weaker than it had been at the beginning of all this. Minding the deep mud in front of the bench, Amy sat beside him.

"Alright, you got me all the way out here, so what did you want to talk about?" Sai asked, looking out at the water.

"Well, I was reporting to Cylus, the Grand Librarian at the citadel, and he asked about my findings in Dione. Long story short, he wants to meet with you."

"Wait, Grand Librarian? Citadel?"

"Yeah, that's the man I work for and where I live, respectively."

"Okay, wait, you were reporting on me? And furthermore, why would he want to meet with me?" Sai looked at her skeptically.

"It's my job Sai," She said flatly. "And well, you and the girl were the only two who survived the attack in Dione. I think he wants to find out if you know anything about it. He may also know something about that note." she explained, trying to soften the betrayal Sai was feeling.

Origins

"I thought I already explained this. I don't know anything more than what I've already told you. I just showed up there at a bad time."

"A convenient time, in Cylus's opinion." She murmured under her breath as she stood up. Slowly, she made her way toward the water's edge. "I don't know exactly what he wants with you, but he ordered me to bring you to him at once."

"To this 'citadel'?" Sai made air quotes with his fingers, and Amy gave a quick nod in response.

"Amy, I can't go with you. I need to stay and check on that girl. She may need my help still. I would help you if I could, but something tells me this is where I need to be for now." Sai looked down at his shoes. He hated disappointing her, even if he hardly knew her, but something compelled him to stay here. To stay with the other girl.

With a disappointed sigh, she turned toward him." Sai, I'm not exactly asking." She placed her hand on the book at her waist and undid the strap that held it in the holster. "Cylus isn't happy that I brought you here instead of to him in the first place. You're coming with me."

Sai remembered the power that the book had displayed in Dione. He stood slowly and waved his hands in surrender. "Okay, Okay! There's no need for that. I don't want to fight you. Not to mention you brought me to this muddy bank without a stone in sight. How would I ever defend myself?" He joked, trying to inject a much-needed dose of levity into the tense air surrounding this conversation. "Can I do one thing first?"

Amy cracked a slight smile before rolling her eyes. She quickly replaced the strap over the book. "Okay, I'll bite. What is it?"

"I'd like to ask the other girl from Dione to go with us." He explained as he grabbed his crutch for support.

"No." She answered flatly. "I was specifically sent after you. How would I even explain bringing her?" She placed her hand on her hip and glowered at him.

23

"Look, she was there that night as well, right? Who knows, she may know more than I do. What happens if you leave her here and then you have to come back because I can't help? She could be gone by that time, and then you've got nothing." Sai explained. "How would your grand librarian react to that?"

"Sai, we ca…"

Finding his nerve, Sai cut her off, "Amy, you either let me go back and try to convince her to go with us, or you can drag my unconscious body all the way back with you. What's it going to be?"

"Hmmm" Amy seriously mulled over this option for a moment before finally breaking down. "Fine, but this better not come back to bite me!"

"It won't. If we run into an issue, I'll take the blame. Now let's head back. After all, I suppose we shouldn't keep this Cylus waiting." Sai turned and began his hobbled stride back toward the hospital, crutch in hand.

Frustrated, Amy let out a small growl and kicked a nearby clod of mud into the pond before following closely behind him.

Chapter 4: Michelle

The two approached the hospital doors and walked back toward the room where Sai had stayed. As they came to the girl's door, Sai glanced down the hall and saw Mel tidying up his old room. For a second, he considered that he might have forgotten something and thought of heading back to check. This thought faded quickly with the realization that everything he owned was on his person.

Turning back to the girl's room, he realized the door was closed this time around. This sudden realization caused him to hesitate. *What if this was the wrong room? What if she had already left?*

Exasperated with this waiting, Amy reached around him and gave a quick knock on the door. The voice that came from the other side surprised them both.

"Come in." The voice was deep and masculine. Sai looked back at Amy curiously before pushing on the creaky door.

The first thing Sai noticed when entering the room was a tall, slender man with a book hanging from his hip, just like Amy. Its bright blue cover caught his attention and caused him almost instinctively to put his guard up.

"Hello." The new tome user spoke calmly and methodically as Sai entered. Looking up from the book Sai noted the man's long, grayish-blonde hair, which hung down over his right eye. His left eye, the only one visible at the time, was a deep brown, and stared at Sai with condescension. Sai took a small step back, bumping into Amy and stepping on her foot in the process.

"Hey, watch it, Sai! What are you doing?" She suddenly caught a glimpse of the man standing before them. "Alister? What are you doing here?"

The man spoke again," Amelia, I'm surprised to see you. Does Cylus have you running errands again?"

25

This clearly angered her. " I'm not running errands. I'm actually on a vital mission! Now again, why are you here? "

"If you must know, I came here to try to gather information on the attack at Dione. Apparently, Michelle lived there and was present the night of the attack." He gestured in the direction of the bed. "I figured she may be a person of interest."

"You don't think I realize that!? I was there, Alister! I'm the one who saved her and Sai!" She was practically shouting as she pointed in Sai's direction. He stood beside her, clearly confused by this turn of events.

"Sai? This is him, hmmm? "Alister pointed at him. "This is the boy you've been prattling on about for weeks?" Laughing, he continued. "Go home, Amy. I have actual work to do, and you are in over your head."

Amy's face flushed with fury. "Shut your mouth, Alister! Cylus sent me to get Sai, and I'm here to bring this girl back with us as well." The tension in the room was reaching a fever pitch.

"Now, now, Amelia, you know what Cylus says about that temper of yours. What's that word he uses to describe you? Started with an A, I believe."

"Don't you dare!" She shouted.

Alister brushed her comment off. "But, I suppose I won't stand in your way since you're running errands for him. This one seems less than helpful anyhow, considering the state she's in." Alister turned smugly and pushed past Amy to take his leave. As he exited, he gave Sai a sharp look. "Nice to finally meet you." His words dripped with sarcasm as he took his leave.

Amy banged her hand on the door frame. "Ugh! That guy is the absolute worst!" She groaned.

Sai place his hand on her shoulder. "Who was that? Clearly, you know each other."

She shook him off before glaring at him. "Alister, he's an inquisitor from the Citadel. I just don't understand why he was here. Cylus asked me personally to come here.

Why would he even make the trip?" Amy mulled this over.

Sai shrugged as they considered what had just transpired.

"Ummm, hi." A meek voice cut through the silence between them.

Turning toward the voice, Sai felt a twinge of guilt. They were so caught up in their conversation that they had completely forgotten about the girl they had come to see.

"Oh, I'm sorry. Hello, I'm Sai."

"You're the boy from that night. The one who saved me."

Sai nodded. "Well, kind of. I pulled you from the building, but Amy's the one who actually saved us in the end." He gestured in Amy's direction, and she stepped forward.

"Hey!" With a half grin, Amy waved nonchalantly.

"Well, thank you. I appreciate it. I'm sorry that you got yourself hurt saving me." The girl looked down at the crutch Sai carried.

Sai walked over to one of the chairs seated in the corner of the room and took a seat. "Don't apologize! I ran in of my own accord. I'm just glad we made it out okay."

The girl looked up with a shy smile and nodded. "I'm Michelle, by the way."

"Sai. It's nice to officially meet you." He replied with a smile.

"Ahem!" Amy cleared her throat and looked over at Sai. "Don't forget why we're here."

"I haven't." With a sigh, he continued. "Michelle, I'd like you to come with Amy and me," Sai explained his memory loss and how he thought she could help with information on Dione.

"I'll come with you."

"You will?" Amy seemed surprised. "That was easy."

Origins

"Oh? It's just I'm here today because of you. Plus, I think someone I'm looking for may be there." Michelle replied.

"Sorry, Sai just took a bit more persuading to get him to agree." Amy smiled wryly. "Something about wanting to stay here for some reason; what was it again, Sai?"

Michelle looked over at him, his face slightly red. "Isn't it about time we got going?" He changed the subject as he stood from his chair.

Amy grinned and nodded." Yeah, we should go."

With a nod, Michelle pulled off her covers and climbed out of bed. She was slightly paler than Amy, and her figure was fuller as well. She wore a light grey tunic and loose-fitting pants to match. Sai recognized the clothing. They were the same as the ones the hospital had provided him within his first few days there.

Noticing the clothes, Amy spoke up," Oh, you don't have any other clothing, do you?"

Michelle looked down at the dull-colored fabric and frowned. "No, everything I had was either damaged or destroyed."

"Hmm." Amy raised her hand, and what looked like a red, pseudo-translucent menu appeared before her fingers. Words such as "inventory,"" status," and "tome" decorated each tab. Tapping on the inventory tab, another box appeared, and a few quick taps later, a stack of neatly folded clothes materialized in Amy's hands. "Here, try these."

The interaction menu seemed wrong to Sai somehow, but he couldn't put his finger on why.

Michelle took the folded pile and nodded with a smile. Then the two of them stood quietly as if waiting for something. Sai stood there obliviously. He looked over to Amy only to realize she was glaring at him.

"Well? Are you going to leave so she can change or…?"

Origins

Sai felt his face getting hot as he grasped what was happening. "S-sorry! It didn't even register!" He turned quickly and stood outside the door.

A short time later, the door opened, and Amy stepped out. Following quickly behind her was Michelle. Sai was at a loss for words as he took in the totally new girl who stood before him. She wore dark leggings covered in light silver armor that ran from her knees to her ankles. Her torso was covered by a long sleeve shirt that resembled the one Amy had brought Sai but in green instead of blue. Covering half her chest and left arm was another piece of armor that resembled the kind that covered her legs. Her long dark hair was pulled back in a neat ponytail, making her blue eyes seem even more striking.

"Rude to stare, you know. You about ready?" Amy placed a hand on Sai's shoulder as she stepped passed him. Sai caught his composure and followed as Michelle passed him as well.

Holland caught them as they headed down the hall. "Are we ready to go?" He questioned, looking over both of his patients. In unison, the two nodded. "If you ever find yourselves in need of my services, please don't hesitate to come back." Holland smiled and let them pass on their way to the front door.

Turning back, Sai spoke," Thanks for everything, and tell Mel thank you as well."

"Don't mention it." Holland waved them away as he made his way back down the hall.

The three marched off in the opposite direction and headed for the door. Together they walked out into the mid-morning light toward the waiting city of Iapetus.

"No turning back once we leave town. Hope you have your affairs in order." Amy said as she turned to face them. "Either way, time to go."

Chapter 5: The Citadel

Sai, Michelle, and Amy walked quickly through the streets of Iapetus. The large red brick buildings loomed over them as they passed. The streets were still abuzz with people going to and fro. These villagers visited shops and stalls and carried on small pleasant conversations.

Sai was almost surprised by how unfazed everyone seemed. Did they even know what had happened just a few weeks ago, no more than ten miles from here? And if they did, how did they go about their lives as if nothing had happened? How easy was it to forget something so tragic? To disjoint yourself from those who had suffered and died? But, what did he expect, for everyone to mourn forever? No, life had to go on, and it did. These people had moved forward, gone back to living their lives. And how could he blame them? These thoughts were driven away as Amy spoke up.

"This way." She said as she rounded a corner and headed toward the edge of town. Soon enough, they came to the crest of a small hill on the other side. A long row of stairs extended down the hillside to an old wooden bridge that crossed a small, shallow creek. Without another word, they headed down. As they crossed the bridge, the sprawling evergreen forest again came into view. At the very edge of this forest sat a small, dilapidated shack. Its windows were shattered, and its foundation was crumbling to dust. Even still, the three strode onward. Sai's ankle ached as he kept pace with the two girls.

As they neared the desolate building, Amy pointed to it. "There it is!" Sai and Michelle both looked at her, confused. "

"What? Where?" Sai squinted as he tried to look past the shabby structure and into the thick forest of trees that lay beyond it.

"What do you mean where? Right here!" Amy approached the old shack and tapped on the rotting door frame. The entire building groaned and creaked as her hand made contact. The only thing that seemed to be holding this place together was the very dust that had fallen from its doorway. The failing foundation made the entire building sit at an off-kilter slant, making its stability seem precarious at best. The front door, which was just a few thin pine boards, hung catawampus by a single hinge in its upper left corner.

Michelle leaned over and whispered to Sai. "She's gonna kill us and harvest our organs, huh?"

"Absolutely, yes," Sai replied seriously.

"Something the matter?" Amy said.

"Ummm, nothing. But, Amy?" Michelle spoke softly. "Is this really where you wanted to take us?"

"Yeah, we must have two completely different definitions of the word citadel," Sai said as he surveyed the extremely shifty-looking structure.

"Of course, this is it! Come on, you'll see." Amy placed one hand on the front door and pushed it open. The rusty hinge that supported the door squeaked as if it hadn't been oiled in decades. The bottom of the door scraped the floor, causing another groan to resonate from the wooden floorboards. Amy stepped inside as Sai and Michelle reluctantly followed. As they entered, Sai couldn't help but note the unpleasantly damp smell of the building. The stench of rotting pine and mildew filled his nostrils. Looking around, Sai noted small beams of light that crisscrossed the room from every angle, no doubt from the litany of holes in the roof and walls. The entire building was simply one big room with a thin cloth rug at its center. Different pieces of busted furniture littered the floor. A couch with a broken leg and massive tears in its fabric backing sat against the back wall. A table that had been toppled over jutted halfway out of the damaged floorboards where it had fallen. A layer of dust nearly an inch thick coated virtually every surface in the room.

Michelle pinched her nose." It stinks so bad in here!"

Sai nodded in agreement." What are we doing here? I thought we were going to see Cylus? There's clearly no one here."

Amy looked back at both of them with a smile. She knelt and grabbed the corner of the rug, flinging it to the side. This created a cloud of dust that immediately choked both Sai and Michelle. The two coughed, trying to clear the dust from their noses and mouths. It settled quickly to reveal what looked like a shiny steel plate hidden underneath. Amy slipped her tome from its sleeve and touched it to the plate. Silently the plate lifted on one side, opening like the hatch to a mysterious underground bunker. A faint warm light poured out as it opened, illuminating the room.

"Let's go." Amy stepped down and onto the rungs of a hidden ladder. Within moments she disappeared into the hole. Michelle and Sai looked at one another, and with no more than a shrug, Michelle stepped forward and descended after her.

Stepping up to the hole, Sai quickly realized he'd have to leave his crutch behind if he was going to follow them. Setting the crutch down, he placed his foot on the rung and began his descent. The soreness in his foot lingered, but he continued on. After heading down a few rungs, he heard a slight click above him. The hatch had automatically shut back, and he could hear the faint shuffling of the hatch concealing its presence once again beneath the dusty, old, tattered rug.

Within a few minutes, they reached the bottom of the ladder and entered a sizeable subterranean tunnel system.

"Come on, this way." Amy motioned them forward. The tunnels wound back and forth for a long while before finally opening up to a large cavernous area with giant stalagmites and stalactites jutting from the floor and ceiling, respectively. At the center of the cavern stood a large half-egg-shaped white and gold structure. Five massive pillars dotted the area around the dome; each ran from floor to ceiling. These pillars looked to be made of polished Ivory with ribbons of gold spiraling up their entire length. Sai figured they might be some sort of support to help with the structural integrity of the cave itself, but there was no way to know for sure.

Origins

"Whoa! All of this was hidden underneath that forest?" Sai said as he examined the fantastic feat of engineering that lay before him.

"Not exactly. As we came down the ladder and even through the tunnels, we traveled through multiple warp corridors. If I hadn't been with you, you could've easily been sent to another part of the continent. It's actually how we get around to different places so quickly. Now come on, Cylus is waiting."

Amy stepped forward, and Michelle and Sai followed after. As Sai stepped forward, the pain in his ankle came back with a force. "Agh!" He knelt and held the pulsating ankle in his hands."

Amy turned to look at him, "Are you okay, and where's your crutch?"

"Yeah, I'll be okay. It just hurts, and I had to leave it up top when we came down," he explained.

Amy gave an exasperated sigh. "Sai, that crutch is specifically linked to you. Check your inventory; it should be there. Have you walked without it this whole way?"

He didn't answer and instead just looked at her perplexed. Swiping his hand down, Sai mimicked the motion he had seen Amy perform earlier, and quickly a menu appeared. This menu seemed slightly shorter than the one Amy had displayed. It was missing the "tome" tab, but the same "inventory" tab he had seen was available to him. Tapping "inventory," another box opened, which displayed two whole items: the note Sai had clung to so desperately and a single item titled "crutch." Sai gave the crutch a tap, the inventory box closed, and the crutch appeared in front of him.

"Just so you're aware, you can also access your inventory by simply reaching in your pockets and thinking of the item you wish to retrieve," Michelle explained. "Just be sure you know what you're looking for if you do it that way." She helped Sai to his feet and back onto his crutch. "Take it easy. You don't want to aggravate that injury."

Origins

She smiled as he lifted the foot and placed his weight on the crutch.

Sai nodded. "Thanks." He felt like a fool. How come he knew so little about this world? Why did it seem like he was the only one who ever seemed lost here?

"Are you good?" Amy spoke up.

"Yeah, sorry," Sai replied.

"Good." Turning back around, Amy stepped forward first and approached the large dome. Once again, she undid the clasp over her tome, raised it above her head, and held it there for a second. A faint light emanated from the book, and simultaneously a loud clicking noise could be heard from the inside of the dome. Suddenly the ground around them began to rumble and shake. The once solid dome seemed to crack like an enormous golden egg down its center. It became immediately apparent to Sai what those support pillars from before were for. Without them, the action of opening this dome might be enough to bring the whole cave in on itself. The two halves of the dome seemed to regress away from each other as they lowered to become flat against the rocky ground. The rumbling of the cavern slowly subsided, and what was left in the center of the room was a vast, white metal plate embossed with an insignia of a solid gold dragon.

Amy stepped onto the platform and waved Sai and Michelle onward. As they stepped onto it, the ground began to tremble again, and the collapsed dome rose to its original shape.

"Last stop, I promise." Holding up one finger, Amy smiled. The platform beneath their feet began to creep even deeper into the earth. Suddenly a light appeared around the edges of the disk. Slowly the light began to grow brighter and brighter. It became so bright that Sai was forced to cover his eyes. When he opened them again, they stood in a large, aboveground courtyard. People buzzed around, each with a book strapped to their hip, some with multiple in their arms. These people paid no attention to their arrival.

Sai couldn't wrap his head around how they had gone down but ended back on the surface. Even Michelle looked confused. The only one who seemed to have any

34

idea what was going on was Amy, and she wasn't spilling that secret anytime soon. Sai figured that at some point, they must have traveled through yet another warp gate and come out upright.

The air and sunlight were warm and welcoming after being underground. In front of them stood a large, two-story brick building. A massive golden dome at the top caused the building to stand out among the many other brick buildings in its vicinity. Two white banners adorned with the same dragon sigil as the one on the disk hung down the front of the building. In between them sat two doors made entirely of stained glass.

"Welcome to The Citadel." A gruff voice from behind them caught them by surprise. With a start, all three of them turned around to see a large, bearded man in dark, hooded robes standing directly behind them. Even as he greeted them, his aura came off as cold and unwelcoming.

"Oh, master Cylus! I didn't expect you to be waiting for us out here." Amy stammered. "I brought the two survivors from Dione as you asked."

"You're late, and I specifically remember asking you to bring only the boy," Cylus replied.

"I'm sorry, he refused to come unless she could come as well, and well, he made a good point. She was in Dione that night. Maybe she can help us get to the bottom of all this." She stammered again as she caught a glimpse of his pale, piercing eyes. " S-sorry"

Cylus stared at her, his pale blue eyes threatening to burn a hole straight through her. "Amelia..." the disappointment in his voice was apparent even to the oblivious Sai.

Without a thought, he cut in. "Sir, it really is my fault. She told me to come with her, and I refused. She even threatened to bring me by force if need be. Don't be mad at her; it was my idea."

Cylus looked over at him. "Well, I suppose you accomplished your task, even if it wasn't in the way I had ordered. I do hope that she wasn't too rough with you."

He turned to Sai. "She has a habit of being a bit abrasive at times." He said flatly.

Those words seemed to tear Amy down even further. "Abrasive." That word had made her so angry before; now, it was clear why. This must've been a term used to describe her often. This time was different, however. It wasn't just some passing comment from a stranger like Sai. This was someone who knew her well. Someone she clearly respected.

Against his better judgment, Sai decided to speak up yet again. "I wouldn't say abrasive. Maybe a better word would be, headstrong." He looked to her for any sign of relief. She blushed slightly with her head still down.

"You'd be wise not to correct me. Now the three of you will follow me." He stepped around them and headed toward the ornately designed building ahead.

Chapter 6: Accusations and Interference

The massive stained glass doors swung open soundlessly as the four of them stepped into the building. The entire floor was open. It was a single large room with bookshelves lining every wall. Thousands of books filled each and every one of these shelves from floor to ceiling. People in outfits resembling Amy's moved around the building, looking over different volumes and articles. At the far end of the room stood a sizeable gilded staircase that wound its way up to the second story.

Without a word, the three of them followed Cylus as he spoke." This is the Grand Library of The Citadel, the place where all tomes originate."

They walked up the stairs at the far end, clearly heading for the second floor, which in all actuality, was just a simple horseshoe-shaped walkway that wrapped around the upper half of the building. More bookshelves lined these walls, and at the center of the room, another walkway affixed to the ceiling via ropes shot out. At the end of this walk was a disk that looked similar to the one they had taken when they left the cavern. It floated unassisted in the air, separated ever so slightly from the long catwalk.

Cylus walked wordlessly around the horseshoe and toward another door that stood at the opposite end. This door was gilded with the same dragon as all the other ornaments, and Sai began to suspect that it had some meaning that he was missing.

Stopping in front of the door, Cylus spoke again. "Amelia, I'd like to speak to Sai in private. Take our other guest and show her around the library."

Amy seemed surprised, but nevertheless, she complied. Something about Cylus seemed to stifle any air of rebellion within her. "Of course, sir." She gave an obedient nod and gestured to Michelle to follow her.

Origins

Michelle quickly glanced at Sai, who nodded as if to say. *It's okay; go ahead.* Hesitantly she turned and followed Amy. They rounded the horseshoe once again and headed back downstairs.

"Come, Sai, let us speak in private." He opened the ornate door and held it.

Sai entered and noticed hundreds of more books lining these walls as he did. Unlike the bookshelves in the other parts of the library, the ones which lined this room were made of rich, dark mahogany. They lined every wall of the circular room and bathed the space in the thick aroma of ancient pages. A grandiose, round, dark wood table sat at the center with several chairs positioned around it, and in the far corner, a dormant fireplace sat, no doubt out of use due to the warm weather this time of year. The room was well-lit by a large, circular window at its western end. In front of this window sat a large desk, also made of mahogany and filled with loose pages and massive books. It took no time for Sai to realize what this room was.

"Your office, I assume?" Sai said as he marveled at his surroundings.

"Yes, it is. Please, have a seat. I want to talk to you about what happened a few weeks ago." Cylus replied.

"Right to it then." Sai pulled out a seat from the round table and sat down.

Cylus sat across from him and spoke again. " What exactly were you doing in Dione that night?"

Sai explained everything. The mountain, the smoke, the fire, and finally, the attack. "That's all I know."

"Yes, as to those details, I am well aware. That would be the same story you told Amelia. My question is, do you truly expect me to believe that you were there by sheer coincidence?"

Sai looked confused. "You think I'm lying? What would I have to gain from that?"

"Perhaps you were working with the attacker. That was a massive blaze; it would be hard to cause that kind of destruction, especially for an untrained tome

Origins

wielder. It would also explain how you could have fought off said wielder with nothing but your bare hands. That should've been a death sentence, but miraculously you walked away."

Sai looked at him, flabbergasted." Walked away? I didn't walk away! I'd be dead if Amy hadn't shown up when she did!"

"Hmmm, perhaps you staged that fight as a way to make contact with our organization. After all, here you are in my office at the heart of The Citadel."

"Look, I don't know what you think is going on, but I assure you I had nothing to do with the attack. I barely even remember my name! How could I have orchestrated any of that? The truth is I went in to save Michelle and bit off more than I could chew."

"If that's true, you'll have no problem telling me all you know about your attacker." Cylus looked at him intensely.

"Of course not! He was wearing a mask that looked almost like a bird's head. It was made of thickly woven cloth or leather. It was hard to tell, but I think he was using it to help him breathe in the thick smoke. He called himself Roark if I recall correctly."

"No doubt a pseudonym." He replied without a hint of emotion. "He was the only assailant you saw?"

"Yes, I found him in the building reading from that blood-red book and attacking Michelle."

"Can you remember any of the lines he read? If so, I may be able to isolate the tome." Cylus probed.

"Yeah, he said something about the middle of his life's journey and the straight way being lost? Then the line 'awaken Inferno." A shiver coursed through Sai's body as he recalled it.

He thought he saw Cylus' eyes almost flash before fading back to their previous dull piercing state. "Hmmm, and you're sure it was those words?"

"Yes, I'm sure of it."

Cylus leaned back in his chair once again. "Fascinating. While I can not definitively prove, you speak

Origins

the truth based on your testimony alone. You do seem strong in your convictions." He added. "However, strong convictions do not prove innocence."

Sai didn't like where this was going. A knot formed in his stomach as he asked, "What's it gonna take to prove I'm innocent?"

"Don't worry, Sai, we have ways of weeding out dishonesties."

Sai looked at him hesitantly.

"You will take the trial of the tome. It will decide if you are whom you say you are. If you're telling the truth, and there's no darkness in your heart, your name will be cleared. If this is the case, I may even find use for you here. However, If even the slightest darkness persists within you, the tome will react to it and consume you. One more shadow will have been expunged from this world."

The floor seemed to fall away as Sai looked at him, horrified. "Consume me? Do you mean it will kill me?"

Cylus looked at him callously." If you are being sincere, you have nothing to fear. Your trial will commence at sun up tomorrow. For now, that is all. If you'll please." He held out a scroll and handed it to Sai. "Give this to Amelia. She will show you where you'll be staying for the night." He stood and directed Sai toward the door.

Sai stammered in vain as he was escorted out of the room by Cylus. "But I" The door closed behind him, cutting him off. His stomach dropped as the door clicked shut. This could be it; by this time tomorrow, he could very well be dead.

Like a zombie, he rounded the long horseshoe walkway and headed down the stairs, where he saw Michelle and Amy waiting.

Amy looked at him, concerned. "Are you okay? You look like you've seen a ghost."

Sai held out the scroll without a word.

Taking the scroll, Amy unrolled it and read the first line aloud. "Trial of the Tome to commence at sun up tomorrow…." She stopped dead. The look on her face was one of sheer fury and mortification. Without a word, she stormed past Sai and up the stairs.

"Amy, wait!" Sai tried to shout, but she was already rounding the corner and heading for Cylus's office.

She burst through the door, this time not holding her tongue. "What the hell are you thinking!?"

Cylus sat a down book that he had been examining. "You would be wise to hold your tongue." He said calmly. She went to speak again, but Cylus's deafening glare shut her down without a word.

"We need to verify if that boy was, in fact, part of the attack or not, or would you prefer I let him go free so he can reduce this place, your home, to ashes as well?"

"Cylus, he was on death's door when I found him! The Trial of the Tome isn't some litmus test; it's an execution!" Her voice shook with anger.

"Amelia, do not forget to whom you speak! I am responsible for the oversight, distribution, and use of all tomes on this continent. We know for a fact that Dione was eviscerated by one of those very tomes, if not more. What would you have me do, wait until these dark users kill every man, woman, and child across Galaxias Kykolos? No, I will not take such a risk. Sai will take the test, and you will remember your place."

"But, Cylus, he doesn't even remember his past! How can we know what will happen?" Amy pleaded with him.

"Enough! I do not know what your obsession with this boy is, but your first duty is to The Citadel. If need be, I will remove you from the equation." He shouted sharply as he drew out a pitch-black book from the sleeve of his dark robe. "Have I made myself clear?"

Amy recoiled and bit her tongue. "Of course, sir, I-I'm sorry."

"Now, go and show our guest where they'll be staying for the night as instructed, and after the trial tomorrow, you are to return the girl to Iapetus." He said sternly.

"Yes, sir." Amy opened the door and trudged defeatedly back to Sai and Michelle.

As he saw her remerge, Sai spoke. "Amy…" He tried to console her as she walked past them.

"This way, please, I need to show you where you'll be staying." The frustrated melancholy tone in her voice was crystal clear.

Michelle and Sai looked at one another with concern before quickly following Amy as she led them from the building.

"He doesn't want to see me?" Michelle questioned.

"No," Amy replied flatly as she walked on.

The group trailed down the steps of the Grand Library and through the smoothly paved streets of the small town surrounding it. Wordlessly they walked across the platform they had taken earlier in the day and headed down another pristine road that cut through a row of tall, black brick buildings. By this point, the sun was beginning to get low in the west, no doubt spilling sunlight over many volumes which lined Cylus' office. They approached a building nestled within the row, and Amy came to a stop.

"This is where you'll be staying." She pointed to a sign that hung above her head which read "Barnaby's." Amy stepped up and opened the door to let Sai and Michelle pass.

"Welcome!" A voice echoed out from behind a bar in front of them. A large man with a fiery red beard stood behind the counter, polishing a fine glass flagon. As she approached the counter, Amy gave him a quick, wordless wave, and he handed her a key. "Room four," he said as he dropped the key into her hand.

"Thanks, Barnaby." And with that, Amy escorted both Sai and Michelle up the stairs. They came to a door which Amy quickly unlocked. The room was warm and lit by the glow of candlelight. It was decorated neatly with a table, a few chairs, and a single, full-size bed at the center of the room. A stack of blankets sat neatly folded at its foot.

"Here you are. This is where you'll be staying for the night. I'll be back first thing in the morning to take you to the trial location." Amy explained. Her tone was disheartened and hopeless.

"Thank you, Amy. Is there any way we can talk about what's going on?" Sai asked concernedly.

She sighed. "I suppose I can't deny you that small comfort. Let's sit." She walked into the room and pulled out one of the chairs from the table. Michelle nodded and took a seat along with Sai.

"I guess the real question is, is there any way out of this?" Sai asked.

Amy shook her head." No, I'm afraid there's not."

Michelle spoke up," Why not just run away? You have nothing to prove to him. I know you had nothing to do with it. I'd even go with you if you wanted me to…." She blushed slightly. She hadn't meant for it to come out like that, but Sai had saved her life, and she knew she'd do anything to ensure he didn't suffer for it.

Amy looked down and shook her head again. "Unfortunately, that's not an option either."

Michelle looked at her, and with a twinge of anger in her voice, she spoke again," Why? Would you try and stop us?"

Amy took obvious offense to the line of questioning. "No, honestly, if there was a chance he could run from this, I'd be one of the first to help him. After all, it's my fault he's here."

"Then why not help? You said it yourself a few hops through those underground warp gates, and we could be on the other side of the continent."

"You could, yes. However, if Sai runs now, Cylus would take that as an admission of guilt and send someone to hunt him down. Then it really would be an execution. At least this way, he stands a chance."

"We could hide. You know, go so far he couldn't find us and…."

Origins

Amy cut across her, " No." she leaned in close and lowered her voice. She looked around with a paranoid kind of glance. "You can't hide from Cylus. Using his tome, he can locate and surveil anyone he wishes."

Sai looked shocked. "Excuse me? You mean he could be watching us right now, and we would have no idea?"

"Keep your voice down!" Amy commanded. "Using his tome; 84, he can view any person he desires at any time. It's how he monitors tome users and keeps control over the vast assortment of us spread out across the continent of Galaxias Kyklos. As for watching us now, I'd doubt it, but you'd never know. The use of that aspect of 84 takes a toll on him; he suffers massive, sometimes blinding migraines if he uses it too frequently. He only uses it when emergency reports come in that call for it. The last time I saw him use it was the night of the attack. It's how he dispatched us to Dione so quickly."

"If he can use that, why doesn't he just use it to find the person who attacked the city?" Michelle asked, perplexed.

"Aside from the side effects, it can only be used if he knows whom he's looking for. He knew a man from Dione, Kacelius, and he used it on him that night in order to gather the information to verify the attack. He dispatched us when he saw nothing but flames, smoke, and bodies burning in the streets." Amy explained. "He simply can't afford to use it on something as trivial as this, even though it is possible." She sat back in her seat again.

"We could…" Michelle sat hunched in her seat.

"No." Sai cut in. " I won't have anyone risking their lives for me, and anyhow you said you thought someone you were looking for could be here. I can't ask you to leave with me and leave that person behind. Looks like I'll be taking that test no matter what. Is there anything you can tell me about it?" Sai asked, looking over to Amy. "I mean, you have a tome. So, clearly, you went through it and came out the other side."

Amy looked down again. "I can't, I'm sorry. I'm expressly forbidden from speaking of how the trial works. The only thing I can tell you is, and this is common knowledge, you want the tome to emit light. If it does, you're worthy of the actual trial. If it doesn't and emits darkness instead, you'll be swallowed up by it."

"Hmmm." Sai rubbed his chin for a moment. "Okay, well, that's that then!" He stood up and grabbed his crutch. "There's no sense in moping around here."

Amy and Michelle looked up at him, surprised. "You're surprisingly chipper about this?" Amy said.

Sai scoffed. "Well, I figure I'm innocent, so not really much to worry about, is there? And anyway, if it's my last night alive, I'm not about to spend it moping around here. He said with bravado. "I'm starving. Do they have food here?"

Amy nodded.

"Anything but fruit sounds amazing," Michelle said with a false little laugh as her stomach grumbled. With all the excitement of the day, the group hadn't eaten anything since the hospital that morning, and Amy had eaten most of that.

Amy stood up." Sure! It's my treat; It's the least I can do, really."

Sai looked over to Michelle, and they both shrugged and threw a quick smile back to Amy. "Not like we had any money, to begin with." Sai joked.

Together the three walked downstairs and back into the main room, where Bartleby greeted them once again. That night they ate like royalty. They had bowls of thick meat stew, succulent pan-fried chicken breast, and some of the largest gooiest sweet rolls Michelle said she could ever recall. They did this all while vastly expanding Amy's tab in the process.

*****

Sai jolted awake. He was lying on a thin pallet that he himself had placed on the floor of his room. His back ached from sleeping against the stiff wooden floorboards with nothing but a single blanket as a cushion. He had forfeited the bed to Michelle last night when Amy conveniently dropped the little nugget of information that the two of them would have to be staying in the same room for the night.

"After all," She reminded him," Cylus had me reserve this room for you, Sai. She's not even supposed to be here, remember?" As she opened the door to head out, Sai raised his hand in protest. She turned, cutting him off. "Oh, and Sai, she's been through a lot lately. So, don't try anything weird, K?" With a wink and a smile, she shut the door leaving the two of them alone.

The annoyance was painted across Sai's face in the least abstract way. He turned to Michelle, who was already sitting on the bed staring at him.

"Sorry if I've been a bother. My coming here seems to be causing quite the burden on you and Amy. I'll make a pallet on the floor, and you can take the bed." She insisted.

Sai waved the comment away. "No, no, I wanted you to come along. It's no trouble at all. I'll take the floor; you take the bed for the night." With that, he grabbed the blanket at the end of the bed and a single pillow and sprawled them out on the floor.

With a thank you, Michelle laid down and fell asleep within minutes.

Sai lay staring at the ceiling, deep in thought about what tomorrow would bring. At some point, he had shut his eyes, and now here he was, being woken up. But by what, he didn't know. He didn't need to consider this long as a blood-curdling scream filled the entire room.

Sai bolted upright with a start; scanning the room, he could see Michelle thrashing violently in her sleep. Making his way over to the bed, he placed his hands on her shoulders and shook her. "Michelle, hey. Wake up!"

Her entire body was convulsing under his hands before her eyes popped open. Suddenly, she sat up in cold sweat and looked at Sai with tears in her eyes.

"Are you okay?" Sai asked, his voice shaking.

She shook her head and threw her arms around him. "No." She admitted through sobs. "Ever since the attack, I haven't been able to sleep. I keep being dragged back into that night over and over. Again and again, that man attacks, and instead of you diving in to save me, I'm… incinerated. I feel myself die each and every night."

Sai was caught off guard by the embrace, but he held her steadily. "Sounds like you're having bad dr___ms." The final word was incoherent, almost as if it were blurred as it met Michelle's ears. He held her for a few more minutes as she tried to slow her breathing.

She looked down, trembling," It's kind of embarrassing, but would you sit on the bed and hold my hand until I fall back asleep? I just need to know I'm not alone." She said meekly.

"Of course." Sai took a seat on the bed and grasped her hand. "I'm here as long as you need me."

Michelle smiled faintly as she laid back down and closed her eyes. She squeezed his hand tightly, and before long, she slipped off to sleep once again.

Sai sat for a while, watching her breath rise and fall. Slowly her grip slackened, and Sai released her hand. Gently he stood and found his way back to his pile on the floor. Laying back down, he went back to staring at the ceiling. He lay there for a long while contemplating everything. Here he was, a boy dead to rights, and he was concerned about this girl's bad dreams. *What am I doing here? What have I gotten myself into? What have I gotten Michelle into? How am I ever going to survive this?* These thoughts kept him up half the night at some point though he had drifted off and slept soundly until sunrise.

Thin strips of light were dancing across the bedroom floor as the curtain covering the window shifted in the light breeze of morning. He awoke with a start as someone pounded on the door to the room.

"Hey, come on, get up. You're going to be late!" It was Amy, and just as Cylus had said, she was there first thing to retrieve him for the trial.

Sai stood up and looked back toward Michelle, who was still fast asleep, sprawled across the bed. Even with all the pounding on the door, she hadn't budged. *She seems to be sleeping better now.* He thought as he turned back toward the loud banging.

Sai cracked the door and popped his head out. "Amelia…" He drawled in his best Alister impression.

Somehow she didn't seem amused by this." Sai, come on, you're going to be late." She pushed the door open and entered the room. "Oh, I see you figured out your sleeping situation." She said, noting the pile of blankets. "How chivalrous of you." The playfully mocking tone in her voice was as grating as ever.

Michelle stirred in bed and sat up. Rubbing her eyes, she spoke. "Is it time to go already?"

"Umm yeah, about twenty minutes ago," Amy responded. "We have to get going. We need to be there in less than an hour.

Silently the two of them packed up what little they had brought with them and headed down to the first floor to get some food. The three of them talked as they scarfed down a quick breakfast of fresh bacon and fried eggs.

"Are you ready for today?" Amy questioned.

"Ready as I'll ever be, I suppose." He replied with a small laugh, his nerves threatening to betray him.

"Well, at least you're in good spirits about it," Michelle said with a small half-smile. She turned back to Amy. "Oh, Amy, is there any way I can come to watch the trial?"

For what seemed like the first time ever, Amy responded with a yes. "You're welcome to come and watch. Trials are always open to the public for the sake of transparency. Not that this one will see much turnout since Sai doesn't have any connections that we are aware of. You'll be able to see at least the initial test. If he passes that part, we won't see what goes on during the second half."

Michelle smiled and nodded, thankful to be included.

"After the trial is over, though. I've been ordered to return you to Iapetus." Amy added.

Not wanting to ruin her chances of attending the trial, Michelle simply nodded. She would willingly go back. After all, Sai wouldn't fail, they would return together, and maybe finally, she could put this all behind her.

The three finished their food and decided to head out. It was still dark when they left the inn, but the sun was beginning to peek over the horizon. It cast thin steaks of light over the horizon, painting it a beautifully dull blue. The morning air was cool and damp as they walked.

It can't be more than 5:30 or 6 in the morning. Sai thought to himself as he followed behind Amy, his crutch clicking against the hard stone street.

"The trial will take place in a special room at the top of the Grand Library," Amy said.

Again they approached the huge ornate building at the center of town. They entered back through the large front doors, headed up the stairs, and around the upper horseshoe walkway toward Cylus's study.

Cylus met them outside his door. "Welcome back," He said as they approached. "Are you prepared?"

Sai didn't speak but instead gave a quick nod.

"Then please follow me." He said as he strode past them and out onto the catwalk that led to the disk suspended over the center of the lower room. He stepped onto the disk, and the other three followed suit. As soon as they stepped on, it began to rise into a dark opening in the ceiling. The room above was clearly the dome visible from the outside of the building. He had seen it on top of the library when they first arrived. Then it seemed to be made of solid gold, but now standing inside of it, they could clearly see out in all directions. The sun coming up over the horizon made the room glow with the faint vermillion light of dawn. The platform stopped, and the group stepped off onto the polished ebony floor.

Cylus spoke again," Now, Sai, before we begin, I'd like to ensure you are given a fair chance." From the sleeve of his long robe, he pulled out a green vial of liquid. "I cannot in good conscience expect you to take on the trial with your foot in that condition." He pointed to Sai's injured foot. "Drink this, and it should repair the remaining damage that was done."

Surprised by this seeming act of kindness, Sai grabbed the vial and looked at Amy for reassurance. She gave a quick nod prompting him to pop the cork and drink down the vial's contents in one gulp.

It was different than he expected. The almost watermelon flavor of it caught him off guard. In an instant, the ankle that had ached every day since the incident stopped hurting. It almost felt better than it did when he had first woken up. In fact, his whole body felt stronger. Whatever was in that vial had cured any ailments he had accumulated since his awakening. He put his full weight on his foot, and for the first time in what seemed like an eternity, and much to his surprise, it felt normal. Opening his inventory, he stashed his now useless crutch and waited for Cylus's instructions.

"It's time." From his sleeve, Cylus drew out what looked like a book. It was wrapped in a white cloth, no doubt to keep the trial from initiating by accident. He held it out in front of him. "Take this tome and step to the center of the room. When you are ready, unwrap the sleeve and place your hand on the book itself."

Sai grasped the book in his hand and did as he was told. Nothing about this book seemed special. Its white cover was blank, and Sai somehow knew the pages were empty as well. For the first time since arriving, Sai experienced something that felt like a memory. The trigger was the smell. It was such a familiar thing; the smell of those bound pages. As quickly as the feeling had come, it faded from him.

Cylus cleared his throat. "When you are ready. Lay your hand on the tome, and Repeat these words. 'Now Awaken!'"

Amy's advice from the previous night rang through Sai's mind. *You want the tome to emit light. If it does, you're worthy of the actual trial. If it doesn't and emits darkness, you'll be swallowed up by it.*

Origins

Staring down at the blank white cover, Sai raised his hand, and without another thought, he slammed it down on the cover as he shouted in the bravest voice he could muster. " Now, Awaken!"

The book flew open, and Amy's face turned a ghostly white as the unthinkable unfolded. Dark black bubbles of what seemed like pitch began to rise from the pages and drip to the floor. Within moments a deluge of foul-smelling viscous goo poured from the pages and began to crawl up Sai's legs. He had been found unworthy and was being consumed by the tome. He hadn't lied to Cylus earlier, but something unknown had clearly caused this violent reaction of negative energy to pour from the pages.

Amy could only turn away, afraid to see the end of the trial she felt responsible for causing.

Just as Sai had come to grips with what was happening and how his fate had been decided, something caught his attention; a blurred image had burst forth from the group of onlookers.

"This time, I'll protect you!" It was Michelle. She had broken past Amy and Cylus and was rushing toward Sai.

The tar-like substance was climbing past Sai's waist and up his chest by the time she had reached him. Without a thought, she grabbed the book in his hands and tried to pry it free. It was no use. It didn't budge as if the cover had fused to Sai's hands. With no other options in sight, she raised one hand and shouted with every fiber of her being. "Now, Awaken!"

A blinding white light exploded from the pages as her hand made contact with the cover, and the darkness seemed to retreat away from it. The shocked faces of both Cylus and Amy were drowned out by the intensity of this miraculous light. Sai was forced to close his eyes as it engulfed and overwhelmed his every sense.

Chapter 7: Eons

As Sai's senses returned to him, the first thing he noticed was the faint chirping of a nearby bird. Opening his eyes, he quickly realized he was no longer in the Grand Library. Amy, Cylus, and even Michelle were nowhere in sight. He found himself instead standing alone on the branch of a giant tree. The smooth white birch bark beneath his feet reflected the light of the intense sun above and gave him a flat smooth surface to stand on. Looking over the edge, he realized immediately how extremely high up he actually was. Millions of equally smooth branches stretched out beneath him. Sai's mind raced, trying to explain how he'd ended up here. Had he traveled through another warp gate? Had the book consumed him after all? Then it clicked. This was it; he had entered into the tome's trial. One thing was for certain: he had been found guilty, and Michelle had saved his life, at least for the time being.

The chirping of the distant bird rang out again and caused Sai to come back to the present moment. He looked around, and his eyes were drawn to a smaller branch that jutted out from the one beneath his feet. A tiny, brownish-grey bird, like a finch, jumped around at the tip of the branch and tweeted as it looked at Sai.

Sai tilted his head curiously at the oddity. "Hello?"

It tweeted again and jumped up into the air before flying right past Sai and into a large, dark hole in the trunk of the tree behind him.

"Wait!" Sai raised his hand as he stepped toward the pitch-black hollow. The bird's chirping echoed from somewhere deep inside the tree's truck. Placing his hand on the outside of the hole, he peered in. He could feel some kind of invisible, intangible force pulling him toward the ominous darkness. Hesitantly he took a step inside. As he delved deeper, it grew darker and darker until he could no longer see his own hand in front of his face. As he walked onward, the chirping of the bird began to grow louder,

Origins

and in the distance, a small light appeared. It grew larger and larger until finally; Sai found himself stepping out the other side of the trunk.

Instead of stepping out onto another branch, however, he stepped into what looked like a vast, dry savannah. The bird from before flew out ahead of him and landed on a small, scraggly tree nearby. He watched the bird as it landed, and though he couldn't quite put his finger on it, there was something different about it this time. *Perhaps the shape of its beak, H*e thought. He walked toward it, and with every one of his steps, the bird hopped to a higher branch.

Suddenly, the bird's chirping stopped, and a soft, disembodied male voice filled the air. *"The works of nature are to those of art."* The ground began to shake, and from the tree's hollow at Sai's rear exploded a stampede of animals charging toward him.

The small opening was rent wide as the animals poured out onto the plain. A proverbial zoo, hundreds of different animals headed straight for him. Every animal he could imagine- Lions, elephants, zebras, deer, bears, red pandas, and many, many more bore down on him. Sai turned to run, and the small finch from before took off ahead of him. He chased after it as the animals gained on him with every step. They were on his heels when the bird dove into a dark hole in the ground just ahead of Sai. Without a thought, he dove in after it just as the animals were about to trample him.

He gasped, trying to catch his breath as he plummeted into the deep darkness. Again, a spot of light appeared ahead of him, and without much choice, in the matter, he fell through it and into a world of ice. He landed on a large pile of snow which cushioned his fall. He tried to rise to his feet which immediately slipped out from under him. As the snow shifted beneath him, he realized he hadn't landed on a flat surface. Instead, this was the steep incline of the side of a glacier. Suddenly, he began sliding down the side of the great mountain of ice and out onto a flat, snow-covered field. Again, he pulled himself to his feet. This time, however, the small finch was nowhere in sight.

The world grew quiet, and the voice came once again. *"We will now discuss in a little more detail the struggle for existence."*

The ground shook again, but this time it wasn't some giant stampede. Instead, a large lumbering animal loomed over him. It resembled an elephant but covered in a layer of thick, brown woolly fur. Its ivory tusks were long and curved. It was apparent to Sai that this animal was far more gentle than the ones from before. Sai met its gaze and almost unconsciously raised one hand to touch its long trunk, which hung low to the ground. Shockingly the gigantic creature let out a horribly pained cry and reared backward. Sai stumbled back just as its massive tusks swung out violently, barely missing him. The massive creature turned to face an unseen attacker. The sound that came next made Sai's stomach drop. It was a deep bellowing roar, unlike anything he had ever heard. Sai scrambled backward in the snow and caught a glimpse of the would-be attacker. It was a huge cat with teeth as big as butcher's knives, and worst still, it wasn't alone. Other members of its pride approached and lunged at the huge creature.

Mammoth, Smilodon. The words seemed to materialize unprompted within Sai's consciousness. He was sure he'd never heard the terms before, yet here they were, and he recognized their meaning.

"No." The word escaped Sai's lips without warning and drew the attention of the largest of the cats. Stepping from around its main course, it slowly made its way toward Sai. Stumbling backward, he fell hard into the fresh white powder. The huge animal got into a low crouching position as it inched closer. Before it could leap, the mammoth ripped around and, with one massive tusk, threw the creature off to the side in an amazing display of raw power.

Sai scrambled to his feet and began to run full bore in the opposite direction. A loud booming cry echoed out of the cloud of whipped-up snow that had been created in the struggle. Suddenly, something exploded from the frozen dust and was charging right for him. As it

Origins

cleared, the cloud Sai could finally make out what it was. This was no smilodon like the others, it was a huge flightless bird, and it was breaking its way through the throng. Sai's mind screamed to run, but his legs wouldn't obey. The bird skidded to a stop in front of him, and the two's eyes met.

It lowered its leathery head, and Sai raised his hand to touch it as he realized he recognized this creature. "You?"

This was the same bird from before. However, this time the changes it had undergone were undeniable. It was at least nine feet tall and had small wings held at its side. It had a large head which was marked with distinctive blue and red skin, which led down to a thick beak that could easily be used to crack open nearly anything it wanted. Its long powerful-looking legs ended in extremely sharp talons which dug into the fresh snow. It was obvious this animal didn't belong here, in this frozen world, but it had been called there by some unknown force to aid Sai.

"Titanis." He named it as the word materialized in his mind, just as it had with the smilodon.

The moment between the two was broken as the mammoth collapsed into snow which was now dyed a deep crimson from the attack. The cloud began to settle as one of the large cats climbed over the heaving mass to spot its next target. One by one, more cats appeared around the dying animal. They moved closer as they geared up for another attack. Sai stepped back in fear. The bird nudged him with its head as it crouched down. Sai looked at its back and then back at the approaching pride. Deciding to take his chances, he threw his leg up over the bird's back and steadied himself by grabbing a tuft of feathers near the base of its neck. The bird sprang up in a fraction of a second, and they were off.

They sprinted off across the frozen tundra at blinding speed. The pride of wild cats chasing them, winding through every twist and turn. They sprinted around the edge of the glacier and burst onto another huge, open plain. Claws drug across the ice as one of the smilodons jumped out from behind a nearby snow drift and straight into Sia's path. The cat's intimidating stance lasted less than a fraction of a second. Without a moment of hesitation, the massive bird lifted one of its large taloned feet and stepped down hard on the snarling monster's neck. The subsequent crunch of bone made Sai's stomach churn as the full weight of the strike registered. The cat went limp instantly, and the bird continued on without breaking its stride.

As they crossed the field, another huge mountain of ice came into view. A large cave entrance was nestled at its base. As they approached, Sai felt the rumbling of the Earth yet again. He looked up just in time to see it. A huge cloud of snow and ice was barreling down the side of the mountain toward the mouth of the cave. They had to stop; otherwise, they'd be crushed under the impending avalanche. Looking back, Sai could see that they were still being followed.

Weighing his options, he realized quickly that if they stopped for even a minute, they'd both be cat food. In that moment, he decided, giving a quick kick to the bird's side, he shouted, "Go!"

The two raced even faster now for the cave's mouth. With no more than seconds to spare, they crossed the threshold just as the avalanche crashed down and sealed the cave entrance. They were safe now, but the titan of a bird kept on running. The cave was pitch black. The avalanche had cut off any and all light that may have been pouring in before, and now they were running blind. Suddenly, they hit a bump, and Sai bounced into the air for only a moment. Gripping at the feathers, he found his hold again and pulled himself back onto the creature. The enormous shoulders felt different somehow, though, much wider, and the feathers seemed less full, yet fuzzier.

They continued to run, but it felt as if they had slowed down. The heavy stamping of the bird's feet had been replaced by even louder thuds. As they ran, another light appeared in the distance, and before Sai knew it, they were bursting through an exit that they could no longer fit through. They exploded out of the trunk of a new enormous tree. An explosion of bark and wood shards showered onto the floor of a dense forest covered in ferns

Origins

and large conifer trees. The air was warm and wet. Sai felt that it was even harder to breathe here, and looking down, the breath left his lungs entirely.

No longer was he sitting atop the back of a giant bird, but instead, he found himself straddling the neck of a forty-foot-tall tyrannosaurus.

"He must have changed again when I was bucked off for that moment," Sai murmured to himself. This world, however, was to have a much shorter existence than the previous ones.

The voice from before echoed out once again, this time more violently. *"Nevertheless so profound is our ignorance, and so high our presumption, that we marvel when we hear of the extinction of an organic being; and as we do not see the cause, we invoke cataclysms to desolate the world, or invent laws on the duration of the forms of life!"*

At the exit of this line, something much more terrifying than anything before appeared. A flaming mass of stone the size of a city roared across the sky. This time there was no running, no thinking, no escape. The monstrous animal he was riding reared back and sent Sai tumbling head over heels down its back and onto the ground behind it. The impact of the enormous asteroid made all the previous rumblings feel like gentle breezes by comparison. In an instant, the entire world was vaporized before his eyes, and Sai was being carried away by a blast wave that had deafened him before he could even realize what was going on. He had no idea what had happened to his new friend, but it was clear he had shielded Sai with his gargantuan body moments before the impact. Even all of that wasn't enough to prevent him from being swept up by a massive shock wave of dust and fire. All he knew was he was sailing through the air, blasted backward through the same hole they had come through. On every side of him, images flashed in the darkness.

Land-dwelling reptiles with huge sails on their backs. Animals that crawled from the sea onto land. Deep, sprawling oceans full of armor-plated fish, some the size of city buses. All these images flickered by in an instant, but Sai could feel that these weren't just visions. These were each differing eons separated by millions or even billions

Origins

of years, and Sai was flying past each in a matter of seconds. Before long, the strain on his body and mind began to feel like too much to handle, and he blacked out.

After an unaccounted-for amount of time, he awoke. He was lying on a round slab of hard stone with several puddles of unknown liquid pooling around him. A primordial sea stretching out on every side of him

He sat up and grabbed his head which ached from the explosion. He took a deep breath and realized. He wasn't actually breathing; nothing entered his lungs as he inhaled. He wasn't suffocating, though; something strange was happening here. It was almost as if he was here in the moment but also not at the same time. He could feel the ground beneath him, but it didn't feel like he was affecting it in any way. He got to his feet and walked toward one of the nearby pools which laid all around him.

Then the same voice rang out again much more affectionately. *"There is grandeur in this view of life. Whilst this planet has gone cycling, from so simple a beginning endless forms most beautiful and most wonderful have been and are being, evolved."*

Sai knelt down to touch the strange liquid, and although his hand made no impact on the substance, something became clear to him. Even here in this desolate land of nothingness, life existed, struggled, and grew. Closing his eyes, he could feel the presence of life's most simple single cellular forms.

As he opened his eyes, the presence faded from him, and he found himself lying once again on the floor of the observatory atop the Grand Library. A light green colored tome lay clutched in his sweaty palm.

Chapter 8: No Harm

The book in his hand wasn't the only thing that had changed. As he came to Sai became aware of the tension in the room and something else. The entire room had taken on a slightly darker hue of red. It was almost as if he was looking at it through a thin crimson curtain. Then he noticed something else, something soft and sweet, was pressing against his lips. He gasped as he became fully aware of the situation at hand. Amy was kissing him!

Amy pulled back and looked down at him. "Oh, thank the gods, you're okay." the relief on her face was evident.

"W…what's going on?" Sai sat up, confused.

"Sai, your heart stopped… I had to give you CPR." She explained breathlessly.

"So, that wasn't a kiss?" The words came out of Sai's mouth before he could register what he was saying.

Amy's face went beet red, and she shouted at him. "Of course not! Why would we… Why would I?" She struggled to find the words. "You were dying, and I was trying to save your life, that's all." She looked away from him.

Sai placed his hand on his chest, which felt sore from the ordeal. *My heart stopped?* He could feel his pulse which resonated hard within his chest. "Thank you for saving me." He smiled at her gratefully. Then his focus shifted to the book under his left hand. He lifted it to read the title. "Origins." He muttered to himself. Suddenly, he remembered Michelle and how she had charged in in order to save him. "Wait is Michelle okay!?"

Amy nodded and tilted her head to the left, where Michelle still lay unconscious on the floor. The tome in her hand pulsated with a dim light. Sai looked at her for a minute, and the light began to fade as the book turned to a golden yellow color in her hand. Her chest rose as she took a deep breath and opened her eyes.

Origins

Sai got to his feet and made his way over to her. Amy followed closely behind him. "Are you okay?" Sai asked as he knelt down beside her.

"Shouldn't I be asking you that?" She replied in a wispy voice as she sat up.

Sai shook his head. "I'm fine; why would you do something like that?"

"Sorry, I just couldn't stand by and watch it consume you. Not after everything you've done for me." She explained.

He exhaled sympathetically. "Thank you, and I guess that makes us even." He rubbed the back of his head, closed his eyes, and smiled.

Michelle returned the smile and sat up.

Amy interjected." Thanks to Michelle, you not only survived, but you both ended up with tomes of your own. Congratulations!"

The two of them looked down at the books in each of their hands. An air of relief hung over the group for the first time since coming together.

This reprieve was short-lived as Cylus spoke up. "One saved by the light of another. This is unprecedented." Though his words were encouraging, his tone dripped with displeasure.

Sai looked over at him and stood. "We passed your test. Are we done here?"

" I would hardly count that as passing." A different voice caught Sai's attention. Turning toward the elevating platform at the center of the room, he saw a familiar grey-haired figure standing beside it.

"Seriously, you again?" Sai snapped back at Alister.

"You've got quite the mouth on you. Big words for someone who would be dead if it weren't for a little girl." Alister stepped toward the group. "Cylus, this boy is clearly guilty. He would've been consumed if it wasn't for that one." He pointed one accusatory finger at Michelle.

60

Origins

"Hey!" before he could think, Sai was in Alister's face pointing one finger at him in return. "I'll show you guilty."

"You little whelp! I'll teach you the meaning of respect." He raised his hand in a backhanding motion before being stopped.

Cylus gripped his wrist firmly before releasing it. "Enough, Alister; you are not the one in charge of making such decisions. He was chosen even if it was only due to the girl's interference. He still passed and was chosen by the tome. Now, are you going to tell me the meaning of this disruption?"

Alister lowered his hand and turned away from Sai. "I need to discuss important information with you regarding disappearances in the city of Elara."

"Please, let's talk." Cylus gestured for Alister to speak to him across the room.

The two walked away from the group and spoke privately. Sai tried to listen in, but they were too far away to hear. Sai walked back to Amy and Michelle and explained what he had heard Alister say.

"He said people are disappearing?" Amy spoke in a low voice, trying not to be overheard; Sai nodded.

"What do we do now?" Michelle asked.

"We'll have to wait and see what Cylus decides," Amy explained. "I doubt we're off the hook yet."

Alister and Cylus approached the group once again.

"An important matter has come up that I need to attend to. Michelle, and Sai, you both have passed your test. You are no longer under investigation in regard to the attack on Dione. However, Alister is correct in saying that you would've failed. If it hadn't been for both the efforts of Michelle and Amelia." Cylus threw a disapproving glare at his young disciple. "Therefore, I am ordering you to stay under observation for the time being," Cylus explained.

Sai was annoyed by this turn of events. What was Alister's problem with him? Even though this upset Sai, he could understand why Cylus had concerns. The

Origins

book had tried to cull him. Clearly, something was amiss, and this may be the only way to get to the bottom of it.

Amy spoke up, " Cylus, haven't we put Sai through enough al..."

Sai cut her off. " No, Amy, it's okay. What do I need to do?" The confidence in his voice surprised Amy. Something within him had changed. He seemed almost stronger, more determined even.

Cylus's stoic expression faltered only momentarily as a small smile crept across his face. "Good, thank you for your cooperation. I would like you, Amelia, and Michelle to travel with Alister to investigate the source of some rumors going around the city of Elara."

Michelle looked surprised. " All of us?"

"Yes, after all, each of you interfered in Sai's test. You with your light, and Amelia with her use of life-saving measures to bring him back from the brink. The three of you must prove your fealty to me."

"Why not send just us, then? Why does Alister have to go?" Amy questioned.

"Amy, you're strong. However, on your last mission, you failed to stop the enemy, and you directly disobeyed my orders when sent to tie up your loose ends. You need an experienced inquisitor to keep you in line. I can't risk you going in alone with two that have no idea how to use their tomes."

"Don't worry, Amelia, you three will be safe in my care," Alister assured her. Somehow the line made the three of them feel even more uneasy.

"And Alister." Cylus turned on him. "I'm sure I don't need to remind you, but you are to be as vigilant as possible. If any of them are harmed in any way, it's on your head."

The threat seemed to shake Alister to his core. "Of course, Master Cylus. No harm shall befall them; you have my word."

"Good, you are to leave shortly. Please convene downstairs and go over the plan. Michelle, will you hang back for a moment? I wish to speak to you about Dione."

Origins

Michelle nodded. Amy gave her a reassuring look as she and Sai were escorted back downstairs by Alister.

*****

"And that's all you know?" Cylus sat behind his large desk and glared across it at Michelle.

Michelle nodded solemnly.

"While I am deeply sorry for your loss, you must understand the position you've put me in due to your interference with the trial."

Michelle nodded again. "I understand; you have my apologies."

"Then you are dismissed. Please join the others downstairs." He turned in his chair.

"I-" She faltered for a moment. "I have one more question to ask you."

Turning back, he spoke. "Yes"

"Three years ago, my brother, Virgil, made a pilgrimage here in the hopes of becoming a scribe. I haven't heard from him since. Would you at least tell me if he's here?" She spoke meekly.

"Virgil, you say?" He trailed off as if to scan his memory. "The name does sound familiar. Yes, as I recall, he did act as a scribe here for a time. However, over a year ago, he decided to take the trial of the tome for himself. Unfortunately, he was found unworthy. I'm sorry, my dear; it seems you may have come too late."

Michelle exhaled sharply, trying her hardest to hold back the overwhelming pain of these words. She had lost everything, and now the only family she had left was gone as well. A small tear rolled down her flushed cheek.

Cylus stood and walked around his desk to place a hand on her shoulder. "I know the pain of losing a loved one to the trial. But, we must remember these trials create order, even when we do not agree with the outcome. "He released his grip and walked to the door.

"Go now. Your team awaits." He said callously.

Without a word, Michelle stood and took her leave.

*****

Origins

For nearly an hour, the other three waited downstairs as Cylus spoke to Michelle. Sai flipped through the pages of his new tome. Each page was completely blank, which confused Sai to no end.

"What's going on with this book? Aren't these things supposed to have words?" Sai asked.

"Tome." Amy corrected. "I'm sorry, normally you'd receive more formal training than this, but given the circumstances, I'll try to explain this as best I can. The short answer is yes, they're meant to be read, but not at first. The more practice you have with it, the more words will appear. The largest factor, however, is the amount of emotion you pour into reading the lines of the tome itself." Amy explained.

"I'm not sure I understand. Again, mine doesn't seem to have any words at all." Sai questioned.

Amy pulled her tome from the pouch on her hip. "Watch closely. First off, you don't look through the book and find the words. Simply close your eyes, focus on the tome, and let it speak to you. The tome should open to the lines you're looking for." Just as she said, the tome's pages flew open, and a single line appeared. "Once you've found your line, you need to pour a single emotion into the reading of it." She continued. Tracing her finger across the line, she began to speak. "Be strong, saith my heart; I am a soldier; I have seen worse sights than this. Awaken Odysseia!" Just like before, the tome vanished, and the sword and shield appeared in her hand. "See?"

"Oh! That's the same line you used when you rescued us!" Sai exclaimed.

"Mmhhmmm, that line summons an impenetrable shield and an unblockable…."

She was cut off suddenly. "Amelia, you shouldn't tell just anyone the secrets of your tome. Especially someone, we don't know if we can trust." Alister scolded her in a harsh tone.

"Alister, he passed the test. If we want to succeed on this mission, don't you think it's best that he knows our strengths and at least the basics of tome use?"

Origins

The annoyed look that seemed permanently painted on Alister's face looked even more obvious after that comment. "Perhaps, but be careful. However, Do you think it's prudent to practice tome activation here? Not all tomes are as concentrated as yours, you know. What if Sai's tome were to activate as an offensive burst? That could prove disastrous for the many tomes stored here, correct?"

This comment made Amy feel two-foot tall. "Of course, you're correct. I'm sorry." The next thing out of Alister's mouth surprised both of them.

His expression softened ever so slightly. "Don't worry about it. You're right. If we hope for this mission to succeed, Sai and Michelle will both require training."

"Wait, really?" Sai was shocked by this turn of events.

The annoyance reappeared on his face within an instant. "Do not misunderstand me, boy. I still don't trust you, but if you are to come along on this mission, I would prefer not to have to carry your dead weight."

Sai just looked at him and shook his head in disbelief. "Man, you are just the worst."

Amy's eyes widened as if to say *shut up!*

Alister looked like he was about to explode. His fury was stopped in its tracks as Michelle and Cylus descended the staircase into the lower library. It was clear that Alister did not wish to evoke Cylus's wrath.

"I hope all is going well down here," Cylus said sternly.

"Of course, sir," Alister replied quickly.

"Good now; I need you to pack up and head out right away; our contact in Elara is awaiting your arrival."

The four of them nodded in unison and headed for the door of the library. Exiting the building, Alister spoke again. "You have ten minutes; go back to your room and pack your things. Meet me at the warp corridor when you're done."

Amy, Michelle, and Sai began to break off, but Alister stopped Sai by firmly grabbing his arm as he passed, stopping him in his tracks. "One step out of line…"

This was all he said, but the veiled threat was crystal clear. Their eyes met, and Alister released him. Without a word, Sai headed away after his things. Minutes later, the group reconvened. They headed down the square, boarded the huge lifting platform at the center, and headed down into the underground caverns.

The group walked through the dark tunnels for a time before coming up to a ladder that appeared to lead to the surface. Climbing up, they emerged out of a hatch and into a tubular-shaped room that looked to be made of faux wood. Feeling around the blank walls for a moment, Alister found a small handhold and gave a forceful pull revealing a hidden door which slid open with a loud groan. Stepping out, the four of them entered a sprawling forest of giant redwood trees. Looking back, Sai realized the cylinder-shaped room they had come from was actually a hollow space inside the trunk of one of these trees. The sun was high in the sky, and the temperature had risen drastically from when they had set out.

"This is incredible. I've never seen anything like it." Michelle looked up at the huge, looming trees as they walked.

"These forests are thousands of years old. Each of these trees grew from something as small as this." Alister explained as he knelt down and grabbed what looked like a small pine cone. Shaking the cone, tiny brown seeds poured out into the palm of his hand. "Each of these has the potential to grow into one of these great sequoias."

The group looked around in awe. Sai spoke up. "These all came from something that small?"

"Yes, it just goes to show you no matter how insignificant something may seem. It could still hold the potential to become something truly incredible." Alister held out the seeds and offered them to Sai.

He took the seeds and rolled them over the palm of his hand. Feeling that he grasped the metaphor, he

Origins

shoved the seeds into his pocket and responded. "Hmm, I think I get it."

"There's nothing to get. Not every seed will become a great sequoia. In fact, most just die here on the forest floor. The least worthy ones, that is."

This was an obvious jab, and Sai knew it. "Still, I appreciate the wisdom." He said calmly. He wasn't about to be baited into another fight.

The group continued to walk for a long while. This denseness of the forest seemed almost endless. In every direction, the giant trees shot up toward the sky and formed what looked like solid walls all around them. Finally, after walking a good distance, they stepped out into a large rounded clearing.

Stopping in front of them, Alister spoke up. "This should do."

The rest of the group looked at him confusedly.

"What exactly do you mean? We're still a ways off from needing to make camp for the night." Amy said.

Alister turned around, and in his left hand, he clutched the deep blue tome that had previously hung on his waist. He opened his mouth and began to speak. "It is not down on any map; true places never are. 'Now Awaken Moby Dick!" There was a vicious roaring sound as a low wave of water poured through the forest behind him.

"What are you doing, Alister?" Amy shouted as she summoned her sword and shield. The wave crashed into the clearing and threatened to sweep the group away. She stabbed the blade into the ground in an effort to anchor herself and held the shield high to deflect the water away from her upper body and face.

Michelle and Sai weren't so fortunate. Caught by the wave's unexpected power, they were swept off their feet and pushed back toward the tree line of the dense forest. Sai reached for Michelle just as the wave hit. In a stroke of luck, he was able to grasp her wrist the moment they were carried off. The two spiraled in the water before stopping abruptly as Michelle caught the trunk of one of the massive trees with her free hand. Holding on for dear life, they waited as the current slowed and eventually stopped. Even though it was no longer flowing, the group still stood in at least a foot of briny, foaming water.

Amy lowered her shield in order to locate Alister, but in that instance, a foot met with her stomach just below her ribs and threw her back into the surf away from her sword and shield.

"You should really be more careful when letting your guard down." Alister plucked the blade from the ground and threw it into the deep water and out of sight. Holding his tome in one hand above his head, he prepared for another attack. " Call me Ishmael." The tome transformed suddenly, and in his hand, he held a massive harpoon. A thick braided rope wrapped its way down his arm and into the sleeve of his shirt. He lowered it and stepped toward Amy, who sat in the water gasping for the air that had just been forced from her lungs.

Meanwhile, back at the tree line, Sai and Michelle had found their feet. Sai looked over to see Alister approaching Amy, harpoon in hand.

"Sai, we have to do something." Michelle pleaded.

He nodded." Okay, I'm going to distract him. While I'm doing that, you need to grab Amy and get her out of there. Are you ready?"

Michelle gave a quick nod, and the two took off across the flooded plain.

Alister raised the harpoon above his head and threatened to bring it down on the writhing body before him when he heard a shout.

"Hey!" Sai dove into him from the left and tackled him into the water. Wrestling with him, Sai tried his best to give Michelle as much time as possible to get Amy to safety.

Alister flailed underneath Sai and forced his head above water. "You really do have some fight in you, boy!"

"I thought you swore that we would come back unharmed. What the hell are you trying to do?" With all his strength, he forced Alister back beneath the shallow waves. *Is he trying to kill us? Am I going to have to kill him?* These thoughts just had time to register in Sai's mind before something sinister shook his confidence. Alister stopped struggling; instead, he was grinning as Sai grasped his throat with all his strength. The next realization almost came a moment too late. The harpoon in his hand had vanished, and suddenly it was erupting from beneath the water, flying out in a direct line for Sai's left eye. With milliseconds to spare, Sai jerked his head to the right as the harpoon cut a deep gash across his cheek. Holding his bleeding cheek, Sai leaped back and onto his feet. Thankfully his diversion had been enough. Michelle was able to help Amy back to the tree line and out of harm's way.

"You'll need more than raw strength in order to beat me, boy," Alister scoffed as he rose from the water. Yanking back on the rope, the harpoon sailed seamlessly back into his hand. "Now let's see what you're really made of." He charged at Sai, harpoon in hand. Sai dodged left and right as he back peddled away from the harpoon, which lashed out furiously. Suddenly his back met the trunk of a tree with a thud.

"Got you!" Alister yelled as he plunged the harpoon forward with all his strength.

Sai dove to the ground, just narrowly avoiding the empaling blow. The harpoon sunk deep into the tree's trunk, which gave Sai enough of an opportunity to kick Alister's legs from beneath him. This knocked him back into the water and disarmed him all in one swift motion.

This time Sai didn't try to jump on top of him. He knew he didn't have the strength to overwhelm him, but if he could just get rid of that harpoon, just maybe he could even the playing field a bit. Getting to his feet, Sai threw his entire weight into the shaft of the harpoon, which still stuck out of the side of the huge tree. With a loud snap, the shaft broke in two. The handle fell into the water, still attached to its wielder by the thick cord. He had done it. The harpoon's tip was still buried in the tree rendering it completely useless.

Origins

With lightning-fast reflexes, Alister spun around underwater and ripped Sai's feet out from under him just as he had done moments before. He quickly found his feet and was standing over Sai. To Sai's horror, the harpoon in his hand was once again perfectly intact. Alister bent over, grabbed Sai's shirt, and pulled him from the water.

"Impressive strength, especially for someone your size, but it takes more than that to destroy a tome construct." He released Sai's shirt, raised the harpoon, and brought it down with all his might.

Sai closed his eyes and braced for an impact that never arrived. Instead, he heard a metallic clang. Opening his eyes, he saw Amy was covering his body with hers. Her shield lay over her back and deflected the blow. Her red hair hung in his face, and his shocked expression had never been more apparent.

"Thanks." He said breathlessly.

Alister staggered backward from the deflection.

Sai and Amy got to their feet just in time to hear Michelle speak. "A bear roaming the woods in search of berries happened upon a fallen tree in which a swarm of bees had stored their honey. Awaken Fabels!"

The imposing buzzing that followed sent shivers down Sai's spine. Dozens of semi-translucent honey-colored bees flew from Michelle's tome and charged at Alister. They Landed on his clothing and popped like bubbles upon contact, leaving sticky, oozing pools of honey wherever they burst.

"What is this?" Alister questioned as more and more bees exploded all over his body. Every move he made caused him to become more entangled in a web of viscous goo." So, you're a defense type?"

"Guys, run!" Michelle shouted. Amy helped Sai to his feet, and they sprinted to her side.

Alister began to swing his harpoon wildly, trying to swat the bees before they could land and make his predicament worse.

"Whoa! Michelle, that's amazing!" Sai exclaimed.

70

Origins

Amy shouted at him," Sai, focus up! I don't know what's going on here, but he isn't playing around. That attack before would've killed you if I hadn't blocked it."

Sai nodded. "Sorry, you're right; what's the plan?"

"We're going to need to coordinate our attacks, and you need to activate your tome." She explained.

"Okay, but…" Sai pulled the book from his side hesitantly.

"No buts! You have to do it! Remember, Sai, focus on one emotion. Pour it all into the words." Amy readied her tome and recalled her sword from beneath the rippling pool. Like a flash, it appeared in her hand just as Alister's had.

Sai closed his eyes and concentrated. *I want to protect them; They've both helped me so much. I need to protect them!* The thoughts screamed through his mind. His tome flew open, and a single line appeared. Opening his eyes, Sai read the line with as much determination as he could muster.

"Natural Selection, as we shall hereafter see, is a power incessantly ready for action. Now awaken Origins!" A huge plume of smoke erupted from the text, and from it flew a single brownish-grey finch. The bird chirped and landed on Sai's shoulder. "You!?" Sai recognized it as the same bird from when he took on the trial.

Amy looked shocked and then almost disappointed. "What the!? What kind of attack is that supposed to be?" She shouted at Sai.

"Huh? How am I supposed to know?!" Sai yelled back.

"Sai, How does a bird help us?!"

"Guys! Come on; I can't hold this forever." Michelle shouted as she strained to hold Alister's trashing body in place.

"Right! We'll just have to figure it out! Sai get into position. We have to flank him from both sides."

Sai nodded, and the two dashed to opposite sides of their increasingly sticky target.

"Ready? Now!" Amy shouted.

As if by instinct Sai stretched his arm out and pointed. "Go!" The bird flew from his shoulder, and Amy charged from the other side. As he watched the bird's flight path, he remembered the larger bird that had saved him in the tundra, and before his eyes, the finch was enveloped in dark smoke. When it broke free of the cloud, it had completely transformed into the same nine-foot-tall behemoth from those ice plains, and it was barreling toward Alister. Greying feathers dropped to the flooded plain as the giant bird sprinted on. "Titanis!" The shout left his lips without a thought. They had simply appeared in his mind yet again as he stared at the fantastic creature before him.

This turn of events shocked even Amy, but she didn't flinch. Instead, she gripped more tightly on the hilt in her hand and charged forward. She cocked her arm back and swung her sword furiously. As she swung, the giant bird leaped into the air and kicked at the nearly encased Alister.

"For hate's sake, I spit my last breath at thee." The words that came from Alister's lips put an end to the oncoming attack. A dark circle appeared beneath his feet, and a giant whale made of water erupted from beneath him. Amy and the titan of a bird were rag dolls in the torrent of water. The massive creature transformed back to its original form and was thrown out of sight. Without warning, the whale came crashing back down to Earth directly on top of Alister, causing a tidal wave which swept Michelle, Sai, and Amy away.

"That's enough, I suppose." Alister's harpoon disappeared, and the tome rematerialized in his hand. He held it above his head and spoke. "Recall!" The water rushed back toward him and was sucked into the pages of his tome. Sai, Amy, and Michelle all lay heaving on the ground at the edge of the clearing. "Congratulations, now each of you are capable of activating your tome."

Origins

Sai sat up. "Are you out of your mind!? You could've killed us."

"Boy, if I wanted you dead, you'd be dead. Do you think an enemy will hesitate to kill you, given the chance? You must learn to fight every battle as if it's your last."

Amy and Michelle both sat up.

"Sai, he's right. He could've given us some warning about what he was trying to do!" Amy shouted with emphasis. "But he is right. You can both use your tomes now. We accomplished at least that today." Amy explained as she got to her feet.

She helped Michelle to her feet. They then walked over and helped Sai up. Michelle wiped the blood on his cheek away with a damp cloth, which she quickly returned to her inventory. She pulled out a bandage and gently placed it over the wound.

Sai's finch flew down out of one of the nearby trees and landed on his shoulder.

"Oh good, you're okay." The bird gave a cheerful chirp as Sai gave his head a quick stroke with his finger. "Now recall." With these words, the bird hopped back into the pages of the book.

"Sorry, I doubted you. Your tome turned out to be really strong after all. Looks like you have a specialist type tome." Amy explained. "I supposed yours must be a defensive type, Michelle."

"You are correct," Alister spoke as he walked over to the group. "His tome is similar to your own specialist type."

"What does that make yours?" Michelle asked.

"My tome, Moby Dick, is an offensive type. Essentially, all of its lines create differing attacks, each deal damage whether I use them for protection or not."

"Moby Dick, yeah, that seems fitting," Sai mumbled under his breath.

Amy hit him in the ribs with her tome as she stifled a laugh. "Shut it." She said through gritted teeth.

Michelle spoke up," Maybe it's time to set up camp now? I'm exhausted after that."

"That's a good idea." Alister opened his inventory, and a few short taps later, four single-person tents were set up and ready for the night. They each turned in early after the exhausting day.

Chapter 9: Oswald

Day in and day out, they traveled and trained. All the while shielded by the impenetrable walls of the redwood forest. One day around a week after they had entered the perpetually endless wood, the tree line ahead of them seemed to thin, and before long, they left it behind. The ground began to gradually slope upward as they walked until they came to the crest of a large open hill.

Looking down, they could see the city of Elara, which stretched out much like the other cities Sai had visited. It spiraled around in a large circle of grey stone buildings before them. It was smaller than the city of the Citadel, but it couldn't have been by much, Sai figured. The group headed down the hill and through the large rounded city gate made of polished black stone. They passed dozens of people as they made their way to the city square.

"So, Alister, what exactly brings us here?" Amy feigned ignorance.

"There have been reports of people disappearing around town. Rumor has it the culprit is a possible tome user." Alister explained. "We think it could be in connection with the attack at Dione. It's our job to find out."

"So, where do we start? Asked Sai.

"We have an informant in the city who has been feeding us information. Recently the disappearances have increased, and he's asked for our assistance in rooting out the perpetrator. We're meeting him by the fountain at the center of town."

They walked on until a large black fountain came into view. It was ornately decorated in the same shimmering black stone as the city gate. Three Enormous winged beings that resembled angels stood back to back at its center. Each held a long, pointed spear that poured water from the tip. In front of the fountain stood a tall, muscular young man who looked to be around his mid to

Origins

late twenties. His short blonde hair was well-kept and neatly combed back in a stylish fashion. His white and blue sleeveless shirt revealed his massive biceps. The Adonis that stood before them raised his hand and gave a quick wave.

"Is that our guy?" Amy asked in surprise.

Alister nodded before waving back to the man as they approached him. "Oswald, It's good to see you!"

Up close, he was even more imposing. He was at least six and a half feet tall, with shoulders nearly double the width of Sai's. His pale blue eyes shone with kindness and enthusiasm for their meeting.

"Good morning Master Alister; it's good to see you as well. I hope your journey went smoothly."

"It did, thank you. These are my charges: Sai, Amelia, and Michelle." Alister pointed to each of them in kind.

"Master?" Sai whispered to Amy, who ignored him. The title seemed odd somehow since Sai hadn't heard anyone refer to Alister as master; sure, he was a skilled tome user but a master? Sai shook this question away as they each held their hand out in introduction.

"It's good to meet you," Oswald said as he quickly shook Sai's hand. Next, he grabbed Michelle and Amy's hands and planted a soft kiss on top of each of them. "Excuse the formality. Local customs, you know." He smiled charmingly.

The girls both blushed profusely and nodded wordlessly. This was the first time Sai had ever seen Amy speechless, and it rubbed him the wrong way somehow.

Sai cut in." Anyway, don't we have something important to discuss?" Alister and both girls looked at him, annoyed.

"You're absolutely right! Sorry about that. Come on, let's go back to my house so we can talk about this in private." Oswald turned, and the group followed him down the cobblestone street to the biggest and nicest house in the area. It was a grey stone building, just like all the others in town. It was two stories tall with a fine black door at the top of its stone staircase. The lawn that

76

surrounded it was a deep green, and hedges on each side were trimmed up and well-kept. He pulled a key from his side pocket and unlocked the door. "Welcome to my home."

  The door swung open, revealing a massive well-lit room with a fireplace directly at the center of its back wall. Fancy furniture and paintings decorated the entire room, and one exceptionally massive painting of Oswald himself hung over the mouth of the enormous fireplace.

  "Please make yourself at home. There are five rooms upstairs where you may stay for the duration of your trip." He explained as he pointed to a staircase attached to the eastern wall. "The one at the far end of the hall is mine, but you're welcome to any of the others."

  "Thank you, you're so sweet!" Michelle exclaimed nervously.

  "And clearly a bit full of yourself." Mumbled Sai staring at the massive painting.

  "It's the least I can do. You're all helping me, after all."

  Alister, weary from the long journey, made his way over and took a seat in front of the empty fireplace. "You've made quite the life for yourself since leaving the Citadel, haven't you, Oswald?"

  "Wait, you were at the Citadel before you came here?" Sai asked in surprise. "So, you're a tome user too?" Sai took a seat across from Alister. The girls followed after him, finding a seat on the couch to Sai's left.

  Oswald gave a hardy laugh. "Not exactly. It's true that I used to live at the Citadel. I even trained under Master Alister here, but no, I was never a tome wielder."

  "What, afraid you're not worthy?" Sai said.

  Amy tilted her head and gave him an annoyed and confused look. "Sai…"

  "No, no, it's okay. I decided not to take the tome exam. I was actually a scribe until I visited this town on one of our missions.

  "Yeah, this place was in pretty rough shape when we arrived. The village leader had made some poor dealing with a shady organization who had recently begun siphoning off the city's supplies. We worked with the city's officials and drove the group out."

"And you decided to stay?" Michelle asked.

"He and both of my other students, actually," Alister interjected. "When you all asked to stay here and help build this place up, I was surprised, but it seems you have really made something of this place. Who'd have thought you'd have such an impact in just five years and after everything that happened? I'm glad to see you're thriving."

A pained look came across Oswald's face at the mention of his teammates.

"I'm sorry; I know Sibyl meant a lot to you. Believe me, when I say I understand the void that can be left when you lose someone you love." Alister tried to console him.

"You had students before us?" Sai asked but was ignored again.

The annoyance Sai had felt toward both Alister and Oswald seemed to soften a bit. It was like a castle of resentment washed away by the tides of empathy. This was a side of Alister Sai had never seen. He was compassionate and seemed to genuinely care about the people he once called students. Maybe this had something to do with the way he acted, a facade perhaps, to mask his pain?

"It's okay. It's been over a year since she's been gone. Even still, I loved her, and this place meant the world to her. It's important for me to carry on her legacy and take care of this place in her memory. That's what she would have wanted."

"So, Sibyl's gone?" Amy questioned. "And you had another student as well?"

Pain and anger seemed to wash over Alister's face all at once.

Oswald placed a palm on his old master's shoulder and quickly changed the subject. "Perhaps it's best if we focus on the matter at hand."

Alister's tension seemed to ease. "Well said. We should discuss the current mission and how we're going to stop these disappearances. We'll talk more later. " His solemn, natural tone returned as he looked up at Oswald.

"For a little over three weeks now, citizens have been vanishing all over town." Oswald walked over and grabbed a file folder from a table that sat on the other side of the room. "This file contains information on each one of the missing people." He handed the file over to Alister, who thumbed through the pages.

"Do you have any leads as of yet?" Alister questioned, still looking over the papers.

"Not much, unfortunately, and the people who have reported sightings have given wildly differing reports on who or what they saw. Some have reported seeing a huge antlered monster stalking the streets at night. Others have told of sightings of a dark-robed figure, possibly carrying a tome, in the immediate areas where the victims were last seen. As you can tell, these accounts are extremely different, and it's hard to know which to actually believe if any. One thing's for sure though the townspeople have gone to calling whatever the kidnapper is;' Ijiraq."

"Ijiraq?" Michelle questioned.

Alister tilted his head back and shifted his eyes toward the ceiling as if trying to recall some ancient information. "It's a name taken from an old world legend. I feel like I read about it once, back at the Grand Library." He pondered the memory for a moment. "If I recall correctly, Ijiraq was supposedly a monster, some kind of hybrid between a caribou and a man. It was said to kidnap children and stash them in hidden places. The question, however, is, did that name begin floating around town because of this creature's appearance, or are people seeing this monster because of the nature of the disappearances?"

"So, you know this creature?" Oswald seemed taken aback.

"I think so, yes. But, as far as I'm aware, it was only ever a legend." Alister contemplated this for a moment.

Origins

"Could a tome bring such a creature to life?" Amy interjected.

Alister scratched his chin as he spoke. "It's entirely possible, I suppose." Pulling a few pages from the files, he began to pass them around to each person in the room."Have a good look at these tonight, and study up on each of them. Tomorrow we will begin conducting interviews around town. We're going to get to the bottom of this, one way or another."

"Right!" The group gave an answer in unison, spurred on by Alister's steely determination.

The day wore on as they spoke and got familiar with all that had been going on. Before long, the sun was setting. Alister retired first. He bid the group good night and headed to the room right across from Oswald's. "Don't be up too late. We have a long day ahead of us."

"Don't worry, I'll be sure they get to bed soon," Oswald assured him. As Alister vanished from sight up the stairs, Oswald got to his feet." Would you all like some tea?"

"I would love some! Two sugars, please, and thank you." Amy replied cheerfully. Sai and Michelle both agreed as he walked into the kitchen.

As he walked off, Sai questioned Amy. "Why are you acting so weird?"

"Huh, what do you mean?"

"You're being oddly sweet. No sarcasm or jokes? Far less abra..." Sai caught himself before personally signing his own death warrant.

Amy could feel her face getting warm. "What do you mean? I'm always sweet, and he seems like a nice guy, so I'm just being nice in return."

"Oh, always sweet, are we? Seems kind of flirty to me." Sai retorted.

"Excuse me!?"

"Two sugars, please, and thank you!" Sai tried to imitate her in a high-pitched squeaky voice.

Origins

"Okay, first of all, it was sweet to offer, and secondly, why do you care if I'm being flirty? Which I'm not, by the way!"

Sai's face got red in return. "I don't!"

Michelle cut in. "Guys." As she spoke, Oswald was making his way back from the kitchen with a tray full of steaming glasses of tea.

"Everything okay?"

"Yeah, of course; thank you so much!" Amy said with a cute little giggle. To which Sai rolled his eyes.

"Say, Oswald, do you have a girlfriend by chance?" The question from Sai nearly made Michelle and Amy both choke on their tea.

"Sai!" They both chastised him simultaneously.

"What? He's an attractive guy; surely he must have people falling all over him, right?" He was clearly trying to rile Amy up.

"No, It's okay. You'd be surprised how often I get asked that." Oswald replied with a charming closed eye smile. "No, I don't have a significant other to speak of at the moment. Not since Sibyl." His smile faded, and he looked nearly depressed yet again. This made Sai feel like trash for even asking. Because of his arguing with Amy, he had forgotten the earlier conversation about Alister's former student.

"Sorry, I…" Sai tried to apologize.

"No, Again, it's all right. It's been nearly a year, and I'm sure she would want me to move on and be happy, but it's hard." Amy stood up to comfort him. This little line of questioning had blown up in Sai's face in the most spectacular fashion.

"Losing someone like that must be awful," Amy said as she stood and placed one hand on his broad shoulder.

"I recently lost several people I loved as well. I get it. Do you want to talk about it?" Michelle asked, staring down into her tea.

81

Origins

Oswald nodded. "It would be good for you to know. It may even help you to understand Master Alister a bit more."

This caught Sai's attention. *How could a story about Oswald's loss help us understand Alister?* He thought. *Sure, they were his students. But surely a heartless guy like Alister wasn't that sentimental.*

"As you know, Sibyl and I were students of Master Alister. We went on several missions as well as trained together daily. After about a year of the three of us being a team, we were sent on a mission to the city of Ganymede. It's a tiny little place over on the west coast. The city had been raided and occupied by pirates. We were sent in to help stabilize the region, but before we even arrived, the pirates caught wind of our coming. In a bid to cover their tracks, they burned the entire village to the ground before we could get there."

Michelle closed her eyes as the memory of her own burning village resurfaced. She exhaled softly, trying to hold back tears.

"By the time we arrived, there was nothing left except for one survivor, Oran."

"Oran?" Amy asked.

Oswald simply nodded. "He told us what had transpired and how the pirates had killed his family while he hid. He also said that he knew where they were docked, and if we hurried, we might be able to catch them before they set sail. We followed him, and sure enough, heading out of the bay were six massive galleons."

"They got away?" Sai looked at him curiously.

"No." He shook his head. "There's a reason Cylus sent Alister. With one line from his tome, Alister created a massive white whale that sank the entire fleet in a matter of seconds. He ensured they paid for their crimes right then and there. From there, Alister took Oran under his wing, treated him like a son, and he became the fourth member of our squad. That proved to be a mistake he will have to live with for the rest of his life." Oswald looked directly at Sai.

82

Origins

"About a year passed, and in that time, Oran gained a tome as well. Then we were called here. We cleaned up the town, and things seemed to be getting better. We had rid the area of the gang leader that was terrorizing the town, and Alister was called back to the Citadel as the region stabilized. Oran, Sibyl, and I asked to stay behind to ensure the power vacuum we created didn't give rise to any more violence. What we didn't realize at the time was that the Oran had been playing both sides from the beginning. With his and Sibyl's tomes, we had rid the area of corruption, but he used his power to assume the leading role and took over the town's criminal underbelly right beneath our noses."

"What happened from there?" Michelle asked.

"Well." He continued. "When Sibyl found out about his betrayal, she went to confront him without my knowledge." Tears welled up in his eyes. "She confronted him and found out that he was actually the son of the pirate leader Alister had drowned. He was left to infiltrate our group but hadn't accounted for Alister's command over the sea. Sibyl pleaded with him as a friend to stop. When he refused, she had no choice but to fight. By the time I realized she was gone, it was already too late. When I finally tracked them down, I found Oran dead, and Sibyl wasn't far from it. As I held her in my arms, she told me what had happened and made me vow to carry on her legacy of protecting this town. She died in my arms that night." As he concluded his story, the room fell silent.

"I'm so sorry. I…" Sai couldn't find the words.

Oswald wiped the tears from his eyes. "Again, It's okay. Alister lost just as much as I did that day. I only hope that my story can help you understand him a little more."

He feels guilty about not being there for his students and guilty about bringing a wolf in sheep's clothing into their group. Sai felt awful for how he had treated Alister and Oswald. *No wonder Alister didn't trust him. How could you ever trust anyone after that?*

Amy, Sai, and Michelle all nodded as if to say *we understand.*

83

Origins

Oswald stood and put on a more confident face. "We should call it a night. Thank you for listening to me. It's good to talk to someone about all of this for once."

They all nodded again, and after talking for a bit longer, each retired to their rooms for the night.

With the rising sun came a knock on Sai's door. Sai found his feet and cracked the door slightly.

Amy and Michelle both stood on the other side. "Are you ready? We need to start making our rounds." Michelle looked exhausted. No doubt she hadn't slept since she was alone in her room. Every night since they had set out, Sai had been sneaking over to her tent to stay with her until she fell asleep.

Sai rubbed his eyes and nodded." Yeah, let me get around." He shut the door and reemerged a few moments later. His hair looked like a bird's nest, as he came out with a yawn. "Ready."

Michelle gave a quick laugh at his haggard appearance. "You're kinda hopeless, huh?"

Sai gave a quick shrug. "Probably so." He said as he rubbed the back of his head and yawned.

"Come on, Alister and Oswald are already waiting downstairs." Amy turned on her heels and headed down the nearby staircase.

As they reached the bottom step, Oswald spoke up. "Good morning! I hope you slept well. His left hand was bandaged, but other than that, he looked as perfect as he had the day before.

"Oh, what happened to your hand?" Amy's concern both surprised and annoyed Sai.

"Oh, this? I burned it while making breakfast this morning." He gestured to a large table which was laid out with a beautiful array of breakfast foods: eggs, pancakes, bacon, and glass containers full of milk and coffee.

"Wow! That looks incredible. Thank you so much." Michelle walked past him, took a seat, and began to eat.

"Would you like me to take a look at it?" Amy questioned. "I have some healing potions. One might help?"

He pulled his hand back. "No, thank you, it's okay. I know how expensive each of those potions can be; it isn't too bad."

"Okay." Amy nodded with a smile as she and Sai took a seat at the table next to Michelle. As they ate, Alister went over the plan for the day. "Today, we need to split into groups and question anyone in connection with the kidnappings."

"Okay, so why don't Michelle, Amy, and I go as one group, and you and Oswald can be the second," Sai suggested as he shoved a wad of pancakes into his mouth.

"I actually had another idea." Alister sipped his mug of coffee as he spoke. Sitting it down, he spoke again. "Sai will go with me. Amelia, Michelle, you will go with Oswald."

"Huh, why do they both need to go with Oswald." Sai stood up from his seat in protest.

Alister gave Sai the signature look of annoyance that he wore so well. "First of all, you're still under observation Sai. Secondly, that gives each team an experienced tome user to act as a leader, Amelia and myself.

"But Oswald's.."

Alister raised a hand, stopping Sai in his tracks. "Oswald is not a tome user, or are you forgetting that detail? Do not forget I'm the person in charge of this mission, Sai. If you have a problem with this plan, prove yourself to me, and become a leader of your own team. Then you can make the plans."

Sai was quickly realizing that this wasn't a battle he wasn't going to win. He sat back down with a huff. "Yes, sir."

The rest of the table carried on the mission conversion. They discussed the logistics of where they would go and how they would question each person when they found them.

Origins

Amy leaned over and whispered to Sai. "Don't worry; I'll keep him away from Michelle for you." She elbowed him in the ribs a couple of times for emphasis.

Instead of getting embarrassed as she had anticipated, Sai flipped the joke on her. "Oh, thank you so much, and tell me, who's gonna keep him away from you?" he looked at her with a tilted glance.

She blushed furiously."Who said he… why do you… shut up!" after stammering for a moment, she turned back to her food and continued eating nervously.

Sai rolled his eyes and went back to his meal. It was a joke when it left his mouth, but something about the way it came out almost convinced even himself that he meant it. The others in the group seemed to not notice the exchange. He didn't want Oswald flirting with Michelle for sure, but he also felt the same way about Amy. It was all very confusing. For some reason, one he couldn't even put words to, it bothered him to no end to see Oswald flirt with either of them. The very thought of it made him jealous at best and, at worst outright angry. He didn't have long to contemplate these admittedly complex feelings. Before he knew it, everyone was standing up and taking an empty plate to a nearby sink to be cleaned. Sai scarfed the rest of his food down and followed the rest of the group to the door.

Chapter 10: Inconsistency

"Are you ready, Sai?" Alister questioned as he slipped a map he had been examining back into his pocket.
Sai gave a quick nod in response, and the two headed for the door.
"Okay, everyone, we're headed out, so listen up," Alister announced. "We are just doing interviews today. If you, by some chance, have an encounter with our person of interest, you are by no means allowed to engage with them. Call for help and wait for backup; am I clear?"
Everyone nodded their head in agreement as the two groups split up. Sai took one last look back at the girls who stood talking to Oswald about their plans. He noted the giant painting above the fireplace once again and let out a small envious sigh before closing the door behind him.
"So where to first?" Sai asked.
"Looks like our first lead lives on the outskirts of town, just east of here. Goes by the name Samuel Flax. His wife was apparently one of the victims." Alister explained, looking over one of the pages from the file. The two walked quietly for a while before coming to a small, nicely built log home with a stone foundation. "Here we are." Alister knocked on the door, and a plump, old man with greying brown hair answered.
"How can I help you?" The man asked, scratching his round stomach.
"Are you Samuel Flax? We're here to ask about what happened to your wife."
"Oh, you're the help Oswald promised to send. Please come in." He escorted them inside, where they all took a seat at a kitchen table.
Alister opened the page of information he had. "How long has your wife..."
"Mary, her name is Mary," Samuel interjected.
"Yes, my apologies. How long has Mary been missing?"

Origins

"She's been gone for nearly three weeks now." He explained.

Alister looked at him, puzzled. " Three weeks? My records show a week. How long did you take to report her absence?"

"I reported it within a day of her not coming home."

"It says here that Oswald found no evidence of her being taken or attacked?"

"Yes, that's correct."

"Can you run me through the events of the day? Had you fought? Might she have left of her own accord?" Alister weaved his way through this line of questioning masterfully. Sai watched on as he narrowed down each possibility with ease. It was clear that he had done this before and often. He did all of this while jotting down notes on the back of the page he had pulled out.

"No, we hadn't fought. She had told me that evening that she was headed into town to grab some food for an upcoming party she was helping to host. She visited the local market just before sundown and talked to several of the vendors there before heading back for the house. The workers can confirm that as well. After she didn't come back for a few hours, I went to look for her, but it was no use. She'd vanished, almost like a ghost."

Sai cut in." So she met with several people and then just disappeared? All of the things she bought just vanished as well?"

"Mhhhmm." Samuel nodded as he closed his eyes. "That's all I know. There were no witnesses to her disappearance or even any sightings of who or what could've taken her."

"Thank you, sir; we'll do whatever we can to locate Mary and bring her back to you safely," Alister said as he put his pencil away, folded the page up, and slid it back into his pocket. He stood from the table and gestured for Sai to do the same.

Sai stood, and they both shook Samuel's hand before heading for the door and back into the street.

Origins

"That poor man. I hope we can help him." Sai could only sympathize with the loss he was sure the man must be feeling.

Alister gave a quick nod. "It's always a shame when people lose someone dear to them. However, I doubt we'll find Mary."

Sai looked at him, shocked. "You're already giving up on her? It's not even been a month."

Alister shook his head." Never, but when someone is gone for that long with no leads, the odds of finding them at all are low, let alone finding her alive."

Sai's heart sank. "That's so cold."

"Sorry, when you've seen as much as I have, you must learn to be realistic."

Sai looked down at his feet. "Oswald told us about your former students." Alister seemed to tense up at the very mention of it. Sai decided to end the conversion there. It was clearly not a subject he wanted to broach.

They simply headed quietly across the town square and to another large home. They met with another person and heard yet another similar story. A family member headed out, the sun went down, and they never came back. This story continued with every home they visited throughout the day. Several claimed they were taken by the monster they called Ijiraq, others had no leads, and a small few claimed to have seen a cloaked figure speak to their relatives during the day before they vanished. The sun was getting low in the sky at this point. They had been interviewing people all day but seemed to be getting no closer to having a solid answer for what was going on.

The two walked on and found the home of the last interviewee on their list. It was another small home, this time made of light grey stone. Alister knocked on the door, and a woman with ashy blonde hair who looked to be in her late thirties answered the door.

"Are you Sarah Albertson?" Alister questioned as he took a step back from the opened door.

"I am. And who might you be?"

Origins

"My name is Alister. I'm an inquisitor from The Citadel, and this is my student Sai. We're here to investigate the disappearances around town. Do you mind if we come in and talk to you about your son Alex?"

The woman simply nodded and turned around, holding the door open for her new guests. "Oswald had said he called for assistance and to be expecting you."

The course of this conversation was very similar to how the last interview had gone. She explained how her son was around thirteen years old with blonde hair and brown eyes. He had gone out just before dark to meet some friends, and friends had reported him missing when he never arrived to meet them. This investigation, however, took a turn the others had not.

Sarah continued," When Oswald searched the area of town he was headed to, I joined him, and we found evidence of a large struggle. Busted store barrels and torn-up cobblestones from the street were obvious signs that some kind of fight had occurred."

Alister jotted notes down. "These friends he was meeting, did they see him at all that night, or might they have any idea of what might have happened?"

She shook her head. "No."

"Our files show that you also found large hoof prints dug into the torn-up street?" Alister asked as he wrote.

"Ijiraq." she murmured.

Alister cocked his head to the side. "I've heard that name several times in the past couple of days. Tell me, where did you hear such a thing?"

"It's just something Oswald had mentioned. Sorry, I'm sure it's nothing." She waved her hand in front of her, trying to dismiss the thought that some imaginary creature had carried her child away in the night. Tears formed in her eyes as she looked away from them.

Alister placed his hand on hers. "I'm sorry for what you're going through. Believe me when I say I understand your loss."

She looked up at him angrily and pulled her shoulder out from under his touch."Don't say that! I'm sick of everyone saying that to me! Pretending as if you understand, how could you? Have you ever lost a child!?" She shouted.

He took a deep breath. "Sai, would you mind stepping outside for a moment?"

Sai, not wanting to be present for the increasingly tense conversation, stood wordlessly and headed for the door.

Alister continued, and Sai could just overhear the conversation as he left the room. "I have. Nearly a year ago…" What came next hit Sai like a freight train. "I lost my daughter Sibyl."

A fog suddenly lifted from Sai's mind. Like emerging from a dark cave into the light of day, everything became clear. This was why he had been so hard-pressed to push the topic of his past student away. Yes, she was his student, but moreover, she was his daughter, and she was gone. The thoughts seemed to click in his mind like puzzle pieces falling into place. This was the reason for his negativity and distrust. He bore invisible wounds that would never heal. He had done the right thing in saving Oran, but in the end, his trust in the boy had cost him the person he had loved most in the world.

Sai closed the door behind him and waited in front of the home. Their muffled voices were too quiet to make out at this distance, and at this point, Sai didn't think it prudent to eavesdrop.

Nearby two boys stood and talked openly across the cobblestone street.

"Is she okay?" One boy asked.

"She's fine. I don't believe she fought off Ijiraq. It's supposed to be huge; how could she? I bet she's just saying it to get attention."

Sai spoke up. "Hey, do you mind if I ask you what you're talking about? I'm here helping with the investigation and could use any information you could give."

"Sure. Doubt it's much help, though." The taller of the two boys announced as Sai stepped across the street.

Origins

"You know someone who fought this Ijiraq creature?" Sai questioned.

"Well, this new girl in town, Alicia, says she did, but I don't really know that I believe her."

"Why's that?" Sai asked.

The taller boy went on to explain that no one he knew had even seen the monster let alone fought with it and come back. "Alicia claims to have fought with the creature last night and escaped."

"Wait a second. Last night?" Sai was shocked. An attack had occurred last night and right under their noses.

"That's what she says." The shorter boy replied.

"I know it's getting late, but can you take me to meet her? I want to hear her side of the story."

The tall boy shook his head." No, the sun's going down, and I'm not looking to be the next one to go missing. I can point you in the right direction, but then you're on your own."

"That'll work. Thank you."

"She lives three blocks in that direction." The tall boy pointed to the east. "In a big house with a small shabby picket fence surrounding it."

"Big house, small fence, got it! Thank you so much." The boys went back to talking, and Sai headed back to talk to Alister.

Heading back into the house, he interrupted the ongoing conversation. "Sir, I have…"

Alister stopped him." Sai, please I asked you to wait outside." The vibe surrounding the room was downright depressing. The strong feelings that had been discussed seemed to permeate the very air itself.

"But sir…"

"Go," Alister said sternly as he continued the conversation with Sarah.

Sai gritted his teeth and spoke," Right. Sorry, sir." He turned back around and headed out the door. *If*

Alister won't listen, I'll have to go and speak to her myself. He thought as he headed across town.

Meanwhile, Alister's conversation continued. "I'm so sorry for snapping at you like I did." Sarah placed a hand on his. "I just have no idea what to do."

Alister shook his head. "It's okay, my daughter's gone, and I must live with that fact. However, it's possible that your son may not be beyond saving. Is there anything else you can tell us?"

She wiped her tears as a newfound confidence swept over her. "After I spoke to Oswald, he couldn't make heads nor tails of what had happened. He came back a few days later and explained that he thought a creature called Ijiraq might be the culprit. He said it was an ancient monster that was said to kidnap people and that this creature is consistent with the evidence found at the scene."

"This information came directly from Oswald? There's nothing about him reaching that conclusion on file." A look of surprise came over Alister's face. This hadn't been the first inconsistency they had come across today.

"Mmmhhmm, I'm sorry, that's all I know, really." She explained.

Alister stood. "That's okay. You've been a tremendous help, and Sarah, I promise we will do everything in our power to bring your son home safely."

"Thank you so much!" She escorted him to the door, and he took his leave.

By the time he left, it was already dark out. An air of concern hit him as soon as he noticed Sai was no longer waiting outside. He looked around for a moment, but the streets were completely empty. *No doubt these Ijiraq rumors are making people more cautious about being out after dark.* He thought as he continued to look around each side of the home.

"Sai?" He projected his voice so it could be heard and then awaited a response. When none came, he decided that Sai must've headed back for Oswald's house when he noticed the sun setting. With this idea in mind, Alister did the same and headed off into the thick fog that was quickly filling the streets.

*****

Sai reached Alicia's home just as the sun fell below the horizon. The thick fog had begun to crawl through the city streets as the warm air of the day was replaced by the coolness of the evening. Sai passed through the gate of the rough picket fence that surrounded the house, headed up the steps, and knocked on the front door. After waiting for a good five minutes with no answer, he gave another more forceful knock.

"Hello? Is anyone home!?" He shouted at the top of his lungs, but still no answer. He looked over to one of the widows and could see a light was on. Then out of the corner of his eye, Sai thought he saw a curtain move in the window just to the left of the one he was looking at. Although, when he looked over, nothing was there.

"Alicia? A friend sent me. I'm here to help." He shouted in the direction of the window, and again the curtain moved just slightly. A female face appeared and stared at him.

"Hey! I'm Sai. Can we talk?" Sai leaned over and spoke at a lower volume this time.

With those words, the figure darted away again.

"No, wait!" Shout shouted.

Suddenly, He heard the clicking of locks unlatching, and the front door creaked open slightly. A girl with unnaturally blue hair appeared in the empty space between the door and the frame. "What do you want?"

"Oh, I guess you couldn't hear me. I'm Sai and.."

She stopped him. "I heard you, and keep your voice down. Are you looking to get taken?"

"Oh, no. I'm sorry! I'm actually here with a group that's looking to put an end to those very abductions. We have almost no leads to go on, even after talking to everyone in our files. I was hoping you could help me clear up what's actually going on around here."

She opened the door, and for the first time, Sai could see whom he was talking to. She was a tall girl with shoulder-length blue hair and brown eyes. He figured she must be around her mid-twenties. Her hands were wrapped up in white bandages that ran all the way up her arms and into the sleeves of her pale yellow tunic.

"Thank you." Sai stepped inside, and she locked the door behind him.

"Let's talk in here." She walked ahead of him and took a seat in a large living area with only a couple of pale blue cushiony chairs.

Sai followed suit and took a seat on the plush chair across from her. "So, what can you tell me about last night?"

"First, I need you to promise me one thing. You can't call me crazy." She looked him directly in the eyes and spoke as seriously as possible.

"Of course. I would never."

"Everyone else did. My family, my friends, everyone…." She looked down as tears filled her eyes.

Sai stood and placed a hand on her shoulder. "I don't think you're crazy. If I did, would I be here?"

She looked up at him, peering into his eyes for any sign of deception. "Okay."

"Thank you, let's start with why you were out last night."

"Okay, well, every other evening for the past few months, I have been volunteering at the orphanage here in town. Sometimes, I'll bring them groceries or healing potions when they need them. Well, last night, I received news that one of the kids had gotten hurt, and they didn't have any more potions to help treat them. I had heard about the abductions and even the monster, but I thought they were just rumors." She began to fidget anxiously, wringing her wrapped hands back and forth.

"Are you okay?"

"Yeah, sorry." She took a deep breath. "Anyway, I had headed out to gather the potions from a nearby shop. After I retrieved them, I was approached by a large man in a dark cloak. I couldn't see his face because he had it covered by a shroud."

Origins

This explanation confused Sai. "Wait, I thought you were attacked by this 'Ijiraq' monster. Was it actually the cloaked figure who attacked you?"

She shuttered. "I'm getting to that. As I rounded a corner about a block away from the shop, he approached me, tome in hand. I felt like I recognized his voice, but with his face covered, I couldn't tell who he was." She began to paint a vivid image of the event.

*****

"You, I sense amazing potential in you. I can unlock that potential for you. Come with me." The mysterious figure held out his hand, beckoning Alicia to take it.

She stepped back, noting the dark grey tome that he held in his other hand. "What are you on about? Who even are you?"

"Someone who needs you. Now please come with me." Forcefully he reached toward her.

Dodging the hand, she took another step back as the oil lantern in her hand swayed back and forth. "Back off, creep! I'm not going anywhere with you! Now leave me alone." She stepped past him and began walking away quickly.

"Why do they always refuse?" The man growled. "Behind every exquisite thing that existed, there was something tragic. Now Awaken Dorian Gray!" With these words, the cloaked figure transformed into a giant monster. Massive antlers sprouted from his head, his feet were replaced by enormous hooves, and his once human face took on the visage of monstrous deer. On top of all of this, he was huge, at least ten feet tall, and he was lunging for Alicia.

She turned just as the monster thrust one giant hand in her direction. As she pivoted, his hand connected with the oil lantern she was carrying. In an instant, the lantern exploded. Shattered glass sliced into her hands as flaming oil doused her arms up to her elbows.

The giant creature wasn't spared either. His hand was slashed deeply, and a large amount of oil ignited across his palm. He reared back, howling in pain. As he recoiled, Alicia found her footing and took off as fast as she could. As she ran, the howls grew fainter and fainter until she could see the fence surrounding her home. She burst through the front door and *collapsed on the floor of the entryway. Her hands were bleeding profusely. The pain was blinding. Her palms felt white hot and began to blister. Before she could even gather the strength to stand and staunch them, she passed out cold.*

*****

"I woke up in a puddle of my own blood. My bleeding slowed but hadn't stopped, and my hands and arms felt like they were on fire. Somehow, however, none of the glass had been embedded itself in them. I was able to get the potion from my inventory, but as soon as I grabbed it, I dropped it from the intense pain. It spilled all over the floor. Luckily I was able to place my palms in what remained of the potion, which closed my wounds and slightly healed my burns. Unfortunately, it wasn't enough; I was forced to wrap them up and let them heal the old-fashioned way." She held out her bandaged hands in front of her and examined the rough wraps.

"I'm so sorry. I know someone who has a few of those potions. I'll bring you one first thing in the morning." Sai said kindly. As he continued, that smile turned into a much more serious look. "You said you recognized his voice?"

"Yes, I know I've heard it before. I think he's someone who lives here in town." She explained.

"And you haven't talked to Oswald about this? He's the guy running the investigation."

"No, again, everyone I've told thought I was lying or crazy. I was beginning to think so myself." She looked down at her bandages again. "These wounds are the only proof I have."

"I believe you," Sai said reassuringly. "So we're looking for someone with a large injury on their ha…." Sai stopped mid-sentence as his mind raced back to breakfast that morning and Oswald's burnt hand. "Wait, do you know which hand you injured?"

"It had to be…. the left? I'm not exactly sure; it all happened so fast. I'm sorry."

Sai stood quickly as the realization of what was actually happening broke open like a dropped egg. "I have to go!" Sai bolted for the door as he remembered the joke he had made at Amy's expense. *And tell me, who's gonna keep him away from you?* Sai shook this thought away as he sprinted on.

"Wait… Sai!" The shout fell on deaf ears as he burst out into the cold, foggy night. He sprinted full bore through the streets toward Oswald's home.

Chapter 11: Untimely Revelation

As Alister arrived at Oswald's home, he quickly realized that the place was completely empty. Neither Sai nor the girls and Oswald had made it back yet. The light of the full moon illuminated the front room as Alister looked around for matches to light the few lanterns that hung around the walls. Riffling through a drawer in the kitchen, he stumbled across a lone match. Scraping it across the countertop, it ignited, and he carried it over to a handheld lantern which he promptly lit. He shuffled through a few papers that lay on the kitchen table, finding a few ads, flyers, and simple town notices but nothing of any real significance.

He sat the pages down and walked toward the living room. Near the fireplace, something peculiar caught his eye. Looking up, he raised his lantern to illuminate the large portrait. The gorgeous figure from before had all but vanished. In its place stood something far more horrifying.

Suddenly, the front door slammed open. A gust of wind threatened to extinguish the small flame of the lantern as he turned toward the disruption.

"Alister! It's Oswald!" Sai's voice was a razor blade slashing through the darkness.

"I know." Alister, pale as a ghost, turned back to the portrait again, which revealed a monstrous deer with glowing red eyes. "We need to go now!" He rushed to the door, and the two darted off into the streets in search of their missing comrades and the kidnapper they had gone away with that morning.

"Where could they be?" Worry clouded Sai's every thought. This was a scenario no one had predicted, and it had been hours. They could be anywhere at this point.

"We'll start by checking the final few places they needed to go. If we're in luck, we may find them before he makes a move against them." Alister explained as calmly as he could, but it was clear he was worried too.

"He could be long gone with them by now. How do we know he didn't take them right off the bat?" Sai stammered.

"All of the attacks have taken place after dark. Oswald has too much of a reputation in this town to risk being outed as the monster. The odds are that he hasn't taken them yet, because the sun only went down a little while ago. Now that it's dark and visibility is low, all bets are off. We need to hurry!"

They rounded the corner and headed for the shopping district. As they turned another corner, they entered a largely empty street lined with shops that were all but abandoned.

They scanned the open street but spotted nothing. "Amy! Michelle!" Sai's shout echoed off of the vacant walls.

"Help!" A scream ripped through the high street.

Instantly they scrambled in the direction of the scream. Before they even made it to the alleyway, the sickly sweet metallic smell of honey and blood filled their nostrils. As they flew around the side of a nearby shop, they saw what they had feared the most. Standing in the alley between two of the shops was a hulking mass of fur and muscle. Over his massive right shoulder dangled an unconscious Amy. Behind him, he dragged Michelle. Her jet black hair gripped tightly in his clearly injured left hand. She thrashed and screamed as he dragged her toward a solid brick wall at the other end.

Sai charged in without a thought. In a full-on sprint, he pulled his tome from its holster and shouted. "Natural selection, as we shall…." He was cut off as he took one step too close.

The monster let out a blood-curdling howl as he pivoted on his hooves, swung Michelle by her hair, and slammed her body into Sai. The blow ripped him off his feet and threw him into the stone wall of one of the shops. His vision rippled as the air was ejected from his lungs. The snapping of nearly every bone in his body echoed in his ears as he slumped down against the wall helplessly. Blood flowed from his mouth, and he watched the monstrous Oswald turn away once again, Michelle's limp body trailing behind him. Wordlessly he headed once again for the back wall.

Just as he reached the end of the alley, Alister shouted," Oswald, stop!" He drew his tome forward before realizing he couldn't attack without also harming Michelle, Amy, and now Sai.

The monster halted momentarily before looking back at his former master. The cold merciless look in his eyes shook Alister in the worst way possible. "If you want them, come and get them." He said flatly.

"Sai, Please..." Michelle reached her hand out with her last bit of strength. She passed out just as the beast stepped seamlessly through the wall with both the girls in tow.

Sai's bones creaked as he stood with the sheer force of his will. So much pain echoed throughout his body, but hollow as a drum, he inched forward. Slowly he found his way forward. His vision drifted in and out of focus, and he held out his hand as he approached the wall. The tips of his fingers barely touched it, only to find it was solid once again, and the last bit of strength left his body.

"No..." The word fell out with a whimper as he crumpled face-first into the wall, sliding onto the cold, dusty ground.

*****

Sai awoke to find himself lying on the floor of his room back at Oswald's house. Sitting up, he saw something he didn't expect. Michelle was sitting at the foot of his bed, staring at him.

"So, you're finally awake?" She smiled as she spoke in a calm, soothing voice.

"Huh, was I dreaming," Sai questioned as he looked her over. "Was none of that actually real?"

"Shhhhh!" Michelle scolded," We don't want to wake her now, do we?" She pointed to the bed. "She's so cute when she's sleeping."

Origins

Sai looked at her curiously as he found his feet. In his bed lay Amy. Her fiery red hair stood out against the white pillowcases. Suddenly, she stirred, which caused Sai to take a step back.

"Oh, Now look what you've done; you really are hopeless, Sai," Michelle said as she stood up from the bed.

Amy sat up and stared at him. "What are you doing in my room?"

"What, no, this is…" Sai was cut off by a loud pounding on the door.

"Sai!" A voice from the other side shouted.

Turning toward the door, he heard another shout behind him, this time from Michelle. "Sai!"

He whipped back around just to be shouted at again but this time by Amy. "Sai!" This shout echoed off the walls and seemed to amplify in volume with each passing ricochet. Before he could even make heads or tails of what was happening, he was being bombarded by increasingly loud shouts. They echoed back and forth over and over again. They were coming from all directions now, and Sai was forced to cover his ears out of sheer pain. He collapsed to the floor and writhed there for a moment before a loud bang cut through all of the other noises.

He sat up with a jerk, and presently he found himself in his bed at Oswald's house. He looked around, but the room was completely empty, with neither Amy nor Michelle in sight. He held his head for a moment remembering the events of the previous night. The girls were gone, and he couldn't do anything to save them.

Then another loud thud caught his attention. It seemed to come from downstairs. Dropping his feet to the floor, he steadied himself as he stood. His body felt insanely sore, but other than that, he was uninjured. Making his way to the door, he could hear murmuring as someone riffled through the downstairs drawers and cabinets. He stepped out of the room and headed down the hall toward the staircase. About halfway down the stairs, he found the culprit.

"Damn it!" Alister threw a load of papers from a drawer near the kitchen, and they scattered across the living room floor upon impact. He looked disheveled like he hadn't slept in days. Placing his forehead on the kitchen counter, he took a deep breath before noticing Sai descending the steps.

"You're awake." He murmured as he straightened up in an attempt to seem composed. "Last thing we need is to lose you too."

"How long have I been out?" Sai questioned as he stepped down into the disaster that was the living room. Looking up, he noticed that the painting above the fireplace had turned into a simple white framed canvas. Its image had disappeared along with Oswald.

Alister stepped out of the kitchen and into the living room. "Two days. After you charged in after him, Oswald broke nearly every bone in your body and damaged most of your vital organs. I administered 'Typhon 'to you, which brought you back from the brink."

"Typhon? What do you mean?"

"It's an extremely rare and powerful elixir. It's used to heal people who are far beyond the point of saving." Alister picked up a toppled chair near the table adjacent to the fireplace. "It's extremely dangerous, however. Most people will succumb to its powerful effects, which can cause the heart to stop."

"If it's that rare, then why would you give it to me? You could've been rid of someone you can't bring yourself to trust. So why?" Sai's tone was somber and serious.

"I was wrong. I'm always wrong." The sudden admission surprised Sai. "I doubted you, the boy who charged blindly into the fray to save his friends. The boy who stepped up to fight even when I, a master tome user, stood frozen by my own sentiment. I trusted Oswald, and it cost us dearly. So, for now, I'm placing my trust in you. Don't make me regret it." Alister sat back in the chair as he spoke.

Sai stepped forward with a newfound vigor. "Well, that's a long way from friendship, but we need each other. So master, what now?"

Origins

Alister rubbed his aching head. "Well, first, we need to find some trace of where Oswald took the girls. That's why I've been tearing this place apart. I'm looking for anything that can help us. It's clear to me that he's working with someone. Since he's not a tome user, he must have someone helping him to transform into that creature."

"No, He has a tome, or so I've been told." Sai rebutted.

"Excuse me? For all the years I've known him, the boy has never been a wielder. What makes you think he's one now?" He asked skeptically.

Sai went on to explain where he had gone the other night, how he had met Alicia, and how the information she had given him had revealed Oswald as the culprit. As Sai reached the point in the story about the tome and the lines Oswald had read from it, Alister's eyes became piercing daggers of white-hot rage.

"Impossible!" Alister spat through his teeth. "Awaken Dorian Gray? She was certain he said those words exactly?" His voice dripped with disdain.

Sai was taken aback by how angry he seemed. "Yes, I'm certain that's what she told me. Do you know that tome somehow?"

"I did…"

"Well, I promised the girl who told me that I would come back and bring her a healing potion. We could go do that now, and you can ask her yourself if you like."

"Yes, let's." Alister brushed a few loose hairs out of his face. Reaching into his inventory, he pulled out a vial of green liquid that was similar to what Cylus had given Sai before his trial. Sliding the vail across the table, Alister spoke again. "Let's go." He stood and walked past Sai in the direction of the door.

Sai grasped the bottle and followed him. They headed across town toward Alicia's house. Sai stepped up the stairs and gave the door a quick tap. And once again, Alicia poked her head out of the curtain in the front room. Sai gave a quick wave as he saw her, and she vanished as quickly as she had appeared. The next thing Sai knew, he could hear the locks on the front door unbolting.

She cracked the door slightly. "You again?"

"Ummm yeah, I brought you that potion I promised you." Sai held up the clear vial so she could see it.

"It's been days. I thought you weren't coming back." She said, looking toward the floorboards.

"Sorry, we got kind of tied up fighting the monster that attacked you."

All the blood seemed to drain from her face at the mention of Ijiraq. "You fought him? And you're here? Does that mean you were able to stop him?"

Sai shook his head as he looked down. "May we come in and talk?"

With a nod, she opened the door and let the two men enter.

"This is Alister; he's my squad leader on this mission." Sai gestured to Alister, who was already looking a bit better than when they had left the house. He certainly knew how to appear put together even while he was falling apart inside.

"Hello. It's very nice to meet you. Sai told me about how you helped him out. Thank you for that." Alister's voice was calm and concise.

Alicia looked at him blankly. "Of course. I was hoping it would help you get to the bottom of all of this." She looked at Sai as she placed her hand down on the back of a chair without thinking. "Arggg!" The pained sound slipped out as she winced.

Sai jumped at the sound. "Are you okay?"

She lifted her hand from the surface and gripped it with her other one. "Yeah, I'm all right, but would you mind giving me that potion now?" She said with a slightly pained smile.

"Oh. Yes, of course!" Sai popped the cork out of the vial and handed it to her.

She gulped the liquid down and let out a sigh of relief as the pain in her arms washed away. Reaching up, she grasped at the wraps that ran up into the short sleeve of her tunic. With a tug, the wraps began to loosen before falling down her arms and to the floor. Her arms looked perfect. Not a burn or a scar remained on her olive skin.

"Thank the gods." She examined her palms as she touched the once-tender areas with the tips of her fingers.

"Now, since we've done you a favor, would you mind answering some questions for me?" Alister asked with an oddly charming smile.

"Yes, I'll help in any way I can." She explained as she crossed her arms. "What would you like to know?"

"Why don't you start from the beginning? I'd like to hear this story directly from its source."

"Sure." Alicia relayed the same story she had told Sai. How she had headed out after dark, how Oswald had attacked, the tome, its exact lines, and how miraculously she had escaped.

"You're certain those are the words he used to activate the tome?" Alister questioned.

"Yes, I'll never forget them. I hear them in my sleep even," she replied as she looked toward the floorboards vacantly.

"I'm sorry you've been through so much." Alister placed his hand on her shoulder. "We're going to put an end to this. No need to worry anymore." His concern and drive seemed genuine. This was no ordinary promise from a stranger. This was an oath of absolution for the sins of his former student.

"Sai, it's time to go; we're heading back to the mansion. Thank you for everything you've done." Lowering his hand, he turned and headed for the door.

Sai followed quickly after him. "Thank you for everything, Alicia."

"Hey, wait!" She shouted. "You didn't tell me where you were going before, and now you tell me you fought that monster. What happened?"

Origins

Sai's breath caught in his chest as he stopped in his tracks. Without turning around, he gripped the front of his shirt tightly as he spoke. "We lost."

The long walk back to the mansion was quiet. Alister had transformed yet again. The anger within him was palpable, surrounding him like fog over a moor. As the two rounded the block, the large mansion came into view, and on the front step sat a figure clad in fine white robes. Her chest and left arm were covered in blue and gold-plated armor. She wore a matching white and gold helmet which obscured her face. When she noticed them approaching, she stood up slowly.

"Alister, there you are. Where have you been?"

"Umbra? Did Cylus send you as backup? Sai and I were just speaking to a lead in our case." Alister explained quickly.

"Not exactly; he feels that you are too close to your target. He asked me to bring you back to The Citadel."

"And what of my missing students? Oswald has…"

She put her hand up and stopped him flat. "Cylus feels that we have bigger fish to fry. You're coming back with me, and another inquisitor will handle this case." She spoke sternly.

"Hold on; you expect us to just abandon my friends!?" Sai shouted.

Alister put his hand out and gestured for Sai to be quiet. "Watch your tone. You're speaking to a Grand Inquisitor." Lowering his hand, he continued. "Very well, we'll go with you. We'll need some time to gather our belongings and any evidence we have here on the case. Can you give us a day to get our affairs in order before we head back?"

"Cylus's orders were for an immediate return." She replied forcefully.

"While I understand that if we leave without all our evidence, Oswald may return and destroy what little we do have. I implore you to give us the rest of the day. We can go first thing tomorrow morning."

She sighed in exasperation. "Fine, but as soon as the sun comes up, we're on our way back, with or without your evidence." She commanded.

"Of course. Thank you for your patience and understanding." Alister bowed slightly.

With a quick wave, Umbra walked past him.

"I'm going to find a secure place to stay and contact Master Cylus, be ready first thing tomorrow morning."

Alister straightened up and, without another word, walked up the steps and into the home.

Sai followed behind him, anger bubbling in his chest," So, that's it? You're giving up on them just like that? You're a coward."

Alister glanced back at him hollowly. "We must follow our orders. Go and pack your things."

"What is wrong with you people?! Orders this and orders that. That mentality nearly got Michelle left back in Iapetus. The girls need us, and you give up on them just because you were told to?!"

"Our Orders…"

"Screw our orders! My friends, your students could be dead by the time backup gets to them!

"Cylus would never allow."

Sai cut him off again. "And screw you! I thought you'd changed!" Sai grabbed a brown bottle full of liquid from the table and, without a thought, threw it as hard as he could into the canvas that hung above the fireplace. It shook violently before collapsing to the floor, the frame shattering upon impact.

He grabbed Alister's collar and yanked him forward, his rage blinding his every sense. "You'd leave them for dead just like Sibyl?" Sai realized the line he'd crossed in an instant.

"And what the hell do you think you'd know about it!?" Alister grabbed Sai's arm and squeezed with an enormous amount of strength. Sai's grip failed as he was lifted off the ground and sent reeling head over heels into the empty fireplace. Stepping around the table, Alister approached slowly. "You will keep my daughters' name out of your damn mouth." Sai knew it was over. Alister had had enough, and nothing could put those words back. Then suddenly, Alister stopped. His attention was drawn elsewhere as he stared at the space where the painting once hung. A new revelation fell upon him. A crude wooden door hung conspicuously at the center of the chimney where the old portrait had once been.

Sai moved to find his feet and scrabbled out into the room, caught off guard by Alister's abrupt stop. "What, have a change of heart?"

Alister took a deep breath to compose himself. "Enough, have a look at this." Alister pointed to the raised door. "Hold on." He stuck his head into the fireplace," Look here."

Looking up, they could see that the chimney was actually sealed off a few feet above the entrance. "It's a false fireplace?" Sai asked.

"Looks like a hidden room. Grab a chair; let's see if we can get that door open." Alister said as he stepped out and stood.

Sai did as he was told and handed him a chair from the nearby table. Sliding the chair over, Alister stepped onto it and gave a tug on the rope handle that was fastened to the door. It swung open easily to reveal a pull-out ladder. He extended the ladder, and the two entered the room above.

Several books and loose pages were littered all over the floor. Many small tables also covered in papers sat along the walls. A large desk sat at the far end of the room with a single piece of paper and an ink well at its center.

Sai walked over and picked up the singular page. On it was a note addressed to Oswald.

Oswald,

Our goal is within our grasp. We just need a few more tomes. Fortunately for us, it has come to my attention that your former master has made contact with the girl from Dione.

There is no doubt that if she's with him, she will surely be making her way to The Citadel. I'm asking that you draw them to Elara. There I need you to capture the girl and, if you can, Alister. Do this for me, and I will fulfill our contract once and for all.

- R

"Alister." Sai held the note out. "This R? Do you think it could be Roark."

Grasping at the note, Alister looked it over carefully. "They were after Michelle and me?" He slammed his fist on the desk. "Why would they want the girl, and what do they mean they need a few more tomes?"

"We have to go after them. Oswald is working with the man from Dione, and he's going to give Amy and Michelle over to that maniac!" Sai shouted.

"And he's using Sibyl's tome to do it." Alister's voice shook with rage.

"Wait, Sibyl? I didn't think it was possible to use someone else's book?" Sai questioned.

"I didn't think so either, but somehow he is. 'Dorian Gray' was her tome. She used it to change her appearance, among other things, and now I think he's using it to help this madman kidnap possible tome users from this town."

"But why?" Sai questioned.

"I don't know."

"So, what are we going to do?" Sai said sharply.

Alister paused for a moment. His mind swam with memories of his former students. Grief, rage, and sadness all culminated in his chest to form his next words. He straightened up and spoke decisively. "Orders be damned, we're going."

Chapter 12: Zaman

Together Sai and Alister scoured the hidden room, gathering anything and everything they could use to identify and locate Oswald and Roark. As they dug, Alister took a small step back and straightened his back. As he stood, the floorboard beneath his left foot squeaked loudly. Regarding this as odd, he bent down to inspect it. He knocked on the board and could hear a hollow echo reverberate back from the other side. Running his fingers across the edge of the floorboard, his index finger caught a small divot, and with a slight tug, the board creaked upward, revealing a small hidden space which held a violet crystal. The crystal was fastened snugly into a cushioned slot built into the floor. Next to it was another slot that sat empty. He grasped the gem and stood once again.

"Sai, look at this."

Sai stepped over with an armload of papers and books. "What is that?

"It looks like a warp crystal." Alister reached back into a pouch attached to the back of his pants and drew out a similar-looking blue crystal. He held it up next to the other stone. "It's a different color, but I'm certain that's what it is."

Sai looked at both questioningly. "A warp crystal?"

"It's an item used to open a warp gate anywhere. It can essentially teleport its user anywhere it's been linked to."

Sai's expression was one of shock. "So, that wall wasn't a normal warp gate Oswald used? Is that why I couldn't pass through? Does that mean what I think it means?"

"If you're thinking we can use it to follow him, then perhaps, yes. At least, I believe so." He clutched the crystals tightly before returning both to his storage.

Origins

Suddenly Sai's tome began to shake violently at his hip. A faint chirping noise could be heard coming from the pages.

"What on earth?" He took the tome from its holster, and it popped open in his hands. With a small puff of smoke, the tiny brown finch burst out and landed on Sai's shoulder. "Oh, Charlie? How did you get out? I didn't summon you." The bird continued chirping loudly on his shoulder.

"You named it?" Alister looked at him unamused.

"Of course. He and I are partners, aren't we? It's only fitting to give him a name." Sai explained matter of factly as the bird's chirps began to get louder and louder.

"Well, whatever the case, what's its problem?" Alister covered his ears as the bird's volume continued to amplify.

"How should I know? I don't speak bird." The sentence had just left his mouth as an idea popped into his head. "Oh wait!" Sai placed one hand over the animal as he concentrated.

"Man selects only for his own good: Nature only for that of the being which she tends. Awaken Origins!" The same smoke from before enveloped the finch, causing yet another transformation. As the smoke cleared, The finch's brownish down had been replaced by bright green feathers. He was slightly larger, and most importantly, his chirps had been replaced by nearly human speech.

"Oh good, another bird," Alister said mockingly before turning away in exasperation to gather more evidence.

"He's a…" Sai paused as the word took a second to materialize from somewhere far off in his consciousness. "Parrot! They can mimic human speech." He wanted to explain further but was cut off by the birds squawking.

"Eighty-four! Eighty-four! Watching! Watching!" Charlie screeched repeatedly.

Alister's eyes got wide as the truth of what was happening poured over him like a waterfall.

Origins

"He can sense it!? Quickly Sai, return him to your tome and gather anything you can. We need to leave now!"

Sai did as he was told and scrambled around the room, gathering any and all evidence he could find that could help them. As they shuffled around the room, they heard a sudden pounding on the front door.

Alister turned back as he heard the noise echo throughout the house. "Looks like we're gonna have company. Ready yourself, Sai!"

The two of them packed what they could into their inventories and leaped down into the living room just as another round of hits struck the door. They each drew their tomes and readied themselves; Sai, his closed tome, and Alister with his harpoon. What came next took the wind out of their sails instantly. The doors flew open, and instead of an armed inquisitor, they saw someone that shocked them even more.

"Oh, thank the gods." Alicia stood in the gaping doorway, her blue hair glowing incandescently in the bright sunlight." They're coming; we need to hurry."

Sai lowered his tome." Alicia? What are you doing here?"

"We don't have time. I'll explain later!" She rushed toward them as she reached into a pouch behind her back.

"Awaken Observations!" A bolt of ionized gas ripped through the air, blinded the group, and made contact with a small metal ornament that sat atop the door frame. The following explosion of sound and heat blasted the group backward toward the faux fireplace.

"You dare defy Master Cylus!?" A black silhouette floated down through the smoke and landed on the ground outside of the mansion. It was Umbra. In her left hand, above her head, was what looked like a large diamond. In her right was what seemed to be some kind of small key-like object. Her voice broke through the thick smoke which was filling the room by the second. "You will pay for your insolence! 'When electrical fire strikes thro' a body, it acts upon the common fire contained in it." She raised the small metal object in her hand and pointed it at the group. "Now, Awaken!"

Before she could finish the incantation, Sai felt a hand grip tightly on his bicep. He looked over just in time to see Alicia with a green crystal clutched between her teeth. Her other hand was gripping Alister's shirt as she bit down hard on the stone. The visceral crunching sound that followed made it abundantly clear that this was not the proper way to activate a warp crystal. Sai only had seconds to contemplate this as the stone shattered with a blinding flash of emerald light, and they seemingly fell through the floor.

The first sensation that registered with Sai was the sound of a hooting owl in the distance, then came the cold. As Sai opened his eyes, he realized it was pitch black out and It was freezing. They were sitting in at least a foot and a half of snow, and as he looked over, he saw Alister, harpoon in hand.

He was straddling Alicia with his hand on her throat. "Who the hell are you!?" He raised the harpoon threateningly.

"Can't… Can't breathe." She gasped beneath his grip.

Getting to his feet, Sai threw his shoulder into Alister's side, knocking him off of Alicia. The girl coughed and writhed on the ground.

"What are you thinking? She just saved our lives." Sai shouted.

Alister groaned as he dug himself out of the deep snow. "Your new friend's clearly not whom she's claimed to be." He rose to his feet and approached her before Sai stepped between them.

Putting both arms straight out, Sai shouted. "Alister, stop! Think about this for just a second! Yes, maybe she's more than she let on, but she at least bought us time. Cylus can't use Eighty-four again for a while, right? We can use that time to find and save Michelle and Amy. We need to give her a chance to explain. We owe her that much, at least."

Alister growled through his teeth. " Fine, I'll trust your judgment this time, but don't think for one moment that I trust this girl." He turned toward Alicia, who still lay gasping in the deep snow. "If you give me so much as an inkling that you are working with Oswald, I will put you down without hesitation."

Alicia sat up, rubbing her swollen, sore throat. "Man, I'm sure glad I brought you along."

"You'd better start talking, or you'll be a whole lot less 'glad' about it." Alister snapped." Why drop us in the middle of nowhere? All you've done is prolonged the inevitable."

"For your information, we're not in the middle of nowhere. I do have an actual plan." Alicia got to her feet and knocked the snow off her pants and shirt. "Come on, follow me." She trudged through the thick snow for a few yards before coming to a large spruce tree.

She placed her hand on the side of the trunk, found a grip, and gave a forceful tug. With a massive creak, the trunk opened like a door to reveal a hollow steel interior. The floor inside was nothing more than a small platform with an attached spiral staircase that descended into the darkness. As the group made their way down, it got warmer and warmer until they reached the bottom. The staircase opened to a small room with a rectangular doorway built into the side of a stone wall. Within the stone frame sat a heavy steel door with a sliding metal grille about three-fourths of the way up.

"We're here." She gave the door three hard raps as she spoke. The small door grille opened, revealing a pair of jade-green eyes. "I brought the wielders you asked about." The grille slammed back shut, and the sound of multiple locks and latches could be heard from the other side.

The door opened slowly, and before the group stood a tall, blonde-haired woman. She looked to be in her early thirties and wore a tight, form-fitting red sweater and blue jeans. Over the sweater, she wore an open lab coat which hung loosely around her buxom frame. At first glance, Sai thought she seemed like the exact opposite of

Cylus. Where his aura seemed cold and menacing, hers instead seemed warm and welcoming. Even her voice came across as charming and charismatic.

"Welcome; I'm glad Alice made it in time. My name's Zaman. Please come in." She stepped to the side to let the group pass.

"Alice?" Sai questioned.

"Just a nickname," Alicia replied.

As they entered, the room came into full view. It was decorated in the style of a quaint little cabin. The walls and floor were made from well-treated pine, which gave the entire house the scent of an alpine forest. A small fire burned in a nearby hearth with a large hardwood mantle. A beautifully ornate hourglass sat atop the mantle among other mementos. One of these items caught Sai's attention. It was a large wooden ring with an intricate, almost spiderweb-like pattern of strings running through its center. *"dream…."* The word appeared in his mind and faded just as fast. His attention was soon drawn to the fire, which was warming the immediate area and keeping the home livable in the harsh environment. Fine cushioned chairs and a coffee table with an ornamental tea set sat in front of the fire.

"Please, have a seat. Can I get you some tea?" Zaman gestured toward the area in front of the fire.

Sai and Alister took a seat as Zaman poured a steaming amber liquid from the teapot into several cups positioned on the table. She gently lifted the glasses and handed one to each person before taking her seat in the largest of the chairs.

Sai took one sip of the tea, and his eyes lit up. The floral flavor and heat filled his mouth and warmed his entire body as he swallowed. "Wow! This is amazing."

Zaman sipped her tea. "It's some of the finest in the world. I had to have Alice travel all the way to Callisto to find some."

Alister was beginning to get annoyed and placed his glass on the table. "Okay, enough." He sat back in his seat. "What are we doing here? Do you even realize the kind of danger you just put yourself and your associate in?"

Zaman pulled the cup from her lips and placed it on the table. Sitting back in her chair, she crossed her legs. "Danger, huh?" She seemed almost amused by this concept. "You assume Cylus knows where you are or that he can even find you here?"

"You know, Master Cylus? Then you must also know that he's all-seeing, correct?" Alister looked at her skeptically. "By bringing us here, you've signed your own death warrant."

This drew forth an audible laugh. "Is that what he told you? Yes, he can see any and all things, but only along the time stream that he is locked within. And only across the main continent, really, but that part doesn't matter in this circumstance."

By this point, Sai was completely lost. He could keep track when Cylus was simply able to see anything in the world at any time, but with these new revelations, his mind was swimming.

"Huh?" it wasn't his most elegant response, but it was all he could muster at the moment.

"Yeah, okay. What makes you an expert on his abilities?" Alister rolled his eyes incredulously as he rubbed the bridge of his nose with a groan.

She laughed again." Yeah, I suppose I wouldn't believe me either. Especially not if I lived my whole life under my grandfather's thumb."

Sai choked on his tea, and after a brief coughing fit, he responded. "Grandfather? You don't mean Cylus?"

"Actually, I do. Well, he was before he sacrificed me to the tome. When it consumed me, he accepted that I had darkness in my heart and turned his back on me."

"You're saying you escaped a tome after it consumed you? Is that even possible?" Sai leaned forward as her words gripped his attention. He threw a questioning glance at Alister.

He shook his head in response. "No. When you're taken by the tome, that's it. You're trapped within it eternally."

"Trapped? I thought it killed you?" Sai shouted. Alister just shook his head again.

"And I suppose Cylus told you that as well?" She smiled, her emerald eyes gentle as ever." It doesn't really matter if you believe me or not at the end of the day."

"We're going in circles. Why bring us here? What do you want?" Alister slammed his hand on the table for emphasis.

Zaman lifted her teacup again and took a long sip before speaking. "I want to help you."

"Help us? What are you playing at? Get to the point already!" Alister said as he leaned forward in his seat.

"Are you always in such a hurry? You should learn to relax, unwind for a minute." She spoke in a nonchalant and unburdened manner.

"Stop wasting our time with this nonsense!"

Sai placed his hand on Alister's shoulder. "Look, we appreciate your help, really we do. But, a couple of our friends were taken recently, and we're really in a hurry to help them."

"But that's just the point. I'm not wasting any time. Time's not even something you should be concerned with." She sat her cup down once again, and from beneath the tail of her lab coat, she pulled a gold-colored book.

Alister flew to his feet at the appearance of the new tome. "You're a tome wielder?"

She set the book on the table." Yes, I am. I already told you I took on the trial of the tome. Of course, I'm a tome wielder, an unchosen one even." She smiled up at him. "This tome is capable of creating concentrated temporal fields within a given area." She raised her hand and pointed to the hourglass that sat on the mantel above the fireplace. "I have done just that within this room. When you entered, you walked into my temporal field. However,

Origins

that hourglass is seated just outside of it. Tell me have you seen a single grain of sand fall since you've been here?"

Sai stared at the glass intently. Not a grain seemed to budge. Not even the ones that seemed to be mid-fall. They hovered in the lower half as if suspended by some invisible force. No matter how long he seemed to stare, the particles didn't so much as vibrate.

Alister looked back at her with a serious glare. "So this is what you meant. Cylus can't see us here because it's out of sync with the natural time stream. You've frozen time within this field."

"Close, but no cigar. You see, this room is designed specifically to create a feedback loop focused on the temporal field of my tome. It allows me to displace this area in time indefinitely. Furthermore, I can make time within this area pass at a much more accelerated rate. For reference, right now, for our purposes, I have it set to where one minute in the outside world is equal to roughly ten hours here. For all the time we've spent talking, barely any time has passed out there." She explained as she stood from her seat. "My thought is I can use my tome to allow you two to prepare and improve before you have to face this 'Oswald' again. That would greatly increase the odds of saving your friends, would it not?" That same charming smile crept across her face.

"It would!" Sai beamed with excitement. The newfound air of hope was hard for him to contain. "But how do you know about Oswald?"

She simply gestured to Alicia, who stood behind her. "Alice has told me all about it."

"What's the catch?" Alister's voice had a way of cutting down any sprigs of hope that were trying to crop up.

"Oh, no catch whatsoever. All I ask is that you put a stop to Oswald and the person he's working for. If those two aren't dealt with soon, they could become a real pain."

Alister's skepticism was graffitied across his face."May Sai and I have a moment to discuss this?"

119

"Please do. Alice, will you help me clean up these dishes?"

Alicia gave a quick nod and gathered dishes, which she swiftly carried toward the small kitchen area.

Alister gestured for Sai to come in close in order to speak. "There's something fishy going on here."

"You may be right, but I don't see that we have much of a choice here. Not to mention your judgment lately hasn't exactly been its sharpest." Sai spoke hesitantly. "When was the last time you slept?" Sai looked at him with concern.

Alister grimaced before easing back. "Three days." He growled. Taking a deep breath, he spoke again. "Perhaps you're right. I don't trust her, but we have basically no choice. We have to find the girls. That's making no mention of the inquisitors who are surely hunting us now."

"So, we trust her for now and use this time to find the strength to save Amy and Michelle?" Sai asked.

Alister agreed, and the two broke apart just as Zaman was coming back from the kitchen. "Have you decided?"

"Yes, we would appreciate your help. We will, however, need a much larger area to train." Alister's expression seemed much calmer and more composed now. It was clear he was trying as hard as he could to be rational.

"Good, we'll pack supplies, and we can use the forest above as your training ground. However, I must warn you the larger the temporal field, the less time I can maintain it. I can perhaps buy you six hours of training time on the surface."

"So six hours in the real world, huh? If one minute is equal to ten hours inside, that would be…" He held up his hands as if he was counting on his fingers.

"Roughly five months outside," Alister said matter of factly.

"Approximately one hundred and fifty days, give or take." She replied. "You also need to realize that given the energy required to pull this off, my tome will go dormant for nearly double the amount of real-world time you spend inside. That means you get one shot at this. Afterward, I will need to return here and will be unable to offer you further assistance."

"Understood." Alister and Sai both nodded in unison.

"With all settled, I suppose it's time we prepare," Zaman instructed.

After all the supplies and materials were gathered and packed away, the group sat down once again and went over how the training would proceed. First, they would make their way to the surface and find a suitable location in the woods. Next, Zaman would activate the temporal field. They would then set up their tents and train day in and day out. Zaman and Alicia would accompany them during their training to offer support as well as hide their presence from The Citadel. The discussion of plans went on for a few hours before they were all on the same page.

They continued to talk for a bit, sipping on their tea as they did. Before long, Alister's head lolled slightly as he began to nod off. Three days was all he could muster without sleep, and yet he was still fighting it.

"Alister, why don't you go ahead and get some rest? We're going to need you in top shape going into this." Sai suggested.

Alister just stared at him flatly.

"Yes, perhaps you should." Zaman echoed in agreement.

"I'm fine." He snapped.

"Look, trust me or don't; it doesn't matter to me. But, if you don't rest soon, the effects of it will get far worse."

"Yeah, and what makes you such an expert?"

"Experience, actually." She retorted. "Let me take a wild stab at this. Judging by the bags under your eyes, you haven't slept in a few days at least. The first night without sleep, you began to feel extremely tired and irritable, right? After about two days, you began to forget minor details of the things you observed, and your decision-making seemed to be impaired. Now you're going on, what day, three or four? You can feel it can't you? Your stress levels are building to a fever pitch. You're even beginning to feel slight paranoia creeping up on you? I'd assume that's part of why you're so combative even."

"Nah, that last part's just him normally." Sai nudged him sarcastically.

Alister gave him a disapproving glance. There were no flaws in Zaman's argument, and he could clearly see that she was right. Since the girls had been taken, he hadn't slept a wink. He had lost his cool while digging for evidence, jumped Alicia after she had saved their lives, and now he was being belligerent to every word Zaman uttered.

He let out a begrudging sigh before standing from his seat. "Fine."

"Good." Zaman nodded with a smile. "Alice, would you mind showing him to his room?"

"Yes, ma'am," Alicia replied as she gestured for Alister to follow her to a room just off from the main one.

The two walked to the far end of the room and went through a wooden door. It creaked loudly as it closed behind them.

"So," Zaman spoke as she leaned the side of her head on her knuckles. "He's a basket of fun to have around, isn't he?"

Sai chuckled. "I used to think like that too, but lately, I've been learning a lot about him. He's been through a lot, and not just these past few days; I'm starting to think his whole life has been one trial after another. Gotta keep telling myself to take it easy on him."

"You don't say?" She asked curiously.

"Well, from what I understand, a while back, he lost his daughter. Then this week alone, he lost two of the wielders he was told to protect. Not only that, but the person who took them turned out to be his former student, Oswald. That's making no mention of the fact that Oswald is somehow using the tome of Alister's deceased daughter,

Origins

Sibyl, to do it." Sai explained, looking down at the floor. "Honestly, I think Alister feels guilty. I think that he feels like it's his fault Amy and Michelle are gone."

"Sounds like he's been through a lot." She looked down at her teacup solemnly and watched as the ground leaves danced around the bottom of the glass. "Do you think that's why he accepted my help, desperation?"

"I'm not sure. It surprised me, honestly." Sai looked up at her. "My guess is he wants to make things right. So much so that he was willing to defy the orders of a man he knows could and likely would destroy him in an instant." Sai caught himself as he realized he was talking to that very man's granddaughter. "Oh, sorry…"

She laughed momentarily." Oh, no worries, You didn't offend me. You're right; my grandfather can be very callous and merciless to those who disobey him. After all, we are talking about the man who sacrificed his nine-year-old granddaughter to the trial of the tome." Her tone was light-hearted as ever, even as she spoke about this atrocity.

"You were only nine?" The thought of it made his stomach churn.

"Yeah, back then, I remember I would have such bad dreams. Sorry, I mean images that would appear when I would sleep." She explained.

Sai looked at her, confused. "I know what dreams are." He said, confused.

She tilted her head in surprise. "Oh? Well, that makes things easier. Each night they would come to me, visions of entire cities burning. People were dying in the streets as monstrous clouds of death created by the flames filled their lungs. For years I'd suffered from these nightmares. Until one day, my parents brought it to my grandfather's attention. He called it 'corruption.' He said it appeared in very rare cases over the years, and in every case, the person would eventually be driven mad by the dreams, and in the end, they would cease sleeping altogether and eventually die because of it. He suggested that we try something desperate. He insisted I take the trial

123

of the tome. He told my parents that it would find the light in my heart and use it to drive out the corruption."

"It didn't work…" Sai said solemnly.

"We're not there yet," Zaman added. "Feeling that it was better for me to live with corruption than to risk my life in the trial, my parents refused. As time went on, the dreams got worse, and I began to fear falling asleep altogether." Her tone was focused and sullen. "I refused to eat or drink. I thought starving had to be better than being tortured to the point of madness every night. As my constitution worsened, I ended up hospitalized, and my parents made the decision that would ultimately cost them everything. They asked my grandfather to administer the trial as some last-ditch effort to save me." A visible tear rolled down her soft cheek dripping off of her chin and into the glass of tea below.

Sai reached out and placed a hand on top of hers.

"I had gone an entire week without sleep when he came to me in the hospital. He told me to repeat after him, and in my exhausted stupor, I didn't argue. 'Now Awaken…' as those words spilled out, the tome exploded in a wave of darkness. I remember sitting there so disoriented that I didn't move as it crept over me. My father was shouting for me to fight it, and I remember him lunging toward me. My grandfather stopped him before he could reach me. The coldness of his words have been what drove me forward from that point on. 'Darkness has swallowed her. The tome has chosen, and she has been found unworthy.'

Sai cut in. "So, it really did consume you?" At this question, she simply nodded in reply. Sai was completely enthralled by this point. "So, what happened after that?"

"The next thing I remember was waking up in a dark forest with a small lever-like object grasped in my hand. I was lying on the cold, damp ground staring up at a massive full moon that shone through a hole in the canopy above me. The tiredness that had taken up residence in my body for months was suddenly gone, and I figured I must have passed on to the afterlife. As I sat up, a mysterious

Origins

voice cut through the air. 'Face this world. Learn its ways, watch it, be careful of too hasty guesses at its meaning. In the end, you will find clues to it all.' Then came the monsters. They charged through the darkened forest toward me. Before I could find my feet, one of them was upon me. As it gnashed its teeth at me, I swung the lever violently, connecting hard with its temple. It was just enough to knock him off of me. I got to my feet and took off as they pursued."

"I ran for quite a ways before coming to the edge of the forest. A rocky outcropping stretched out about twelve feet in front of me before dropping off a steep cliff side. I knew it was over as I heard the creatures reach the edge of the forest. Then something made them stop. They refused to leave the shadows of the tree line. They stood there growling from within the darkness. Then something surprising appeared within the darkness."

"Stop! Get back!" A voice startled me as the light from a torch swung wildly from side to side. The creatures seemed to recoil from it as it arced toward them. Before long, a man emerged from the woods and approached me. "Are you okay?"

As he held his hand out, I scrambled backward toward the cliff edge.

"Whoa, whoa, slow down. I'm here to help." He assured me. "What's a kid like you doing all the way out here? Aren't you afraid of the Morlocks?"

"I-I don't know where I am."

He knelt down and let the torchlight illuminate his face. "What's your name?"

"So, I told him. He revealed to me that he wasn't from that world. He was a time traveler, and he had come there by accident as well. The lever in my hand was actually a missing piece to his time machine. He took me under his wing, and together we traveled through time on many different occasions."

"We continued to travel, and every time that voice came, a new challenge would arise. I met the Eloi: a peaceful group that had taken him in, and I formed connections with them. I stayed with the traveler for nearly fifteen years. We fought the Morlocks on more than one occasion. We traveled to lands no man would have ever seen, a future where the planet had stopped spinning, and the sun had become massive. We even visited beaches where these giant crab-like monsters roamed. As we jumped further into the future, we watched the world die an icy, timeless death, and after all of this, we climbed back into the time machine, hoping to head back to our life with the Eloi, but reality had other plans."

"As we traveled back, the ride became increasingly turbulent. It threw the machine from side to side violently, and with one massive jerk, I was thrown out into the void. Moments later, I woke up alone. This was gripped tightly in my hand." She held out her tome. The words "The Time Machine" were embossed neatly on the cover.

"I had aged at least a couple of decades, but I awoke near my home only a few years after I had left." She placed the tome on the table in front of them. "The traveler, my parents, my life, it was all gone. Only one thing remained, my grandfather."

"That's horrible," Sai said. "So, even though the tome rejected you, you still entered the trial and came out the other side?

"Seems like it. Although, I clearly went the long way around," she replied. "How long did your trial last?"

Sai thought for a minute. "Hmmmmm, it couldn't have been more than a few minutes here. But, inside the tome, it was literally eons." He explained.

"Mhmm." Zaman nodded and sipped her tea. "And you didn't age at all? Fascinating." She said, shaking her head. "Honestly, that seems to be pretty standard for a successful trial."

"But it wasn't successful," Sai added.
"What do you mean?" She asked.
"My friend Michelle intervened."
"Intervened?" She looked at him curiously.
"Yeah, the tome rejected me as well, but my friend, Michelle, one of the girls we're trying to save, jumped in at the last second, and her light somehow

overrode the darkness. We both entered different trials, and both came out with tomes by the end of it. It still almost killed me, and I'm sure without Amy's help, it would have."

"And Cylus was okay with that kind of interference?" She looked almost hurt.

Sai shook his head." Not exactly. For helping me, both Michelle and Amy ended up on this mission to prove they could be trusted. So, if it's anyone's fault they're missing, it's mine, not Alister's."

"Yeah, that sounds like the old man. You broke the rules of his test, and now he doesn't know what to do with you. I'm sure at first he didn't quite trust you, and now that you're thinking for yourselves, he's come to the conclusion that it'd be easier to simply eliminate you as a variable. Do you know why it rejected you?" Zaman asked.

Sai shook his head and swallowed hard. "I'm not sure. My memories of my past are missing. It could have been anything." He went on to tell her the events he had gone through up to that point.

"And you can dream." She muttered as she placed her glass back on the table.

"Huh?" Sai couldn't really hear her.

"It's nothing, sorry." Zaman waved the question away.

Sai let out a deep breath. "Do you think we made the wrong choice by refusing to follow orders?"

Zaman laughed loudly," Of course you did! My grandfather could end both of you in a heartbeat."

Sai looked down, ashamed.

"But, he's not gonna get that chance!" She said assuredly.

"Do you really think that by going through with this plan, we can get the strength we need to save my friends?"

"I do, but strength alone isn't going to be enough. Let me tell you a secret, Sai, true power comes from the strength of our resolve. Since you woke up here,

Origins

it seems like your choices have been thrown to the wind by one command after another, tethered to the whims of the people around you. So, let me ask you one last thing." She leaned in with a smile. "What is it you have resolved to accomplish?"

Sai looked into her immaculate green eyes and found his nerve, "I'm going to find my friends and ensure Roark and Oswald never hurt anyone ever again."

"Now, that is an admirable goal!" Zaman commended him. "Let's run that down together, shall we?" She said, raising her glass to toast to his ambition.

Chapter 13: You Idiot…

Nearly three days prior…
　　Cool, dry air brushed across Amy's face as she lay on the cold, rough wooden floorboards of the cage cart. Her hands and feet were bound tightly to prevent her movements. She lay motionless on the floor of the cart, which was driven by a now-human Oswald. It moved gracefully as it was pulled across the moonlit desert by two slate grey mules. Below it sat two wide skis which glided smoothly across the shifting sands. Suddenly, the ski on the left side passed over a large stone jutting out of the sand, which caused the whole cart to sway. This sudden jolt woke Amy as her head bounced off the hard wooden boards.
　　"Ughhhh…" She groaned as pain washed over her entire body. Opening her eyes, she could see large jagged pillars of stone in the distance illuminated by the light of the full moon overhead as they strode onward. *What's going on? Where am I?*
　　She looked around the cart just to see an unconscious Michelle lying beaten and covered in blood in the far corner. "Michelle…" Her voice was stifled by the pain in her chest and the dryness of her throat. She struggled as she found her hands bound behind her back and feet tied tightly together.
　　"Finally awake, I see." An odd raspy voice came from the front of the cart.
　　Rolling her head in the opposite direction, she could see Oswald's back facing them. "You, you killed her." She groaned.
　　"Oh, calm down; she isn't any use to us dead." He replied coldly. "That's not even her blood."
　　"Then whose?" It took everything she had to speak even this much.
　　"I would assume that's from your little boyfriend. I didn't exactly have a free hand when he

charged into that alley, but that one made a competent enough fly swatter." He remarked.

She didn't even have the energy to rebuff the boyfriend comment. "Sai?"

"He's most assuredly dead. You should have heard the snapping noises his bones made, like tree branches in a hurricane. But don't worry." He continued. "I gave her a potion immediately as we crossed the portal. So, she's sustained very minor injuries." He was so callous when he spoke; it almost made Alister's condescension sound downright charming.

"You're a monster. You're gonna regret this." She struggled as she tried to reach for the tome holster on her hip. Only to realize the book wasn't there.

"Sorry, sweetheart, I'm not the monster in this story. Nah, we left him in the alley." He glanced back at her for only a second. "You think I'd be stupid enough to let you keep your tome?" He laughed at how preposterous it sounded. "Don't worry; I've got both of them right here." He reached into a burlap sack in between his feet and pulled out both books. He held them up, so they were easily visible.

Amy suddenly became aware of how dire their situation actually was.

"You caused quite the fuss back there in town. Not to mention the number you did on Roark back in Dione. You're truly not someone I wish to tangle with, Miss Amelia."

"Why don't you untie me, and I'll show you just what kind of fuss I can cause?" She snapped as best she could.

"Hmmph, not gonna happen, sweetheart." He looked back at her again, but this time she noticed something different. His face had changed; his hair was a deep raven black, his eyes were almost violet, and he sported a long, full-length beard. His body type had even been altered. As she got a clearer view of him, she noticed he was much skinnier and, dare she say, shorter? By no means would she call this man handsome.

"You changed your appearance?"

"My, aren't we observant?" He said sarcastically.

"Yes, I did. Alister knew that face. Can't exactly go around looking exactly the same now, can I?" He explained.

"So is this your true face then? Not nearly as becoming." She remarked with a cough.

"No, the face you saw before was the original. Can't say I ever wanted to use the tome's power like this, but we do what we must."

"Is that a hint of remorse, I hear?" Amy questioned.

"Tch! Quiet, I need to focus." He took his attention from her and focused his eyes straight ahead.

The cart came to a halt as they reached a rocky slope that led down into a large mountainous gorge. A narrow pathway led down between the red stone walls of the gorge, and a little way down opened on one side to a deep chasm. Oswald reached down once again and pushed forward a lever that sat next to the burlap sack. Suddenly, the cart seemed to raise ever-so-slightly as retractable wheels from underneath it appeared and locked into place. The skis they had used on the sand were pulled up and folded into the side of the cart. They wouldn't be much use on rocky terrain like this, after all.

As the cart rattled into the canyon, a drastic thought ran through Amy's mind. She propped her back against the wooden bars that surrounded the cart. Gently she rubbed her bound hands against the cart where the beam connected the floorboards. As she shifted, she found the head of a small square nail that wasn't hammered flush with the wood. Quietly she rasped the ropes binding her hands against the nail's head. She prayed that the clomping of the mules' hooves and rattling of the cart would be enough to drown out the small tearing noises which emanated from the rope. With each consecutive motion, the bindings seemed to loosen more and more until, suddenly, they snapped. She quickly unbound her feet and then sat motionless with her hands behind her back for a while as she contemplated her options.

Looking under the seat where Oswald sat, she could see the sack with the tomes. But, any hope she had of getting ahold of those was dashed as Oswald lifted his foot and placed it firmly on top of the bag.

The incline steepened as they descended further into the gorge. The brakes holding the wheels back from spinning freely creaked with the added strain. She knew now she had one option, and it wasn't a good one. Slowly she inched toward the front of the cart and gingerly reached her hand through the wooden slats underneath Oswald's seat.

Slowly, silently her hand stretched out farther and farther until she was mere inches from the lever. She was up to her shoulder in between the bar as her fingers made contact with the wooden rod. Just as she wrapped them around the lever, Oswald's foot shifted and hit her forearm.

"Huh?" This was all he could utter as he looked down just in time to see Amy's hand rip back on the lever with all her might, shearing it clean off in the process.

The cart rocked violently as the wheels shot up, replaced by tractionless, brakeless skis. In an instant, they were picking up speed uncontrollably. The mules sprinted full bore ahead in an attempt to flee from the quickly encroaching cart. They were too slow, however, and within seconds the cart knocked each of them to the ground and mercilessly ran them down as it continued its wild descent. Amy's stomach turned as the mules' bones cracked beneath the weight, but what were a couple of animals' lives compared to their own? Michelle slid violently to the front of the cart and into Amy's arms.

Oswald wailed as the cart skidded against the canyon wall, threatening to throw him from his seat with every hit. The cart was now flying at blinding speeds down the ramp that was narrowing by the second. Out of nowhere, a large rock appeared in front of them and ripped the left ski from underneath the cart, causing it to flip. Throwing Oswald along with the tomes to the ground as the cart pinwheeled with the girls still inside.

Origins

Amy and Michelle were battered back and forth within the cage as it tumbled. The cart nearly came to a halt as it reached the bottom of the ramp. Unfortunately for its unwilling passengers, this wasn't the end of the line.

The path let off onto the still more narrow path with a steep drop-off on one side. The cart slid to the edge of the drop-off and teetered there, one hundred and fifty feet above the void. Amy tried to gain her composure. She grabbed Michelle's unconscious body and tried to drag it toward the edge of the cart that was still on solid ground. With every movement, the cart swayed, threatening to fall at any moment.

A loud roar echoed through the canyon as Oswald, in full Ijiraq form, charged toward the busted transport. One antler was completely broken off, and he was covered in blood. Amy knew that he must have transformed mid-fall, or else he'd surely be dead. In one hand, he carried the sack of tomes. The other seemed mangled and severely injured.

In a split second, Amy was forced to make another horrible decision. She picked up Michelle and, with all her strength, rushed for the unsupported end of the cart. The added weight caused the cart to lurch toward the river that flowed far below. It groaned as it slid quickly over the edge before unceremoniously coming to a grinding halt.

Oswald's monstrous hand had caught a single wooden bar on the cart and began dragging it back toward him.

"You little brat! How dare you!?" He screamed like a crazed animal as he pulled with all of his strength.

He was furious, and his rage had caused him to make yet another vital mistake. The hand he gripped the cart with, the only one usable to him, was also the one in which he held the sack of tomes. It hung just inside the cart as he pulled them back toward him.

This is suicide. Amy thought as she sat Michelle down on the floor of the cart. Sai's stupid smile flashed into her mind. "You're rubbing off on me, you idiot..." She muttered as she steadied herself in the rocking cart. "Be strong, saith my heart; I am a soldier; I have seen worse sights than this." With those words, she bolted directly for Oswald. "Awaken Odysseia!" She leaped forward, one hand extended, and made contact with the bag. A bright light illuminated the cart as her sword and shield appeared in her hand.

"Arrrgggg!" She screamed as she brought the blade down across Oswald's fingers freeing the bag and the cage in one fell swoop. Both tomes fell into the cart along with three of Oswald's digits.

He reeled back, wailing in excruciating pain, and the cart, free of his enormous grip, careened over the edge and toward the water. On the way down, it stuck several trees that lined the cliff's edge, slowing its fall. Even still, the impact was anything but pleasant.

Just before they hit the water, Amy managed to grab Michelle and placed her shield between themselves and the water. The shield's reflective magic softened the blow, but only just enough. The fall hadn't killed them, but the cart was now half submerged and flying down a roaring river. It lurched back and forth as it dashed against the smooth stones of the river bed.

"What… What's going on?" Michelle's eyes opened slowly, and she found herself propped up in Amy's arms. "Where are we?"

"Michelle! Oh my god, you're awake. We're in kind of a predicament. We just escaped Oswald, but now we have to find some way to get out of this river and to safety." Amy explained as she gasped for air.

"Do… do you have my tome?" Michelle murmured weakly.

"Yeah, It's here. Is there something in it that can help us?" Amy held the book above the water in her shield hand.

"Maybe, hand it here." She took the tome from Amy and weakly thumbed through the pages. "A scorpion and a frog meet on the bank of a stream, and the scorpion asks the frog to carry him across on its back. 'Awaken Fables." A dark shadow appeared beneath the waves, and they began to be lifted as a giant amphibian emerged with them on its back. It carried them to the nearby bank and deposited the cage ashore before vanishing once again beneath the waves.

Amy and Michelle both collapsed on the floor of the cage, heaving and trying to catch their breath.

"Thank you, Michelle," Amy said as she cut the remaining bindings from Michelle's hands and feet and extended a hand to help her up.

"Isn't that my line?" Michelle said with a weak smile as she stood.

"Stand back. We're getting out of here." Amy raised her sword, and with a few quick swings, she had cut away the bar enough for the two to crawl out. "We need to keep moving; no doubt he's coming after us as soon as he recovers."

After walking for some time, the two found themselves outside of what looked like the mouth of a large cave. "I think the river created enough distance between him and us. Maybe we should bed down for the night." Amy suggested. "I need to try and contact the Citadel. Maybe they can send help." They entered the cave, and Amy rummaged through her inventory.

"He took all of my communication scrolls. Looks like we're on our own. Unless Cylus uses Eighty-Four on us." She groaned.

All that was left in her bag was a flint striker, a few small torches, and two healing potions. She lit one of the torches, and the two walked deeper into the cave system.

After walking for a moment, Amy noticed a small gap in the wall to their left. With torch in hand, she slowly approached the crevasse and peered inside. On the other side was what appeared to be a small room with a few little stalagmites dotting the floor.

"Hey." Amy gestured for Michelle to take a look. "Think I found a place for us to bed down for the night?"

Michelle poked her head into the room and gave an approving nod. "At least this way, we won't be in the main entrance if Oswald decides to come looking."

"Agreed," Amy replied.

Turning sideways, Amy shimmied through the small opening and emerged on the other side. Michelle did the same; for her, the squeeze was a bit tighter, but she made it through without much trouble.

"I'll need to go grab some wood from the cart. We're gonna need a fire." Amy said as she surveyed the room. Michelle gave a quick nod, and without another word, Amy slipped out again. Before long, she returned with an armload of chopped bars from the cart.

"Any idea where we are?" Michelle coughed as they sat around a small fire. They wore simple beige tunics and black pants. Their armor and previous outfits were slung loosely over one of the stalagmites near the fire. Amy had argued that it wouldn't be wise to remain in the sopping wet clothes as the temperature in the cave was descending steadily.

Prompted by the cough, Amy held up a potion. "Take this, and no, I have no idea. I know we're still in the same hemisphere. After all, it's still night. Other than that, I've got nothing." She replied. "And without any supplies, we're not in good shape."

"I can't believe he ransacked our bags." Michelle panned through her inventory and took stock of all she had left. "Looks like I've got my sleeping bag and some berries from when we were camping, but not much else."

"Well, that beats sleeping on the cold ground. Oswald took mine along with most of my other stuff." Amy grumbled as she took stock of her belongings once more. "Either way, we need to try and get some rest. First thing in the morning, we'll try to head out and find somewhere to get help."

"Good plan," Michelle replied as she pulled the sleeping bag from her inventory and rolled it out on the hard, cold stone floor.

Amy doused the fire and leaned against the wall on the other side of the small alcove. For a while, the coals from the fire kept the cave warm, but as the night wore on, the cold desert air caused the temperature to drop drastically. Amy began to shiver slightly as the cold fingers of night crawled into her bones. She curled up into herself in a feeble bid to keep warm.

Before long, the chattering of her teeth caught Michelle's attention. She sat up in her sleeping bag and glanced in Amy's direction. She stood and picked up her sleeping bag, walked over to Amy, and laid the bag back on the floor at her feet. "Why don't you crawl in with me?"

Amy opened one eye, gave her a suspicious look, and shook her head before rolling over to face the other way.

"Come on; I don't bite. If you don't, you're going to catch your death." She unzipped the bag and motioned for Amy to crawl inside. Reluctantly Amy rolled over once again and slid down into the bag. Michelle followed suit and slid in beside her.

The inside of the sleeping bag was like spring after an eternal winter. With Michelle's body pressed so close to her own, the ice that had infiltrated Amy's veins retreated. As embarrassing as it was to admit to herself, Amy finally felt safe for the first time since leaving Iapetus.

"Amy?" Michelle's voice was barely more than a whisper.

"Yeah?" She said with her face to Michelle's raven hair.

"I'm really sorry…"

"For what?" Amy asked genuinely.

"For all of this. For everything I've put you and everyone else through." She sniffed. She began to roll over before realizing shed be nose-to-nose with Amy if she did.

Amy exhaled. "Don't apologize. You realize I was the one to jump in to save you back in Dione, right? I didn't see you asking me to do any of that. I did that because I wanted to, and I'd do it again in a heartbeat. Michelle, look at me."

Slowly she rolled over till she was staring directly into Amy's emerald eyes. "I just…"

"Stop. We're gonna get out of here. You and I together got it! No more apologizing."

Michelle rolled over again to face the wall. "I just don't want anyone else getting hurt trying to protect me."

Origins

Amy sat up and looked over her with a smile. "Tell you what. When we make it out of here, we'll do some real training. We'll make it to where you won't need to rely on anyone's protection ever again. Not even mine."

Michelle blushed, looking up at her before breaking eye contact. "Thanks, Amy, for everything." She rolled back over gently, and within minutes she was out like a light.

Amy lay staring at the back of her head for a good while. There was no reason to worry her now. For now, they were safe here in their little alcove, if only for a moment she would let her live with that small comfort.

As the sun rose outside the cave, the heat inside began to rise slowly. Before long, the warmth even penetrated the inner room, making it far too hot to sleep soundly.

Amy woke up first to find both of her arms wrapped around Michelle's waist. The realization of this prolonged contact was enough to embarrass her to no end. She pulled her arm out and shook the numbness out of her fingertips. This motion caused Michelle to stir slightly before falling back asleep.

Gingerly Amy sat up and crawled out of the sleeping bag. As she made her way to the cave entrance, the desert heat hit her like a cannonball.

"Dear lord, It must be a hundred and fifty degrees out here." She muttered as she covered her eyes from the immense light of the morning sun.

Moments later, Michelle came up from behind her rubbing her tired eyes. "I haven't slept that hard in a long time." She shielded her eyes and stepped to the mouth of the cave. "It got so hot. When can we leave?"

Amy shook her head. "I don't think we can. Without any way to transport water. We won't be able to leave the riverside for very long at all."

"So, what do we do?"

"I don't know," Amy replied, looking out the cave entrance. "I'm not sure we can leave with the sun beating down like this. We may need to stay here for the time being."

Origins

"Well, if we can't get out, perhaps that means Oswald is having to hunker down as well. We should be safe, at least for a little while." Michelle said while trying to stay positive.

"You're probably right. Unfortunately, we still have zero food or supplies. We need to find some way out of here before he can recover and come looking for us again." Amy explained.

They waited for a while, but as the day pressed on, the heat at the cave entrance only got worse and worse. They only made a couple of trips out of the cave to drink and try their luck at catching river fish, but even that was unbearable for very long at all. The temperature shot higher and higher as the day wore on. The only reprieve came as the sun descended past the western cavern wall.

This reprieve was short-lived. As soon as it got dark out, the temperature plummeted drastically. The girls gathered more wood from the cage cart and hunkered down once again for the night. Sitting around the fire, they roasted the single fish they had caught. It was small, hardly a meal for one, let alone two people.

"We can't do this again tomorrow. Before long, we won't have the energy to keep going." Michelle said as she roasted the fish over the fire.

"You're right. Tomorrow we find a way out of here no matter what."

Inside the shelter of their cavity, they shared the fish and headed to bed for the night. Without being drenched to the bone, the temperature in the room was far more bearable than it had been the night before. Therefore the fire wasn't as necessary to keep warm.

Michelle laid out her sleeping bag as Amy snuffed out the fire. Amy went to take her spot on the ground before Michelle spoke up. "Ummm, Amy?"

"Yeah?"

"Would you like to share my sleeping bag again?" She said, looking down shyly.

"Oh no, I'm okay. It's warm enough tonight that I don't really need to, but I appreciate the offer."

"I was actually asking for me," Michelle said shyly. "I haven't told anyone but Sai this, but ever since Dione, I have a really hard time feeling safe at night." She said sheepishly. "Never mind, it's silly." With that, she crawled into the bag, rolled over, and closed her eyes.

She was surprised when Amy tapped her on the shoulder a few minutes later. She had her tome in hand as she spoke.

"That would explain the sneaking around then, huh?"

Michelle rolled over. "You knew he's been staying with me till I fell asleep?"

Amy gave a small laugh. "Don't think I can tell when that knucklehead is sneaking around camp just after sundown? I just thought you guys had a thing going on or something."

Michelle looked up at her and blushed profusely. "No!" She retorted.

"Sorry. Hope I make a decent enough substitute." Amy joked with a smile, "Scoot over." She crawled into the sleeping bag and placed one hand on Michelle's back. "I didn't realize you were struggling so much. You should've told me. Sleep is actually something I can help with. As long as I can maintain contact with you, you'll sleep." She held up her tome and spoke softly. "Sleep, delicious and profound, the very counterfeit of death' Awaken Odysseia."

Within an instant, Michelle could feel herself being pulled into the blackness of dreamless sleep. Amy sat her tome against the wall while still maintaining her touch with her other hand, and surprisingly out of desire more than necessity, this time Michelle shifted backward toward her. Taking the hint, Amy slid her arm under her ribs, embracing her, and presently they slept. They slept straight through the night, and both woke up sometime after sunrise when Amy finally rolled over and broke the connection. Checking the entrance again, they decided that it was going to be another day of extreme heat.

"We can't survive out here. We're going to need another plan." Michelle suggested.

Origins

"Guess we'll have to try our luck further in. Maybe there's another exit?" Amy walked back into the cave.

Michelle agreed before following closely behind.

"This cave is massive," Michelle remarked as they trailed onward. Every step drew them further into darkness. Eventually, Amy was forced to pull out her final torch. With a strike of her flint, the tip ignited, illuminating the whole tunnel.

"It is. It almost reminds me of the tunnel system that leads to The Citadel." Amy said. As they spoke, they came to a large dome-like room with several cave-like corridors that shot off in all directions. "Whoa! What in the world is this?"

"Looks like the entrance to a larger cave system." Michelle ran her hand along the wall that separated two of the entrances. "Which way should we go?"

"Wait, shhh, do you hear that?" Amy cupped her hand around her ear and listened carefully.

"What is it?" Michelle questioned.

"Shhhh!" Amy grabbed Michelle by the wrist, pulled her into one of the tunnels, dropped behind a nearby stalagmite, and snuffed out the torch. She covered Michelle's mouth and sat stone still.

Michelle shook her mouth free from Amy's hand. "What's going on?"

Amy pinned her against the stone spike, jutting up from the floor, and covered her mouth again. She put one finger to her lips and silently quieted her. Just as she did, Michelle heard the footsteps.

A black-cloaked figure entered the room. They had a glowing stone in their hand, which they spoke into. "Yeah, 'R 'they're down here somewhere. I found the cage cart outside the entrance and the remnants of a fire nearby. 'O's 'searching the eastern cavern. I'll be in contact as I find out more." The glowing crystal vanished in the darkness as the man's voice quieted.

Amy poked her head out and stared at him as the room grew dark once again. As she watched him, he vanished into the darkness. Suddenly, two bright red eyes looked directly at her. She ducked back behind the stone and prayed that he hadn't spotted them. She held her breath as they listened to the man's footsteps disappear down one of the long tunnels.

"That was way too close." She said, releasing her held breath.

Michelle squirmed under her grip. The faint glowing embers of the torch illuminated their faces ever so slightly. "I can't breathe…" She murmured.

Amy pulled her hand away. "Sorry, didn't have time to think."

"It's okay," Michelle whispered. "Thank you. I owe you yet again."

"Let's just get out of here. Looks like Oswald's still after us. Not to mention he's got help. We need to move."

"Going somewhere?" What sounded like hundreds of voices hissed from above them.

Michelle looked up and stifled a scream as she realized there were at least fifty pairs of glowing red eyes staring back at them. "Amy…" She whispered with a hint of panic in her voice.

Suddenly hundreds of bats were swarming them. Before they could react, they were being bitten over and over again. Amy summoned her Sword and Shield and swung wildly at the encroaching horde.

"Amy!" Michelle's scream broke through the swarm just as she was grabbed by a gigantic hand from the darkness. Her fingers skimmed her tome as she was ripped off her feet.

"Mich…" The word narrowly escaped her lips before she was bashed over the head by another shrouded figure.

A large torch ignited and illuminated the dark corridor as Oswald appeared. He looked far worse than the last time they had seen him. His fur was singed from the intense sun, he only had one antler, and he was missing three digits on his left hand.

Origins

He stood over Amy, who fought to remain conscious. "This time, you're not getting away." He placed one hoof on Amy's right leg before applying pressure and twisting it hard, hobbling her in an instant. "Consider that reparations for my hand."

She screamed in agony. Her sword and shield disappeared as they were recalled into her tome. The second smaller figure, a young handsome yet sallow-skinned man, pulled the tome from her side before grabbing her by her hair and, with ease, dragged her into the inky darkness.

Chapter 14: Training

      Snow fell quickly onto Sai's head as he sat in a wide field surrounded on all sides by the dense forest of silver pines. The snow had been rather shallow when he had sat down to meditate, but due to the way the temporal field worked, it seemed to enter it from the outside and pile up at a much quicker rate than usual. Presently, he sat up to his stomach in the frozen white powder. It had been three weeks inside this odd zone, and under the guidance of Alister and Zaman, he had been instructed to focus and meditate.

      "Your devotion to your friends gives you strength, but it's also your greatest weakness," Zaman explained.

      "Every time they've been in danger, you've charged in without thinking. It's almost gotten you killed twice now. You need to learn to shut out the distractions that pull you away from your goal." Alister added sternly.

      "But saving them is my goal," Sai argued.

      "That's true, but if in your haste you get yourself killed, your goal won't matter," Zaman interjected. "You need to learn to calm your mind and find a solution before charging in. Then you may channel those emotions into an effective winning strategy."

      This conversation flowed through Sai's mind as he meditated. *Come back to your breath.* This thought was interrupted as the sound of someone crunching through the snow approached him.

      "You've been out here a while. How's it going?" Alicia's friendly voice had become a welcome sound in these strenuous times.

      Sai opened one eye to see the blue-haired girl standing before him. He closed his eyes again. "Trying to meditate here."

      "I see that," she replied. "Zaman sent me to get you, actually. It's time to eat." She held out her hand

Origins

Sai opened his eyes again and took her hand. She hoisted him up, and he dusted the snow from his clothes and followed her as she trailed back toward camp.

"Gods, it's cold. How are you not freezing out here?" She remarked as they walked.

"I was at first, but recently I've really been getting better at shutting out outside distractions. Even shutting out the cold." He stopped, placed his hands on his hips, and stared off into the distance majestically. As he did, a small pile of dun-colored down fell out from under his shirt and gave him away.

Alicia noticed this little slip instantly but decided to play along. "Well, that's very impressive." She said, laughing at his exaggerated stance.

Sai laughed in return." Nah!" He reached into his thick tunic and pulled out a handful of gray feathers. "I've been collecting these loose feathers from Charlie every day and stuffing them in my clothes. They make great insulation!" He grinned as he showed her the handful of long grayish feathers.

"Well, I have to say that's less impressive. But, nonetheless, resourceful!" The two laughed and continued on toward their small camp.

As they approached, Alister waved to them from the door of a large white tent. "Hurry up, food's getting cold!"

As they entered the tent, the warmth of it surged across their bodies. Zaman had created a small fire in a portable hearth at the center of the shelter, which caused it to remain several degrees above freezing. The smell of frying fish permeated every inch of the living space and brought with it an air of comfort that was hard to come by in the frozen forest. Zaman served up plates, and the group sat and ate together like they had several times throughout their time there.

As Sai ate, his shirt began to rustle slightly. A small lump formed near his chest and worked its way up to his neck. Suddenly, Charlie's small brown-gray head popped out of his shirt collar with a chirp.

"Oh, sorry, buddy! Are you hungry?" Sai picked off a piece of fish and fed it to the small finch, who chirped approvingly.

Zaman smiled that charming smile of hers. "So how goes the training Sai? Have you made progress?"

"I think so. I've definitely felt more at peace and in tune with my tome." Sai rubbed the back of his head, closed his eyes, and smiled.

"Has it strengthened your tome usage any?" Alister questioned.

"Hmm, I'm not sure. The duration of my summons have gotten longer. I feel like I can maintain Charlie's basic form nearly indefinitely now." He fed another small scrap of fish to the chirping bird.

Alister nodded." Good, and what about his transformations?"

Sai looked down. "The parrot and eagle transformations are fairly easy for me now. The titanis form is doable, but maintaining it for any time at all is a feat in and of itself."

"Anything beyond the realm of birds?" Alister probed, hoping for good news.

Since they had entered the temporal field, Sai had explained to them the breadth of the creatures he had seen during his tome's trial. At the citadel, this would've been expressly forbidden, but given that they were already on The Citadel's bad side, what did he have to lose? Ever since then, Alister had been asking about these transformations.

Sai simply shook his head.

"That's okay. The transformations haven't been our focus up to this point. We first needed to get you in the correct headspace for growth. Now comes the real training." Zaman stood up from her chair and grabbed a paper scroll from a nearby satchel. "As I see it, your tome's archive of transformations acts like the branches of a tree." She rolled the scroll out across the table and drew a small box at the bottom with an "X" at the center. From this box, she drew a tree trunk that shot up to the top of the page.

Origins

Many branches stretched off in every direction, each with its own set of sub-branches. At one of the highest branches, she wrote "finch (Charlie)." On a couple of sub-branches just off from "Charlie," she wrote "parrot" and "eagle." She then jumped down ever so slightly and wrote "titanis" on yet another sub-branch.

"I thought perhaps it was the animal's size that was affecting the duration and difficulty of the transformation. However, that might not be the case at all. Instead, it might have to do with how far down the tree you're actually traveling." She traced her pencil across the illustration as she spoke.

"What I'm beginning to suspect is that your tomes' evolutionary abilities almost act like an elastic band." She pulled a thin ring of black fabric from her lab coat pocket and began to stretch it outward. "As you can see, when I first start pulling on this band, it's difficult to stretch even a little bit, and once the strain becomes too great, I'm forced to let go, and it snaps back into place. Are you following me?"

"Sort of?" Sai cocked his head to the side, trying to figure out what all of this had to do with his tome.

"The original position of the band represents Charlie's finch form' no changes have occurred; he just is." She continued. "As we stretch, the band that represents a movement down the tree toward the other forms. Ones like the parrot and eagle aren't hard to reach, but as you get further and further from the original form, the harder it gets to maintain the transformation." She handed the thin piece of elastic to Sai.

He stretched the band a couple of times and let it snap back into place. "So, is there no way to make it easier?"

"I may have an idea for that," Alister suggested. "As you pull on the band, its fibers become looser and looser. Over time it becomes easier to stretch. The looser the fibers become, the further it can be stretched."

Sai tried to follow this metaphor as best he could. "Okay, so we stretch out my tomes ability for longer and longer durations, and that should make it easier to reach and maintain the lower branch transformations?"

"In theory, yes. The next stage in your training will involve pushing you and your tome to new heights." Zaman explained. "I have a hunch that due to how your tome works if its power is completely awakened, you could gain power even beyond that of my grandfather."

Alister looked at her skeptically. "Don't you think that's a bit of a reach?" His tone seemed softer with her now than it had been in the past.

This statement was by no means convincing to Sai. "Yeah, I'm sorry, that seems like a huge leap from simple transformations."

Zaman laughed slightly. "Guess we'll see. For now, we need to focus on reaching these further transformations. Why don't you finish eating and get some rest? We'll start this new training afterward." She picked up her plate and cleaned it in a nearby basin of hot soapy water.

Sai finished up his food and continued to talk with Alister and Alicia. "Have you come any closer to understanding what Oswald and Roark are after?"

Alister shook his head. "I've been panning through all of the evidence we gathered, but the only communication we have between the two is the note we found." Alister pulled the slip of paper from his pocket. "Alicia, you were around town a lot longer than we were. Do you have any information at all?"

She sighed as she leaned back in her seat. "He hid his connection to the kidnappings well. I was observing the town for weeks and never so much as caught a whiff of Oswald's involvement. However, I had been keeping an eye on those connected to the victims. Zaman noted that several of them could have had the potential to become tome wielders." Alicia explained.

"We gathered that much, but how could you possibly know that kind of info?" Alister questioned as he looked toward Zaman.

Origins

"Said it's a skill she picked up while living at The Citadel. You have to understand; she worked under her grandfather for years before she was consumed by the tome."

"I thought Cylus was the only one able to identify possible users?" Sai looked confused.

"It's an essential skill to have when you're being groomed to be the future leader of The Citadel." She explained calmly.

Alister pinched the bridge of his nose in frustration. He still knew so little about these women. "Okay, all of that aside. What else do you know?"

Alicia continued. "Not much. We weren't getting anywhere with the people in town. They all believed he was some sort of paranormal demon, and once that rumor took hold, many outright refused to talk about the kidnappings. In our urgency, we decided to use another possible wielder as bait to lure him out."

Sai looked at her grimly. "You don't mean…"

She nodded. "We decided I would draw him out myself, but we drastically underestimated him. The rumors were true. He was a monster, and I paid the price for that information. I was lucky to escape with my life. Then you arrived, and you know the rest."

"So, you lied to me, and you can wield a tome?" Sai looked at her in surprise.

She just shook her head in reply. "Sorry, and no, I said possible wielder."

"All blank tomes are stored in the private library at the citadel due to how dangerous they can be. That means she judged you worthy but couldn't get a tome into your hands?" Alister added.

"More or less, yeah." She replied.

"So, could they be gathering tome users in order to gain powerful allies?" Sai questioned.

"It doesn't sound like it. They mention gathering tomes, not gathering allies themselves. But why kidnap possible users then?" Alister read over the first line of the note again.

Origins

"What if they're administering tomes and transferring them to their sympathizers?" Alicia pondered.

"That's not possible."

"But, it is. You said so yourself. Oswald is using a tome that once belonged to your daughter, correct?"

Alister sighed indignantly. "That's true. However, my daughter is gone. Do you truly believe they could steal a tome from a living user?"

"I didn't say they were taking them from the living."

The chilling response shook Sai to his very core. "You think they'd really kill them to get their tomes?"

Alister was quick to rebuke this notion. "No, from my understanding, you can't just steal a tome off a dead wielder. Something fishy is going on. Not to mention the note seemed to indicate that Roark wanted Michelle and myself for some reason." He pondered this quietly for a moment. "No, they're not dead, and if I know Amelia, they have their hands full if they do plan on killing them."

Sai thought back to his conversion with Amy and how intimidating she had been at the hospital. He let out a small laugh. "I sure wouldn't want to be on her bad side."

"She's young and brash at times, but she's also extremely strong. A fighter till the end if I've ever seen one. Kind of reminds me of Sibyl, honestly." A small unwilling smile seemed to appear on Alister's face before fading as quickly as it had appeared. "In any case, they weren't in much of a condition to fight." He looked directly into Sai's eyes." You focus hard on your training and leave the tracking to me. No matter what the cost, we're going to bring them back."

After a few hours of sleep, Sai was back to training. It was hard to tell how many days had passed since the sun didn't seem to move across the sky much at all. His days were only separated by his sleep cycle. Day in and day out, he trained with both Zaman and Alister. Alister was great for combat training due to his years of experience. Zaman, on the other hand, offered a wealth of

Origins
knowledge based on time and how organisms are affected by it.

"It looks like you are beginning to better handle these greater transformations." Zaman ran her hand along Charlie's huge body. "This titanis form is rather impressive and, at this stage, very manageable for you. It could be extremely useful."

Sai walked up next to Charlie as well. He brushed his hair out of his eyes. It had become noticeably longer, hanging down in his face most of the time.

"Yeah, but the other form is far bigger and more intimidating. Plus, it's got the power to match!"

Zaman simply smiled at him." And how long can you sustain it?"

"Forty-five seconds!" Sai said proudly.

"Then would that be effective to use in battle at this point?" She reprimanded.

"No…"

"Exactly; remember, we need to focus on stretching that band. It's only been a month, and you're making great progress. Show me this transformation. Let's see if we can stretch the time out further." Her instruction was always so kind and understanding. Basically the exact opposite of Alister's.

Sai pulled out his tome." Nevertheless so profound is our ignorance, and so high our presumption… Awaken Origins!"

Chapter 15: Roark

"Amy... Amy...Amy..." The melodic voice floated through her delirious head. It was beautiful and soothing. "Amy, wake up..." She drifted in a dark ocean, unable to move or breathe. "Amy, wake up!" Her eyes popped open, and with consciousness came an immense amount of pain. Her bloodied and throbbing leg felt like it would explode at any moment. It took everything within her not to scream as the pain radiated throughout her body.

"Amy, oh, thank the gods you're awake." Michelle sat to the left with her hands strapped behind her back around a large wooden post. They sat in a dingy, dark room that was strewn with damp straw.

"M...Michelle? Where are we? What's going on?" The room spun as bright colors floated around her vision.

"They caught us. We're in a dungeon somewhere." Michelle coughed weakly as she tried to explain.

Michelle's face came into view as Amy's vision began to clear. Her left eye was bruised, and she looked to have a large gash across the bridge of her nose.

"Michelle, what did they do to you?" Amy groaned as she tried unsuccessfully to get to her feet. She quickly realized this was a futile effort. The pain in her leg was the first indicator, followed by the tug of short leather bands strapped around her wrist that pulled her back to the floor. "Gaaaahhh!" The cry escaped her lips as the sharp pain ripped up her leg yet again.

"Amy! Please don't try to move. Your kneecap is shattered." Michelle pleaded with her.

Amy rolled back and leaned against the wooden support beam to which she was strapped. She breathed heavily in an attempt to manage the immense amount of pain. Her pant leg was stiffly covered in dried blood, and her knee looked like a grapefruit under the fabric of her leggings.

"Michelle, I'm sorry. I thought I could save us, but I only made everything worse." She looked down, disappointed in her own failures.

"Hey, come on! If anything, you bought us time." Michelle tried to smile through the obvious pain. "I'm sure Sai and Alister are coming for us."

"Michelle…" Her voice trailed off.

Michelle stopped her. "They're coming! I can feel it! Your bravery and sacrifice aren't going to be for nothing." She tried to sound reassuring.

Amy smiled. " Thank you. You're right. We just need to hang on."

Clap! Clap! Clap!" Isn't that sweet? Finding hope even in these dark depths. Isn't that just like you, Michelle?" A voice from the darkness sent a chill down the girls' spines.

Amy and Michelle spun their heads around to face the disembodied voice.

"You?" Amy's voice caught in her throat as the figure stepped out of the darkness to reveal the familiar, tightly-woven, long-beaked mask.

"The name's Roark. It's been a minute Red; I hope the ride over wasn't too rough on you." Icy tendrils seemed to crawl into her mind as he spoke.

"What the hell do you want with us? I thought I ran you off back in Dione." Amy's words dripped with hostility. "Haven't you tortured this girl enough already?"

He knelt down and lifted Amy's chin gracefully. "What do I want with you? The actual instruction was for Oswald to bring me Alister and Michelle, but I suppose you'll do." He said as she jerked away from his touch. "You sure were a handful when we last fought. Didn't think I was going to survive for a minute there." He reached down and gingerly touched her swollen knee with his fingertips.

Amy bit her lip hard, trying not to give him the satisfaction of seeing her hurt.

Slowly he began to run his fingertips up her leg to her thigh. "I must admit I like this helpless version of you a lot better."

Snap! The sound of the bonds holding Amy's hands behind her back echoed throughout the room. With one swift motion, her left fist connected with his temple, and he crumpled into the floor as his mask flew off into the darkness.

"Hands off, asshole!" Amy spat.

Michelle gasped as the man's obscured face was suddenly revealed. He had short black hair, and his face didn't look unlike her own. As the shock of that happened registered, he recovered and turned back to face Amy, his sapphire eyes full of rage. They, too, were the same as Michelle's, blue and deep as the ocean itself.

He raised his hand to strike Amy, but before he could, Michelle spoke. "Virgil?"

He winced in pain at the sound of the name. "Argh!" He exclaimed as he covered his left eye with one hand. "Stay put." He growled.

At first, Michelle thought this was directed at her, but that didn't make sense. She couldn't move, and even if she could, she could never reach him. No, the comment was directed inward, almost as if Roark were talking to himself.

"And you! Call me by that name again, and I'll burn your bones to ash!" He screamed furiously as he turned to face Michelle while still holding his eye.

Amy fumbled with the bands which bound her feet as Roark stood and walked over to where his mask lay on the floor. Bending down, he grabbed the mask and refastened it over his face. As the straps of the mask snapped on, he let out a sigh of relief and made his way back to her.

"You have no idea who you're dealing with, Red." He said calmly. Suddenly he raised his hand and backhanded her hard across the face knocking her onto her side. Grabbing her by the hair, he pulled her back toward the post and rebound her hands. Then making his way back in front of her, he knelt down once again.

Origins

She glared at him as her ears rang from the strike. Suddenly, he slammed his hand down on her injured knee.

"AAAAAHHHH!" The hapless scream echoed throughout the room. The pain made the world spin out of control.

Cold and calculated, he pressed on. "Now, where was I?" He said. "Ah yes, torture. I wasn't out to torture anyone, especially not her. Back in Dione, I was simply going to liberate her along with the other villagers, but you and that boy…." He twisted his grip, which sent a fresh wave of pain throughout Amy's body.

Amy stifled another scream. Instead, she gritted her teeth and doubled down. She'd crack her molars before letting him see her cry. "You mean Sai? You know, he was the boy who nearly knocked your head off."

With this provocation, he put all his weight on her knee and began to scream erratically. "You two are the reason Michelle has suffered! You're the reason you're both suffering now!"

"Please stop!" Michelle lunged toward them only to be pulled down by her bonds.

Roark let off Amy's leg and stood. "All I want is to give these people freedom, but you and that oppressive group from The Citadel are always in the way." He regained his composure and straightened his robes.

Amy writhed in pain as he released her leg. Tears threatened to pour down her face as she spoke. "You think killing these people is some form of altruism? You're a psychopath." She heaved.

Without a word, he knelt down once again and pulled out his tome. He held it up for her to see before tapping it against her forehead. The most excruciating visions of torture and death wound through her consciousness. What, in reality, was only seconds felt like an eternity. She burned and died thousands of times in those fleeting moments. She collapsed, writhing in pain. Her screams filled every inch of the room before she finally vomited onto the hard stone floor.

155

Origins

Bringing his face down to hers, Roark spoke in almost a whisper. "You who are so blind to the truth dares to lecture me? You are but an ant in the grand scheme of things."

"Please stop! You wanted to 'liberate 'me, right? Why not just do it already? I'm here now! Why not do it and let Amy go?" Michelle screamed as she lunged forward again. Tears poured down her cheeks as she hit the floor. "Just do it, you coward!"

Roark straightens up once again while Amy lay helpless in the dirt.

His cruel disposition seemed to snap back wildly. "Sorry, I just lose my head sometimes." He took a deep breath before continuing. "It would have been that simple before, but now you have a tome." He sighed calmly. "No, for now, I need you alive. Once I get your tomes, I'll anthologize Inferno and librate everyone, I promise." His tone sounded oddly sincere. He turned away from them and walked back toward the shadows.

"You've already taken our tomes." Amy's muttered in a pathetic empty imitation of her own voice.

"Not what I mean, Red." With that, he vanished again into the darkness. The sound of a large wooden door closing signaled his exit.

"Amy, I'm so sorry." Michelle sobbed as she lay on the floor.

Amy did all she could just to force breath into her lungs. "H-he's a monster." She said as she forced her head away from the puddle of vomit and pulled herself back to sit against the post. "You called him Virgil? You know him?"

"I do…" Michelle sobbed. "H-he's my brother."

Chapter 16: Scalpel

Boom! An explosion of water shook the forest and blasted away the deep snow and several small trees that dotted the clearing. Suddenly, the newly cleared area seemed to fill up like a glass under a gushing faucet.

"Remember to push it as far as you can!" Alister shouted from the branch of an enormous tree as the water rushed around.

Sai sat with his legs straddling the neck of Charlie, who had transformed into a huge theropod dinosaur. He held tight to the bluish fuzz around the neck of the giant tyrannosaur." Gotta transform again! Awaken Origins!" Sai tapped the book on the huge creature's back. Plum-colored smoke surrounded the animal as the water built up around its torso. They dropped below the waves just as Charlie transformed.

Sai rose up from the dark water holding the dorsal fin of a giant fish. "Go!" Sai shouted as they charged at Alister, who now stood only a few feet above the whirling pool.

"Some kind of whale? Stealing a page from my book?" Alister vaulted from the tree branch and launched his harpoon toward the fish while reaching for Sai.

"Guess again!" Sai's shout echoed out as the harpoon ricocheted off the animal's heavily armored head and spiraled off into the water. "This is dunkleosteus!" The giant brown armor-headed fish leaped from beneath the waves and opened its gaping maw. It had no teeth, but the armor around its skull formed a massive scissor-like structure.

With no time or means to correct himself, Alister ended up right between the jaws, which were primed to snap.

He closed his eyes and smiled. "Checkmate."

Before the animal could close down, Sai tapped his tome on its head and returned it to its finch form, causing both Alister and himself to crash back into the deep water.

The water quickly receded as it returned to Alister's tome. Even the moisture from their clothes seemed to fly back into the pages. Sai held out his hand and helped Alister to his feet.

"Finally got you."

"You've come a long way, Sai. Your transformations are truly something to behold." He stood and dusted off his clothing just as Zaman approached from their left.

"I must say, I'm very impressed. Your strength, as well as your knowledge of your tome, has grown dramatically." She commended him as she walked up. "And Alister, you've actually grown quite a lot yourself." She smiled at both of them.

"Do you think it will be enough?" Sai questioned as he pushed his now long black hair out of his eyes.

"Strength-wise, absolutely!" She replied with a smile. "However, do you remember what I told you before we started?"

Sai thought back momentarily before answering. "It will take more than strength to save them."

She nodded. "You should think of your tome's power as a blade."

"I thought it was an elastic band?" Sai said smartly.

Zaman didn't acknowledge the comment. "What do you use blades for?" She asked intently.

Sai contemplated this before answering. "To fight to protect ourselves and the people we care about?"

"In the case of a sword or knife, I suppose that's true. However, blades have other uses. Take a scalpel, for example." Reaching into her lab coat, she pulled out a small metal wand with a razor blade on one end. It glinted in the sunlight as she held it up. "Scalpels are blades as well, but they simply aren't very useful in a fight. Very fragile and can be broken easily. However, they are indispensable when it comes to saving lives, don't you think?"

Sai simply nodded.

She continued. "You have created a fine weapon out of your tome, but I would hardly call it a life-saving instrument. Do you follow me?"

"Maybe? You're saying that sometimes raw strength isn't the best solution when it comes to a delicate situation." He reasoned aloud as he thought about what needed to be done.

"Much like the one we've found ourselves in," Alister added.

"Exactly, you've all but mastered this macro form of transformation for the time being. I think we need to spend the remainder of our time focusing on the small scale or the microforms if you will."

As she spoke, she knelt down and picked up a pine cone off the ground. She shook it slightly, and tiny dark seeds fell into her palm. This harkened back to the same action Alister had performed when they had first set out.

"I don't want you to focus on changing these seeds into anything new. I want you to try and simply make them grow."

Sai looked at her with skepticism. "Do you think that's possible? Is that even an evolutionary ability?"

Zaman placed the seeds in Sai's hand. "No, I don't think this is an evolutionary ability at all. But, if I'm thinking about this correctly, what you're actually doing with your tome is essentially rewinding Charlie's genetic code and body structure. Then you're throwing it forward into a form found on a branch of the tree. What I'm asking you to do here is simply push the biological object forward without changing it into anything new and essentially fast forward its growth. It's much more precise and possibly much more simple at the same time. If you can do this, you may be able to affect much more than just Charlie with your ability." She tilted her head with a sly smile. "You can do this."

Sai rolled the seeds in his hand, remembering the similar seeds Alister had given him back in the sequoia

Origins

forest. "But, how do you know I can even do anything with plants?"

Alister decided to interject. "Sai, she may be right. Think back to your tome's trial for just a moment. Was it only the animals that were changing as you headed backward across time, or did the plants change as well?"

"Well, I guess the plants seemed to change too."

Zaman tried to guide him through these thoughts. "And when you reached the end?"

"There was nothing. No plants or animals. Nothing except whatever was living in that liquid." Sai explained.

"Exactly." Zaman reached into her pocket and pulled out the scroll with a tree drawn on it. She pointed to the X at the bottom of the tree's trunk. "I think that 'thing ' is our 'X 'here. I think every living thing, including all plants, stems out from that one life form."

"Every living thing? Could you mean us as well?" This realization hadn't even crossed Sai's mind. This implication brought with it many different moral implications.

Zaman nodded her head, and suddenly her tone got serious. "If I were to impose any one rule on your tome usage, I would ask that you never under any circumstances use it to directly affect another human being."

"But, if I could use it on…."

"No, you will promise me this, or else your training will end here." The lighthearted levity that she normally possessed had vanished somewhere below the surface of this dire new rule. Somehow the beautiful Zaman had been replaced in an instant by a deadly version of Cylus.

Sensing the seriousness of this, Sai agreed. "Yes, Ma'am, I'm sorry."

"No need to apologize. If it were to be used on another person in either reverse or forward transformation, it could have dire consequences for that

160

person." She reached into her lab coat and pulled out the elastic band from before.

"Say you took a person so far back they weren't human any longer. What would happen to their soul? You may not be able to reverse it at that point. Furthermore, it could be that Charlie will always snap back due to him being a construct from within the tome."

"Much like when one of my harpoons breaks," Alister added.

Zaman nodded. "Biological entities may not snap back in such a way. Simply put, if you pulled too hard, the band could snap." She stretched it so far that the fibers popped and split audibly. "And if it snaps, there may be no way of reversing what you've done."

"I understand. Thank you for the advice." Sai bowed slightly to show her respect.

"Good, now get to work. Looks like we're gonna have company soon." She pointed behind the two of them to a large storm front that seemed to be building on the horizon. "I'd say we have eight, maybe ten minutes of real-world time left."

Sai looked off into the distance. "A thunderstorm?"

Alister's response was quick and decisive. "Yeah, one we barely escaped back in Elara." He turned slowly and headed back for the campsite. "I'm going to gather my research and see if I can get any more evidence before we're forced to go. Sai, you stay and train with Zaman. Best case scenario, we have one week left here. Use it wisely." He shouted as he vanished into the tree line, leaving only his footprint in the deep snow.

Chapter 17: Parting

Five days passed, and as they did, the thunderclouds grew larger and ultimately more menacing until they all but threatened to cross into the temporal field. Sai sat exhausted beside the trunk of a massive sequoia that had sprouted from the center of the field.

"It's time, Sai." Alicia stood over him with her hand extended. "They'll be here within minutes. Let's go."

Sai grabbed her hand and found his feet. Together they trailed across the field and back toward the camp where Zaman and Alister waited. As they approached, Sai could see that Alister was wearing a large pack on his back while working on filling a second one that lay open in the snow.

Zaman sat in a rough wooden chair beside him breathing heavily. Ever since Sai had begun training under her, she seemed to be getting more and more exhausted as time wore on. It was clear that the constant use of her tome was taking its toll. At this point, she could barely walk and spent most of her time sitting and observing his progress.

"How are you feeling?" Alicia approached Zaman and knelt down beside her.

She waved her hand in protest of the coddling. "I'm okay. Please help Sai and Alister prepare. We don't have much time." Reaching behind the chair, she pulled something out. Weakly she handed the long object wrapped in white linen to Alicia. "Be sure he doesn't forget this."

She noted agreeably and helped gather their things. Before long, the group had two full packs and had deconstructed their campsite. Sai picked up the second pack and loaded it onto his back.

"Hey, Sai, this is a gift from Zaman and myself." Alicia handed the wrapped bundle to him.

"Huh? What's this?" He looked over it momentarily as he rolled it over in his hands.

"Well, unwrap it!" Alicia commanded excitedly.

Origins

He tugged at the tie at the end, and the wraps fell loosely to the ground. As they did, the milky sheen of a polished pine blade came into view. Zaman had created a wooden katana for him from the very trees of the forest.

"This is beautiful! Thank you so much!" He shouted as he threw his arms around Alicia.

The sudden embrace made her blush for a moment as she hugged him back. "Of course, now go!"

Releasing her, Sai latched the sword to his belt and tightened it down. "Do you know where we're headed?" Sai asked Alister.

"Yes." Alister reached into his pack and pulled out the warp crystal they had found in Oswald's home. "This crystal is primed to take us to the edge of the Cyllene Badlands. From there, we can use the clues we found in Oswald's study to find these 'catacombs' that lead to their hideout."

"Time's up." Shakily Zaman stood from her seat and pointed toward a silhouette emerging from the storm front.

Umbra descended kite in hand. She was moving slowly outside of the field, but it was clear that the time dilation within had weakened significantly. She raised what appeared to be a small brass key above her head and seemed to be speaking.

"Everyone grab on. We're going!" Alister's command took no time to register as Sai grabbed his shoulder.

What happened next caught both Sai and Alister by surprise. Zaman and Alicia both gave faint smiles.

"Sorry, no can do. We're staying here; you go and save your friends." Zaman's words almost seemed visible as a slow-motion bolt of lightning reached from the cloud toward Umbra's raised key.

"We aren't going to leave you here!" Alister demanded. His response was full of something Sai had rarely seen from him: concern.

She raised her hand and placed it gently on Alister's cheek. "Is that worry I hear in your voice? You're getting soft, you know." She looked at him with a weak smile. "You have lost so much in the past. It even began to jade your heart, but something in you is changing for the better, and I think I know what." She looked over to Sai for only a moment before switching her focus back to Alister. She raised up on her toes slightly and planted a soft kiss on his cheek. "We're staying to buy you time. Now, go."

Reluctantly Alister nodded. He could tell just by the tone of her voice he wasn't changing her mind. Umbra directed her key toward the edge of the field, and a bolt of lightning ripped out from the tip, flaring out slowly. Alister gripped the stone, which shattered and sent them falling through space.

As they vanished, Zaman leaned on Alicia for support. The bolt struck the edge of the field and caused it to collapse. The following thunderclap was deafening. Umbra landed and approached the two of them as time returned to normal.

"Where did they go?" It was clear by the way she shouted that she was furious from seeing them vanish before her very eyes.

"That's a good question. Wish I knew the answer, but alas." Zaman smiled slyly as her vision drifted in front of her.

"Then tell me. Why shouldn't I end you here and now for assisting traitors?" She raised the small brass key and pointed it directly at the two of them.

Zaman laughed weakly at the threat. "We'd like to be tried for our crimes. Anyone can ask for a trial by tome, correct? " She said with a sarcastic smirk as she raised her arms in surrender.

"You're not a wielder?" Umbra snarled. "We'll just see about that." Sliding her hand through the air, a window appeared. The word "database" was written above a long list of names.

"It's Zaman and Alicia Harcourt, by the way."

"Looks like you aren't in the database." She growled before reciting a few almost scripted lines. " Alicia Harcourt and Zaman, you have been seen aiding fugitives of the Citadel. How do you plead?"

"Oh, guilty for sure." Alicia chimed in.

Origins

"For your crimes, you will be administered the trial of the tome. If it finds you worthy, you will be pardoned and assigned work through The Citadel. If it does not, you will pay with your lives." She placed shackles on both of their hands, and with a long chain attached to them, she headed back with her captives to The Citadel.

*****

Alister and Sai landed atop a sand dune at the edge of the desert. This landing was far more graceful than their previous one due to them being prepared for the teleportation when it occurred. The sun was low in the sky, making the heat far more manageable than when Amy and Michelle had spent their days in the cave.

Sai pulled his hand from Alister's shoulder. "Do you think they'll be all right?"

"Both of them are very strong. Plus, if there's anything I've learned about Zaman, it's that she'll leverage their way out of trouble one way or another."

Sai gave him a wry smile and nudged him with his elbow. "Just how well did you get to know her? Don't think I missed that cheek kiss."

Alister was quick to change the subject. "Sai, focus up. We're in enemy territory now. Not to mention the weather here is famously volatile. We need to get a move on before it gets dark." Alister took a few steps forward and headed down the side of the dune.

"Yeah yeah." Sai followed him down and continued. "I have to ask. How do you think Umbra found us? Cylus 'Eighty-Four vision shouldn't have been able to see us in Zaman's field. Not to mention it should've still been disabled."

"I assume it has to do with the warp crystal Alicia used when she pulled us out. It could've left a trace signature behind. Either way, the Citadel has other ways of tracking targets. Eighty-four is simply the most effective and accurate." He explained as they meandered on.

Sai stopped and looked at him with concern. "So, will they be able to track us again?"

"Yes, Eventually. That's more than likely why they chose to stay behind. If Umbra has her hands full with them, she'll have no choice but to let us go, at least for a little while."

This line of reasoning made Sai feel uneasy, but he knew it to be true. After all, Alister had used this same method of tracking to figure out where Oswald's stone was going to take them after finding it.

Sai picked up speed to catch up again. "So, we need to find the girls, rescue them, and stop Oswald and his accomplices all before Umbra can track us down? Sounds like we're on a time crunch again."

Alister nodded. "Always were."

The two marched on for a while, looking for any signs or clues, but as the sun got lower, they began to realize that the harsh winds had swept away all signs that anyone had even been there. The two of them stopped at the top of another large dune and looked around in all directions. The setting sun seemed to paint the land a deep red. The sea of sand stretched out before them as far as the eye could see. A few small spires of stone jutted up toward the sky in the distance.

"We're losing daylight fast. Sai, why don't you send Charlie out to see if maybe he can find any signs of water or life? Oswald was surviving on something out here. He looked to have little to no supplies when he left." Alister sat down atop the dune and looked out over the horizon.

"Good idea." Sai pulled his tome from his holster and held it out. "I am fully convinced that species are not immutable. Awaken Origins!" As always, Charlie popped out and landed on his shoulder. Sai held up his tome again and transformed him into a large bird with a leathery-looking head.

"The condor form should suit you better out here." The large bird hopped to the ground and awaited instructions. "Can you go and see if you can find any signs of the girls? Maybe look for water sources?"

With these instructions, the bird took off and flew high into the sky. Before long, he vanished behind another dune leaving Sai and Alister to simply wait. By the time he had returned, the sun was well below the horizon, and the temperature was dropping rapidly. He landed at Sai's feet with something clutched in his beak.

"Hey, Alister. Looks like he found something." Sai held out his hand as if to say *drop it*. He retched in disgust as the giant bird dropped a giant severed finger directly into the palm of his hand. Dropping it into the sand, Sai heaved, trying to keep down his lunch. "Oh god, where did you get that?"

"Sai, look at how large it is." Grabbing a handkerchief from his pocket Alister picked up the severed digit. "I think this may be Oswald's, or at least it was." He wrapped the finger up and put it into his pack.

"You think he lost a finger? How?" Sai patted his hands on his pants as if trying to wipe away any traces of finger that still remained on them.

" Amelia the Abraser, I'd say," Alister said with a small grin. "We need to go. Can he take us to where he found it?"

Sai rolled his eyes. "Surely he can, but first, why do you insist on calling her that? You know she hates it."

"Sorry, old habit. A cruel nickname given to her by her classmates at the academy. I'll be sure to drop it as best I can." Alister apologized.

Sai thanked him and agreed to transform Charlie once again into his Titanis form. "Would you mind taking us, boy?" He patted Charlie's huge head with the book and strengthened him beyond his normal carrying capacity. He knelt down to let them climb onto his back. "I owe you any food you want when we get home, buddy."

The two climbed onto his back, and he sprinted across the arid sand. They rode for a few minutes before coming to the large, descending rocky ramp that led into a canyon. No amount of wind could have erased the signs of a struggle here. Two dead mules lay strewn across the stone ramp. Sawdust and huge chunks of wood dotted the path, along with one massive antler. As they descended, they found the busted ski and traces of blood near the edge of the gorge.

"What happened here?" Sai muttered to himself as he looked around.

"Oswald bit off more than he could chew, it seems." Alister peered over the edge of the gorge as he spoke. "Sai, look here." He pointed down toward the river below, where several small desert trees grew from the cliffside. They were snapped and dismembered in a descending line straight down.

"They fell?" A sinking feeling came over Sai.

"Clearly, but look how much damage they caused going down. Were they in something? Perhaps a cart. That would explain this mess as well." He pointed to the Debris behind them. "We need to get down there." Alister straightened up and looked toward Sai. "Any ideas?"

Sai nodded. "Charlie, we're gonna need your help again." He turned around to see the large bird pecking away at the mule carcass. "Oh, gross, man! Come on, that's disgusting!"

Charlie just gave him a sideways glance before standing up straight again and walking over to them.

"Ugh, that stinks!" He tapped Charlie on the side with the tome, and he transformed into a giant, leather-winged pterosaur. "Can you get us down there?"

Charlie, who was now massive, gave a slight huff of disappointment.

"Sorry, bud, the girls need us. You can eat later, I promise." With that, Charlie flapped his massive leathery wings and ascended just slightly. Alister and Sai each grabbed onto each of his monstrous feet, and together they descended toward the river. "I owe you one, buddy."

"I'm amazed he can lift both of us," Alister said as they headed down.

Sai shook his head. "He can't. All he's doing is slowing our fall."

Charlie flapped his enormous wings all the way down. After what felt like an eternity, their feet touched down gently on the muddy banks of the large river. They scanned the shore but only found broken branches that had fallen from above.

Alister knelt down and picked up a small twig. He turned it over in his hand before placing it back on the ground. "There are no signs of blood or pieces of the cart down here."

"Maybe they landed in the water and were pushed down the river," Sai suggested as he kicked a few of the branches around. He looked up at Charlie, who seemed to be trying to pluck fish from the river with his large mouth. "Eat up, buddy; you deserve it."

"I think you may be right. Judging by the trajectory, it's possible that by hitting the trees, they ended up in the river. Let's check down steam." Alister walked along the banks, and Sai followed.

"Charlie, time to rest!" Sai shouted, held up the tome, and recalled the large animal back into the pages.

The two of them trailed on together for a long while. The sun had already set behind the walls of the canyon, making the bank hard to discern from the edge of the water. From this angle, the canyon walls seemed to stretch on into eternity. As the two of them rounded a curve in the raging river, the decimated cage cart came into view.

"Alister, is that what we're after? Sai approached the wooden cart, which had been chopped into several pieces. Several of the bars had been sheered clean in two.

"Definitely the work of Amelia. No hacking. Just split perfectly down the middle." Alister ran his hand along what remained of the bars. "Looks like we're on the right path, and I think we just found our next place to search." He pointed into the darkness of the mouth of a large cave.

"Right, what are we waiting for?" Sai said as they stepped in.

They made their way into the cave, and before long, the scent of ash caught Alister's attention. He poked his head into the small opening in the cave wall to find the abandoned room the girls had sheltered in. "Someone was here and recently." He added. "Must have gone further in." They continued on and entered the room full of corridors.

"Could these be the 'catacombs' that were referred to in Oswald's papers?" Alister directed the torch down each path.

"Possibly, but how do we know which one they took?" Sai peered into each dark entrance as he spoke.

"Good question." Alister looked around once again. "I have absolutely no idea."

Sai knelt down by a nearby Stalagmite that jutted up from the floor. He took in a deep, exasperated breath. "What now.? He placed his hand down on the ground and came into contact with something unexpectedly sticky.

"Yuck, what is that?" As he raised his hand, a thick string of something gooey dripped from it. Bring it closer to his face; he could smell the almost floral aroma wafting off of it. "Honey!? Alister, it's honey. I think it's from Michelle's tome."

Alister walked over to examine the substance. "It is indeed."

The buzzing noise that came next surprised the both of them. Sai turned his attention to his shoulder, where a small, crystalline, amber color bee landed with its wings buzzing just slightly.

"This is one of Michelle's for sure," Sai spoke just as the bee lifted off of his shoulder and flew a little way into one of the caves. It stopped and hovered in the air as if asking them to follow it.

"Michelle, you beautiful genius," Sai muttered.

Alister and Sai followed the buzzing bee down one of the tunnels and through dozens of forked paths. They could even tell they crossed multiple warp points along the way. After a long walk, they arrived at an exit. The air was cool as it poured into the cave's mouth. With it came the scent of cherry blossoms, and the two men found themselves standing in a dark forest of cotton candy-colored trees.

Chapter 18: Eclipsed

  Oswald sat leaning back on the steps leading up to a large Japanese shoji-style home. Still fully transformed, his massive body covered most of the entrance to the building. The wood and paper structure sat in a clearing that had been carved directly out of the middle of the forest. A perfectly symmetrical circle of green grass was all that separated the home from the dazzling pink trees that surrounded the area on all sides. He stared up at the brilliant night sky, which was splattered with incandescent starlight, and held his bandaged hand up to the light of the full moon.
  I'll do whatever it takes, he thought. He examined the hand and its missing digits. *If this loss brings me closer to you, then that's a price I'm willing to pay.*
  A lone owl flew over, silhouetted against the brilliant moon, before vanishing into the forest behind the building. Oswald let out a deep sigh as he lowered his arm to his side. Something tiny clicked as it hit his antler and fell into the fur on his shoulder. Sitting up, he noticed something odd at the edge of the clearing. Around twenty yards in front of him, there was a figure standing at the tree line. Pink petals danced around the concealed being as the wind blew hard through the branches.
  "What, Oswald? Weren't expecting company?" The voice slashed the silence as it flew out across the open field, carried by the wind.
  "So you survived." Oswald stood to his full height. "You must have a death wish coming here alone." He drew his tome with his good hand. "That coward Alister couldn't bring himself to defy his inevitable orders even to save his students? Typical."
  Sai stepped out into the full moonlight, which revealed his long black hair held back with a white tie. It was clear he had changed. He was a bit bulkier than

before, and his clothes seemed to be just slightly shorter on him than the last time they had grappled.

"You look awful, you know," Sai said as he stepped into the clearing. "Step aside and let me through. Wouldn't want you to get hurt any more than you already are." Sai gripped his pine swords attached at his hip.

"Hahahaha! You truly have lost your mind! Your hair may look different, but you're still that same weakling I dispatched in one blow. If you think you have what it takes to even lay a scratch on me, come try it!" Oswald flung his tome open.

Without another word, Sai charged straight for him. Oswald did the same, and the two closed the distance within seconds. As they got closer, Oswald lunged at Sai, who dove into a roll and slid directly underneath the behemoth. They both slid backward and corrected their stances.

Oswald straightened up. "You've gotten faster. I'll give you that, but you're going to need more than speed to beat me!" He threw his powerful arm toward Sai.

With a swift dodge, Sai darted under the massive attack and gave the arm a quick tap before catching a massive hoof with his crossed arms.

"Arggg!" Sai went flying backward across the open ground.

"You weak piece of trash is that all you've got!" Oswald stomped toward Sai. He stood directly over him and raised his fist. "Now die!"

"Awaken Origins!" Sai's shout came just as the fist was about to deliver a fatal blow. Suddenly a full-grown pine tree sprouted from Oswald's shoulder and tore him off of his feet and to the ground. The roots wound down his entire arm, took hold in the dirt, and imprisoned him on the spot. It was then that he finally realized the small object he had heard bounce off his antler earlier was a pine seed which was now dragging him down with its enormous weight.

Sai got to his feet and dusted himself off with a smile. "Sorry, but I don't have time to waste on you." With that, he leaped around the immobilized brute and sprinted for the doors of the building.

"No, you bastard! You think that this is over?!" The earth shook as Oswald began to rip the entire tree free of its root system.

Sai looked back for only a moment before continuing on. "Wow! Stronger than I expected. Guess it's plan B, then!" He shouted.

Just as Oswald got to his feet, he felt something sharp sink into his back.

"What?"

As he turned, he could see a large harpoon that jutted out from his left shoulder. The cord of the harpoon extended off into the dense woods. With fury in his eyes, Oswald spun slightly and wrapped the cord around his arm. With one forceful yank, he pulled Alister from the shadows still attached to the cable. He flew off of his feet and straight into the monstrous hand.

"You are as foolhardy as ever, master." He gloated as he began to squeeze Alister. His confidence didn't last long, however.

With a wry smile, Alister revealed something diabolical. It was a trick stolen directly from Alicia herself. A green crystal sat snuggly between his teeth. With a swift biting motion, he shattered the crystal, and the two together collapsed through a portal beneath their feet. In less than a fraction of a second, they had been transported far away from the cherry blossom wood.

The two men exploded out of the portal in mid-air and fell to a small island in the middle of a massive ocean. The entire island consisted of a single massive volcano, the obsidian beach that surrounded it on all sides, and water that stretched out as far as the eye could see. They both tumbled head over heels down the sheer volcanic wall toward the pitch-black beach.

With the shock of the fall, Oswald unwittingly released Alister. As he hit the steep outer walls of the volcano, Alister summoned a harpoon. He stopped his uncontrolled descent by stabbing the harpoon deep into the craggy surface of the slope.

Oswald, however, was far less fortunate. His much larger mass prevented him from finding a foothold upon impact. Without any way to slow himself down, he plummeted down the entire length of the volcano. Basalt, pumice, and obsidian crumbled under his massive weight as he took a small landslide with him to the beach below.

Alister stood and pulled his harpoon from the rock. Slowly he made his way toward the heaving mountain of fur and stone that now rested at the base. As he moved down, he could see the pile bobbing up and down as Oswald's breath rose and fell. Harpoon in hand, he approached his former pupil.

"What have you done?" Oswald growled as he struggled to rise.

"I wanted to ask you the same question. Or, more accurately, what the hell do you think you're doing?" Alister crouched beside him.

"I'll kill you… I'll kill you and use your warp crystal to get back." Oswald's breath was heavy as he struggled beneath the rubble.

"Sorry. That crystal was my last." He spit, trying to dislodge stone shards from his teeth. "We're marooned here."

"Y- you would doom us both to help those whelps?" Oswald growled, his fury palpable.

"Those 'whelps,' as you call them, are my students. I will not allow them to die even if that means I have to." Alister planted the shaft of his harpoon into the pitch-black sand.

"You think stranding me here changes anything? No, Roark will kill Sai before he can even reach those girls."

"And what do you get from that outcome? What, do you just want the world to feel your pain? You'd sacrifice the innocent for something so childish?" Alister spit in disgust.

"That's rich coming from the man who's killed so many. I heard what you became after Sibyl's death, the dispatch missions you undertook. Your ledger is written in blood." The rubble shook as he began to stand. "You were the one who left us back in Elara. You're the one who brought Oran into the fold! You're the reason Sibyl is dead! Don't pretend that you've ever given a damn about us, about those new kids, about anybody but yourself and the damned Citadel!"

  Alister stepped back and readied his harpoon. "Don't make me do this, Oswald."

  This plea fell on deaf ears as the rubble began to shift and fall as the mass of muscle and rage rose. "Then you should have walked away back in Elara!" He hurled stones which Alister deflected with his harpoon. "I'll kill you!" He lunged at Alister.

  Alister sidestepped him and jumped back into the foamy surf of the nearby sea. "The three of you chose to stay behind. What happened to you?" Alister said, trying to reel the conversation back. He stabbed forward in an attempt to pin Oswald's arm.

  He dodged just in time as the harpoon grazed the outside of his arm. Without a word, he thrust himself forward in an attempt to use his remaining antler for a surprise attack.

  A second harpoon materialized in Alister's other hand and stopped the blow before it could skewer him. This forced him to backpedal a few more steps into the sea, which was now nearly to his knees. He stared at Oswald as the tide beat against him. Pity washed over his mind as he looked over the monster that was his former student.

  "Look at you. It would break Sibyl's heart to see what you've become."

  "Don't.... Don't you dare speak her name in my presence!" Oswald's howl shook the very earth itself as the tome reappeared in his hand.

  "Lecturing me over what Sibyl would want. What the hell do you know about it!?" The book flew open and began to glow. "The basis of optimism is sheer terror! Awaken Dorian Gray!" Suddenly, a transformation seemed to take hold of Oswald. His damaged hand seemed to mend; the busted antler regrew, and any scratch or scar he had vanished without a trace. He even looked far larger than he had before. He was an unstoppable mountain of muscle and sinew.

Tears welled up in Alister's eyes. "Stop this! Do you really think this is what she would want?" He gripped a harpoon in each hand as cords attached to the ends of them wound up his arms and into his sleeves. Without another word, he lobbed the harpoon in his left hand with such force that it caused his joints to crack as he released it.

Oswald juked to one side and dodged the attack as he charged forwards. For someone so large, his speed was blinding. In an instant, he was on top of Alister. His enormous fist poised to crush him like an ant. The water exploded as his fist came down, causing a dense mist to fill the immediate area. Oswald let out a horrific howl as he came to an agonizing realization.

Just before his fist came down, Alister summoned three more harpoons, thrusted their hilts into the soft sea bed, and turned them into pikes. These pikes were all that Oswald had caught when he attacked. Somehow Alister had done all of this and moved to his immediate left, all before the strike could hit. The cables attached to these harpoons fell from Alister's arms as he summoned yet another harpoon and thrust it across Oswald's left calf. He collapsed to his knees in the shallow water. Alister stabbed dozens of harpoons into his back, all within a fraction of a second, till he was dotted like a porcupine in water.

Alister stood upright and spoke softly. "It's the last thing I want, but I will kill you if I must."

"No… No! This will not end till she's back in my arms!" The shout caused the water to ripple as energy pulsed out from every inch of his body. The energy appeared to heal the wounds as he snapped the harpoons and ejected them from his body. He grew larger yet again as he rose. He was at least thirty feet tall now, and with one swipe of his arm, he caught Alister in mid-air and blasted him back to the island.

"Arggghhh!" His back hit the wall of the volcano. He bounced off, and before he could land, Oswald was on top of him. Due to Oswald's newfound size, he misjudged his aim and slammed his fist into the wall of the volcano a couple of feet above Alister's head. Large deep fissures formed in the dark stone beneath his knuckles and began to glow. Oswald had just slammed his fist into the thin outer wall of a subsurface lava tube, which threatened to gush forth at any moment.

Alister collapsed on the ground just below his strike. He heaved as he felt the multiple fractures he'd suffered from just the single hit. While Oswald was recovering from the strike, Alister used his remaining strength to grab a potion from his inventory and quickly heal his injuries. As he glanced up, he saw something glimmer ever so slightly at Oswald's side. Without another thought, he summoned a harpoon and flung it at Oswald's midsection.

In the blink of an eye, he dodged and went in for another strike. Alister dodged by grabbing the cord attached to the launched harpoon, which carried him directly under Oswald's arm and back out toward the ocean. He landed on his feet in the surf and grabbed the harpoon as he readied himself.

Oswald turned, and like a flash, he was back on the offensive. His fists flew with a fury that Alister had never experienced from such a gargantuan beast. Alister swayed back and forth, dodging each consecutive blow. Just as Alister thought he was beginning to understand his patterns, a fist came out of nowhere.

"I will end you!" Oswald screamed as his fist snapped the handle of Alister's harpoon before slamming him in the solar plexus. He went flying and landed at least fifty feet from shore. As he disappeared beneath the deep waves, Oswald turned away from him.

"You damned fool. My power eclipses even yours now." He muttered as he trudged his way back to the island. Slowly, he noticed that the water was getting shallower much faster than it should have. Suddenly harpoons shot out of the water on every side of him. Oswald dodged each of these as they flew past him. As soon as the assault stopped, another came; the cords attached to each harpoon seemed to erupt from the water,

Origins

wrapping swiftly around Oswald and binding him in place.

"Enough!" Alister rose from the wave in a giant whale made of water. Hundreds of harpoons swirled within the aqueous avatar. It flew into Oswald breaking the cords and blasting him back into the same spot he had hit on the volcano. Oswald was suspended within the water as the harpoons tore into him. With only his head free for air, there was nothing he could do.

Alister stood atop the enormous whale and looked down at him. Without a word, the whale began to break down till all that was left was a layer of water covering Oswald. From the fissures on the volcano, lava began to leak out and run over the liquid layer on Oswald's body.

Alister continued to pump water over his body as the lava hardened into stone, encasing him tightly. Before long, the flow had hardened so completely that it stopped dead. Oswald had no room to move with only his head exposed. The noxious fumes from the liquid rock made his head swim.

Alister stood on a rocky outcropping jutting from Oswald's chest, made by the freshly cooled lava. Placing one hand on Oswald's antler, he leaned in to look directly into his eyes. In his left hand, he held up a red potion and a small gold heart-shaped locket.

"I'm done. We're going to talk." He drank the potion down and mended his shattered body.

Chapter 19: Victims

At a full-on sprint, Sai busted through the building's paper doors. "Amy! Michelle!"

The room was empty. Each wall was covered in a thin paper to allow light to pour in from the full moon above. The hardwood floor of the entrance dropped off into a floor covered in thick green tatami mats. His voice seemed to fall flat into the empty void that was the room.

"You seem lost." A disembodied voice called from somewhere above Sai. "Let me help you find the exit." Suddenly a shadow like an enormous bat swooped down, transforming mid-flight to a much more humanoid appearance.

Sai drew his sword and blocked an open palm strike that was aimed at his heart. The force of the blow caused Sai to slide back across the hard floor and back out the door. He tumbled down the steps and onto the lawn.

The figure's bright red eyes shone in the dim light of the room. As he walked toward the door, Sai got a better look at him. His skin was pale, and two fangs jutted out from the top of his snarling smile. He wore a dark pair of dress pants, which were held up by black suspenders. The long sleeves of his button-up shirt were rolled up to reveal his forearms. The figure reached up and straightened his blood-red tie with one hand as he stepped out.

"I must admit I'm impressed you got past Oswald. How'd you do that, by the way?"

"Sorry, I'm not much for small talk." Sai found his footing and burst forward, sword in hand. The menacing figure caught the blade easily. Sai quickly tapped the base of the hilt and caused sharp thorns to manifest all over the sword.

"Arrrgg" He yelped as the thorns pierced his hand. He didn't let go, however, and instead raised his foot and kicked Sai directly in the gut, and as he did, he released his grip. This sent Sai flying back yet again. "You truly have no idea who you're dealing with, do you?"

Sai gripped his sword as he slid back across the field. He rubbed his stomach as he steadied himself. "Can't say I do. Why don't you enlighten me?"

The shadowy figure stepped out into the small porch as he spoke. "You can call me Bram. I'm the head of Roark's vanguard. And who might you be?"

"The name's Sai. So Roark's here, huh? Say, Bram, you wouldn't mind stepping aside to let me through, would you?" Sai straightened up and dusted off his clothes.

"Ha! Sorry, kid, you shouldn't have come here." Bram summoned his tome.

Sai did the same and summoned Charlie, who landed in a tree at the edge of the woods behind Sai.

"There are vampires. They are real, they are of our time, and they are here, close by, stalking us as we sleep… Awaken Dracula!" Bram's book flew open, and a dark wave of bats erupted out. Sai raised his sword and braced for the onslaught of creatures, but this was unnecessary. The bats didn't swarm him and instead landed all around him in the field. Without another word, Bram turned and headed back for the door.

"Where do you think you're going?" Sai dashed toward him, leaping a few of his bats in the process, and he lunged, sword in hand. Before he could reach him, however, Bram transformed into a cloud of mist, causing Sai to pass directly through him; he reappeared once again and snapped his fingers.

"You don't get to fight the head of the vanguard without going through the vanguard itself. That would just be ludicrous." As he spoke, the bats around the clearing were all enveloped in a black fog that transformed them into human beings.

Sai looked around as more and more people with glowing red eyes appeared in the clearing. They snarled as they slowly approached. Bram vanished again, and the Shoji-style doors of the building slammed behind him, leaving Sai in the lurch.

Origins

He backed toward the door as the throng inched ever closer. He readied himself with his sword in hand. *Well, this isn't going as planned, h*e thought. He swung the sword around, causing the thralls to jump back. There were at least twenty-five of them, each with pale skin and fang-like teeth.

One of the thralls leaped at Sai, which he dodged with ease. He looked down to see that the boy had ashy blonde hair and looked to be around thirteen. *He looks familiar.* Then Sai realized where he'd seen the boy. This was Sarah Albertson's son, the one who had been kidnapped by Oswald. Oswald had delivered him here, and they turned him into this.

"Come on, Charlie! Gotta dispatch these guys! Awaken Origins!" Sai held his tome up, and Charlie came flying from the trees, transforming mid-flight. He turned into an enormous dinosaur with three horns sticking out of its frilled head.

"Go!" Sai shouted as the triceratops rammed its way through the crowd. Sai grabbed one of its horns and leaped onto its back. The two charged around in a circle breaking free of the group.

"Be careful; we can't kill them. They may still be able to be saved!" He patted Charlie's head as they curved around for another pass. "Just knock them down, and we'll bind them up with the seeds I have left."

Charlie charged through yet again, thrashing while trying to avoid seriously injuring any of the victims. As they did, Sai threw small pine seeds at the feet of each of them. With a tap of his tome, the trees sprouted and grew around the thralls, encasing them almost completely.

They're not tough. He thought. *There are just so many of them.*

When Sai could see that the final thrall had been contained, he brought Charlie to a halt. He leaped down from his back and inspected the newly formed trees. The thralls growled and hissed at him as he passed. It was just as he had feared all of these hollow, half-dead beings were clearly the kidnapped townspeople.

Origins

"What did they do to you?" He placed his hand on the cheek of one of the victims, who hissed at his touch. Their skin felt like ice, as if they weren't alive at all. "We'll need to come back for them once we save the girls." He placed his hand on Charlie's side, and he transformed back into a finch which landed on Sai's shoulder as they headed back into the building.

*****

Oswald growled as he struggled beneath his stone straitjacket.

"Would you stop struggling?" Alister held up the locket, placed his thumb over the face of it, and began to apply pressure to the locket's faceplate. Oswald seemed to stop almost entirely. "So, you realize what this is after all?"

"Of course I do. How did you get that?" He growled through his massive teeth.

Alister popped the locket open to view the picture inside. "I grabbed it with that last harpoon. This was hers."

"It's all I have left of her." Oswald's menacing tone seemed to falter slightly.

"It's more than that. This was the catalyst she used for her transformations, and now it's yours as well." He rolled the gold heart over in his hand. In the center sat a small photo of Oswald's human form.

"No, my catalyst is the painting back in Elara." Oswald protested.

"You moved too far away from it. When you teleported, it reverted to the nearest previous catalyst." Alister held it up again, letting it catch the light. "I couldn't figure out how you were healing yourself, but I think I understand now."

Oswald breathed heavily. "I've mastered the power she left me. It's a sign that I'm on the right path."

"Power she left you? Mastered it? No, you haven't. She could do something similar. You're not actually healing at all."

Origins

"I just did it. Perhaps your eyesight is failing you in your old age." Oswald scoffed.

"No, you're simply transferring those injuries to the other you." Alister dropped the locket into his other hand. "You realize that by doing that, you've cursed yourself to live out the rest of your life as this? If you transform back now, those wounds will be too much for your human form and kill you."

Shock filled Oswald's eyes. He lowered his head. "You're lying."

"If you don't believe me, transform back. You would be small enough then to get out of this stone cage." Alister placed the locket into his pocket. He stood up again on the rocky outcropping.

Oswald eyed him, contemplating what he could only assume was a bluff. He thought about it for a while but couldn't bring himself to test the authenticity of his claim.

"I've been around that tome long enough to know its workings and pitfalls. Tell me what I want to know, and I'll save you from that fate." Alister stared out at the open sea.

"Piss off," Oswald growled.

"That's fine. Guess we're done here." Alister walked to the edge of the plateau and jumped down to the black sand below. He made his way to the water's edge and pulled out his tome. The water bulged at his feet and lifted him slightly. He put two fingers to his head in a kind of salute. "Goodbye, Oswald."

"You would abandon me here? You would turn your back on me again!?" Oswald's howl caused Alister to turn to face him once again.

He used the water and raised himself back to the plateau. "You abandoned yourself! You abandoned your humanity, your soul! And for what?"

"For her!" Oswald screamed furiously.

Alister stepped onto the platform. "You keep mentioning how you're doing this for 'her.' You mean Sibyl?"

"Of course," Oswald growled.

"Explain." Alister looked at him solemnly.

"Roark promised me that if I brought him enough potential tome users, he would use the power of his tome to bring her back to me." Tears welled up in his eyes. "His tome allows him control of certain aspects of the afterlife."

"Roark is the man who attacked Dione?" Alister held up the note he found in the study.

Oswald let out a low growl again. "So, that's how you found us... but, wait, what do you mean attacked Dione?" This information seemed to surprise Oswald.

"Yeah, he burned it to the ground along with everyone in it. Well, except Michelle, and she's only alive because of Sai." Alister responded.

"I didn't know." Oswald mulled over this new information. "It doesn't matter. He is the only one who can bring her back."

"My daughter, Sibyl? She's dead! Gone! You're telling me he promised to bring her back to life?" Alister looked him directly in the eyes. "You realize how insane that sounds?"

Oswald seemed to compose himself at this line of questioning. "If I hadn't seen him do it once already, I wouldn't believe it either."

This caught Alister's attention. "You've seen him revive another person?"

"Not long after he first made contact with me, he told me of this ability, and I didn't believe him. He offered to prove it and asked me to come to the hideout. When I arrived, he had a man with him. He forced this man to undergo the test of the tome. When the darkness poured out, I was surprised to see that it didn't consume him. Instead, it seemed to stop his heart on the spot. Roark knelt down and placed his own tome on his chest, and the boy rose. Not only was he alive, but he had somehow gained a tome in the process." Oswald laid the entire story out in excruciating detail.

Origins

"And this 'boy,' where is he now?" Alister spoke firmly as he grasped Oswald's antlers.

Oswald flinched as Alister forced him to tilt his head. "Back at the base. He's the leader of Roark's vanguard. Goes by…"

Chapter 20: Vampirism

"Bram!" Sai burst through the front doors of the building. A single tatami mat lay flung against the far left wall. A gap in the floor where the mat once sat revealed a dark staircase that seemed to lead to another level of the building. As he approached, Sai could hear low, pained groans coming from below. Charlie chirped on Sai's shoulder as they both looked down into the void.

"Yeah, can't say I'm a fan of this either, buddy." Sai pulled out a quick light torch, stuck it against the floor to light it, and descended down into the lower room.

The torchlight illuminated the room as Sai entered. He could still hear the noise, but it seemed more present than before. As he panned around, something horrifying came into view. A dark figure was hunched in the far north corner of the room, clutching in its arms a familiar redheaded girl. Bram's mouth was pressed to her neck, and her body seemed to pulse rhythmically as he pressed his teeth hard into her jugular.

Sai's voice caught in his throat "Amy…."

Bram stood up slowly as the voice registered. "I must admit you work fast." His red eyes shone in the darkness. "Do you know this girl? She's my new favorite. Only got her a few hours ago." Bram wiped a dribble of blood from his chin.

"Amy! What did you do to her!?" He walked toward her without regard to Bram whatsoever.

Bram placed his hand on Sai's chest as he approached. "Eh eh eh" He waved a finger at Sai. "She's mine."

Sai grabbed his wrist forcefully. "Get them the hell out of my way!" He yanked Bram's hand off of his chest and threw it aside.

Bram grabbed Sai's collar in an instant and lifted him off the ground with a demonic level of strength. "You want her?" He threw Sai back into one of the many support beams that dotted the store room.

Origins

Charlie flew off into the rafters as Sai tried to recover from the hit. He drew his pine sword and charged back in on an opponent who had turned his back on him.

"Fine then, she's all yours." The words came as Sai's blade made contact with a far too familiar shield. Bram vanished into the darkness as Amy's eyes met Sai's. Her once brilliant emerald eyes were now clouded pools of stagnated blood. Her leg looked swollen and damaged, but she seemed unfazed by the injury. Her movements were lightning-fast, and her strength was greater than before.

"Amy, why?" Sai pressed hard against her enormous strength. She didn't respond and instead brought her sword down in a deadly arc. Sai managed to jump back. His shoulder caught the tip of the blade as it came down. He staggered backward as the cold steel skimmed against the layer of chainmail under his shirt. It left a small incision where it made contact. He raised his sword just in time as Amy swung again. The blade slashed across Sai's sword, which it passed through like butter. The tip flew off as the volley continued. With every strike, pieces of pine split off and littered the room.

"Amy!" Sai lunged forward and slammed her shield. The tattered and now admittedly much shorter blade of the pine sword cracked up the entirety of its length. She staggered backward before righting herself.

"You're voice can't reach her where she is." Bram's voice seemed to pour from the darkness itself. "I'm going to have your friend kill you with her own hands." A menacing laugh sent a chill up Sai's spine. "Then I can add you to my collection as well! That way, you can be together forever!"

Before Sai could regrow the damage to his sword, Amy was on the attack again. Her blade swung at blinding speeds, and Sai took blow after blow as he tried to dodge. With one massive swing Sai took a hit directly across his chest that threw him to the ground. The sparks from his chainmail flashed in the darkness of the room. It cut clean through, leaving a large gash across his chest. She stood over him, blade raised.

Origins

"Think that's about enough. Time to join my collection." Bram's voice reached out of the darkness and seemed to surround him.

A small chirp echoed from above one corner of the room. "Found you! 'Nothing is easier to admit in words the truth of the universal struggle for life. Awaken Origins!" Sai's tome appeared in his hand, and a blinding light from it illuminated the room. It faded with no apparent effect.

"Hahahaha! Not enough power left in that pathetic husk you call a body?" Bram bellowed.

Boom! The entire room shook as an enormous orangutan-like creature fell from the dark ceiling and slammed its fist down into one of the room's corners. Amy collapsed on the spot. The ape stepped back. It was massive; at almost ten feet tall, its head brushed the rafters as it stood over its crippled victim. Between Charlie's monstrous feet, sunk into the cracked stone floor, lay the mangled body of Bram.

"Gigantopithecus," Sai murmured as he collapsed to his knees and looked toward the back of the enormous beast. It was clear this transformation was no easy feat. Within seconds Charlie transformed back into a chirping finch.

As soon as Bram was down, Amy's body hit the floor. Scooping her up, Sai cradled her lifeless body.

Her skin was pale and cold, two puncture wounds adorned her neck, and fangs jutted out from her lips. She was breathing softly, but her pulse was nearly non-existent.

"Amy, please wake up." Sai shook her, but she didn't budge. "Amy, please…" The dread of what was happening began to sink in at once.

A weak laugh echoed out from the corner, followed by a cough. "You broke nearly every bone in my body, you bastard."

Sai turned toward the voice. He laid Amy on the ground gently and stood. Walking over, he grabbed Bram by the collar and lifted him slightly. "You killed her." He growled.

Origins

Bram coughed again. "Close, but no cigar."

"Then you're going to save her." Sai yanked him upward forcefully.

He groaned in pain before laughing again. "She may not be dead, but I didn't say she could be saved."

"What did you do to her?"

"The same thing I did to the others. I turned her into a vampiric thrall. She's not even human anymore. I changed her genetic makeup on a fundamental level. She's mine, and if I die, all of my thralls will as well." He cracked a maniacal smile and began to laugh, which led him into a pain-induced coughing fit.

Sai gritted his teeth. He gripped Bram's collar sharply before dropping him back into his hole. He continued to laugh as Sai walked away and back toward Amy.

Sai knelt beside Amy. As he watched Amy's breath rise and fall, he thought back to the girl who had saved him, the one who had given him a hard time since the hospital, the beautiful fighter who flustered him with every flirtatious line she dropped.

He placed his hand over Amy's chest. "I'm sorry, Zaman, 'This preservation of favorable individual differences and variations, and the destruction of those which are injurious, I have called Natural Selection ' Awaken Origins." His hand shook as it began to glow with a bright golden light that engulfed Amy's body. His mind raced back to her eyes, her voice, the way she walked, every little detail he could remember.

"Come on; please work; I don't want to lose you." Tears poured down his cheeks as he remembered everything he could. "Please!"

His focus broke as a hand reached up and brushed Sai's cheek gently. As she spoke, the spell stopped immediately." Gods, your hair looks stupid at this length."

Sai opened his eyes to see Amy staring back at him, the resurgence of green in her eyes causing him to break down without a word. He squeezed her tightly as the light faded from her body. Her once icy skin was warm and welcoming once again. Her hobbled leg had been restored, and the sharp fangs jutting out from her perfect lips seemed to have regressed back to normal.

She groaned loudly as he squeezed her. "Careful." She laughed in an attempt to hold back tears.

This moment was cut short as a pained noise rose from the opposite corner of the room. "How?"

Sai helped Amy sit up before standing and walking toward Bram. He knelt beside Bram's broken body.

"You lose." Sai rose again and turned his back to walk away.

"Wait, please… You made her human again." He coughed violently. "Roark told me that was impossible."

Sai stopped at the mention of Roark's name.

"Please, take mercy on me. Roark is the one who turned me into this. Can you restore me as well?" He pleaded pathetically as Sai walked away.

Without turning around, Sai gritted his teeth in anger. "You think you deserve mercy!? You were just reveling in the thought of having my friend kill me. Now you beg me to save you!?"

Was it true? Had this man been turned into this against his will? Was it possible that he was yet another victim of Roark's madness? These thoughts clouded Sai's judgment as he contemplated what he should do.

"Please, If you save me, I could take you to Roark and the other girl."

Sai turned to face him. "Do you have any idea what you're asking me to attempt?" He shouted. "You could end up dead or worse."

"It doesn't matter. If you leave me here, Roark will end me regardless. Please take this curse from me." He coughed again as tears poured down his cheeks.

Sai looked back to Amy, who was still sitting, catching her breath. Zaman's words raced through his mind. "Never under any circumstances use it to directly affect another human being."

Origins

I've broken my promise once, but I can't just leave him here. Sai weighed the morality of this choice. Before long, he knelt down beside Bram. "If I do this, what happens to the thralls I trapped outside?"

"I'm not sure. It's possible that by removing my vampirism, you may also remove my hold on them." He said weakly.

Sai spoke sternly. "I'll help you, but once you're human again, I want you gone. I never want to see your face again."

"You don't want my help with Roark?" He questioned.

"No, I want you gone," Sai repeated.

"You have my word." A weak, almost sincere smile crept across his face before coughing again.

"Hold still. This takes an extreme amount of focus." Again Sai placed his hand over Bram's chest and repeated the same line he had used on Amy.

"Awaken, Origins." The golden glow returned to his hand and enveloped Bram. Sai closed his eyes and focused. As he worked, Bram's bones and muscles seemed to move back into place and mend. From there, Sai tried to work backward the way he did with Amy.

Without warning, Bram's powerful hand reached up and grabbed Sai by the throat. He was lifted off of the ground as Bram stood. The glow still surrounding him, he gripped down tightly. "You pathetic fool!"

Sai choked as he tried to speak. "N...no. You said..." Sai tried to maintain focus as the power spilled out of his tome.

"Why would I ever want to return to that weak human state?" He laughed again. "I asked Roark for this gift, and now I'm going to use it to do whatever the hell I want!"

This all happened so quickly that Amy barely had time to register what was happening. "Sai!" She screamed as she scrambled to her feet.

That was it. Her scream was the straw that broke the camel's back. As Sai turned as best he could toward the sound, he lost what little focus he was maintaining. The once precise scalpel was now a chainsaw tearing through Bram's molecular structure. In what seemed like an instant, Bram vanished in a puff of smoke; his clothes and tome lay hollow on the hard stone floor.

Sai collapsed to the floor. As he lay gasping for air, he noticed a lump within the pile moving. Sai shook his head, thinking he was seeing things as the head of a small shrew-like creature poked out of Bram's collar. It sniffed the air for a moment before lunging at Sai, teeth bared.

A foot swooping in from the sides sent the creature sailing into the darkness, where it whimpered and scurried through a small hole in the wall.

"Yikes, what was that?!" Amy shouted as she squirmed with discomfort.

Sai's head swam with guilt. "Bram… I…I…" He put his hands to his head.

Amy knelt down and grabbed his shoulders. She shook him. "Sai! Sai!"

He looked up at her blankly. His breath was labored and panic-stricken. "What have I done? What happened to his soul?"

Smack! Amy's hand landed hard on Sai's Cheek. "No, we're not doing that! Snap out of it!"

The hit jarred him back to reality. "But, I…"

She cut him off. "You saved me!" She threw her arms around him and squeezed him tightly. "He was going to kill us both, and you save me. Thank you."

Sai put his arms around her as well, and they sat huddled in this embrace. This moment was interrupted as an oddly human sound rang out from above them.

The two broke apart, giving each other a confused look. As they stood, Amy grabbed a length of fabric from the floor nearby. She covered Bram's tome and, carefully picking it up, stored it in her inventory. Together they made their way up the staircase to ground level. More and more voices seemed to fill the air as they came to the exit. The realization of what was going on was the best news yet. All of Bram's victims had returned to normal; their vampiric traits had all but faded away.

Origins

Sai regressed the trees, encasing them, and released the captives. In tandem, the busted sword, which Sai had reattached at his hip, grew back to its original pristine condition. The free citizens swarmed and thanked him.

"Everyone gather up!" Sai addressed the crowd. He pulled a green crystal from his inventory and clutched it firmly in his hand as he thought about his next word very carefully. He took a deep breath and held the crystal out to the familiar blonde-haired boy. "You're Alex, right?"

The boy nodded in surprise. "I-I am. Do I know you?"

Sai shook his head. "We're part of a group that was sent to help you. We talked to your mom. She misses you."

Alex's eyes got misty. "I miss her."

"I know." Sai slid the crystal into his hands. "Alex, I need your help. Would you mind?" Alex nodded in response. "This crystal will teleport you and anyone touching you to The Citadel. I need you to make sure everyone gets there safely. They will get you home."

"You're not coming with us?" Alex questioned.

Sai shook his head. "No, we can't. We still have a friend to save." Amy nodded next to Sai.

Without another word, Alex asked everyone to grab hands, and together they teleported to safety. Amy and Sai were left alone in the pale light of the full moon.

Turning back to the building, Amy spoke. "We're not allowed back home, are we?" She asked as she summoned her sword and shield.

Sai shook an obvious air of exhaustion off of his shoulders. "Yeah, I doubt it." Using the tome at this level and frequency was taking a serious toll on him. Drinking down a small potion to heal his wounds, he straightened up. "We need to find Michelle; then we can figure out the rest."

Amy nodded, and together the two headed back into the building.

Chapter 21: Love and Loss

"So, you did all of this to see Sibyl again?" Alister sat on the stone outcropping, jutting out from Oswald, and stared out toward the ocean. "And you blame me for her death?"

Oswald looked on, unable to move. "You allowed Oran into our team. You didn't return when we asked for assistance. If you had been there, she would still be here today."

Alister simply sat silently as he listened to the waves crash onto the beach.

"Am I wrong?" Oswald snapped.

Alister stood up once again. "No, you're not. You have every right to hate me. It's my fault she's gone; I placed my loyalty to The Citadel above my family, and it has cost me everything." Small sparkling droplets fell at his feet. "I truly am sorry."

"If that's true, then make amends and help me bring her back," Oswald commanded.

Alister turned toward him, and as he did, he seemed to transform before Oswald's very eyes. Where the gruff and beaten Alister once stood was now a beautiful dark-skinned, long silver-haired girl. Her deep brown eyes bore straight into Oswald's. "Do you believe that's what I want?" She said softly as she melted back into the visage of Alister again.

Oswald shook his head, trying to comprehend what had just happened. The word vestige came to mind. He'd heard of such a thing in the past, remnants of a tome's past wielder's consciousness clinging to the book after their passing. Was this the doing of Dorian Gray? He shook the thought away. *It can't be. H*e thought.

"Yeah, didn't think so," Alister replied harshly as he turned away again.

Origins

This made Oswald snap back as his blood boiled. "You are still a dog of The Citadel! You could have her back in your life, and you refuse out of what? Fear?"

Alister glared back at him. "Sibyl's death has haunted me every day. But she's gone, and we must both learn to live with that!" He shouted.

"You're weak. You lack the constitution to do what needs to be done. If you ever loved her…"

Turning on the spot, Alister summoned a harpoon and lunged it toward Oswald, stopping only inches from his right eye. He faltered and lowered the harpoon, and once again, the girl appeared, this time behind Alister as he spoke. "When I started out on this mission, all I wanted was to help the people of Elara. The people you and Sibyl swore to protect. I wanted to help you. But then I got saddled with that boy: Sai. He reminded me of Oran in so many ways, and it brought back so much regret. Seeing you reaffirmed those feelings. Sai didn't trust the one person I did most." He continued. "You were like a son to me, and his doubt in you made me dislike him even more. But, then, you turned on us. You hurt innocent people, and while I stood there helplessly, he charged in. Without a prayer of beating you, he jumped in, all to save a couple of girls he had only just met. And for a fleeting moment, I didn't see Oran in him. I saw you." Alister fought back tears. "The real you."

"He's right." The girl added. "I see you in him too."

"Sibyl?" Oswald murmured. He couldn't believe his eyes. This was no hallucination. He could see her there plain as day, but Alister didn't seem to notice. It was clear now she was, in fact, a vestige of his tome.

"And you, my only living student," Alister continued. "You turned out to be the very thing you vowed to stop. After Sai recovered, I found a need to trust him, and someone else appeared before me. Someone who understood the pain of loss. She taught me that we need to let go of the past and forgive ourselves in order to protect those who need us in the present. Sibyl will always be my daughter, and I will always regret not being there for her when she needed me, and I will always love her. But I have students who need me now! Guiding and protecting them is the recompense for all of my past failures."

With a closed-eyed smile, Sibyl vanished again.

Oswald shuttered as she did. "So, you've turned your back on us again!" He shouted.

"I've turned my back on you? Look at yourself! Ask yourself this, if this Roark could bring back the dead, why hasn't he done it for you?"

"He needed more power. He said by gaining others' tomes; he could use their power to strengthen his own. He would anthologize his tome and…."

"Wake up! He's using you! He's playing off of your grief and despair! " Alister screamed.

"He said…"

"You've allowed yourself to be swallowed by your anger, your hatred, your fear!" Alister shouted.

"No… he…"

Sibyl appeared on Alister's left, this time as he shouted. "Listen to me! Even if he could bring Sibyl back. Is that something she would want? And furthermore, do you truly believe she could ever look at you the same way if she did return? How could you expect her to love the man you've become?"

"Now, this is the part he's wrong about," Sibyl added as she stepped forward and placed a hand on Oswald's cheek. "There is always time to make amends. So long as you have breath in your lungs, you can make this right."

His breath faltered as she touched him. "But, I…"

"Oh, looks like I'm out of time." She said with a smile as a small tear rolled down her cheek. "One more thing, though. No matter what you do, I will always love you even as you are now." With this final line, she dissolved in a shower of golden sparks. All of this occurred, and Alister was none the wiser.

The rock encasing Oswald suddenly cracked and began to crumble. Alister leapt back and readied himself for a fight, but it never came. Oswald fell forward, catching himself with his hands. He gripped his tome, and his wounds transferred yet again.

"Oswald, don't." Alister lowered his harpoon and held out his hand. "Please don't make me do this."

Tears poured down Oswald's face, and fell into the dark sand. "No, no, why do I believe you? Why can't I just do what needs to be done?" He slowly shrank down to his original Ijiraq form. He stared at his trembling hands. "How could you ever love me like this?"

Alister let his guard down and approached Oswald. "She always loved you. Oswald, It's never too late to make things right. Come back with me and help me stop Roark and free those victims." He held out the locket. "It's time to become the man she always knew you were destined to be. The man she gave her tome to. Keep her memory in your heart, and use it to help the world she loved so much."

At once, Alister had become a beacon of hope in the darkness that surrounded Oswald's very identity. Slowly Oswald raised his head. He stood to his full height, and Alister stood his ground. He reached one hand out and grasped the locket. The two's eyes met, and for the first time in what felt like an eternity, they stood united.

Chapter 22: Reunion

Amy and Sai entered the building once again and climbed down into the underground room. Amy grabbed one of her remaining torches from her inventory and illuminated the room. Several sconces hung on the wall with unlit torches of their own. She walked around slowly, lighting each one. With the added light, the full breadth of the room came into view. Sacks of grain and store barrels lay around the mostly empty stone room. If Sai hadn't just defeated an extremely powerful vampire here, he might mistake it for a standard cellar.

The two looked around the room for a moment before Sai spoke up. "This place seems kind of anticlimactic for a hidden base." He ran his hand over an open bag of grain. He picked up a handful and let it slip through his fingers back into the sack.

"Most likely to throw off any would-be pursuers. Believe me, from what I've seen of it; it's much more elaborate than it looks." Amy walked over to a wall at the far end of the room and ran her hand along the neatly aligned stones. Applying a bit of pressure to one caused it to sink in, which in turn caused a low humming sound to fill the room.

"There you are." Slowly she lifted one hand, and it passed seamlessly through the wall. She looked back to Sai and waved him on. "Let's go."

Quickly he followed behind her, and the two passed through to another room. It was a simple stone corridor that led to a descending flight of stairs. A faint melody could be heard as they came to the top of the staircase.

"A warp gate?"

"No. Some kind of holo-door, essentially a secret passageway. I'd bet money we're still under the same building." Amy replied.

Origins

The two of them headed down and entered another long corridor. "Mind if I ask you something?" Sai questioned.

"Of course. What's up?"

"You still have your tome. We were under the impression that these guys were gathering possible tome users to steal their tomes. Were we wrong?"

Amy stopped momentarily before continuing on. "No, you're not. I don't know everything, but here's what I gathered. A tome cannot be stolen. There is absolutely no way to steal one. They have to be given by a living user or taken from a person who would willingly give it."

"And that's how you still have yours?"

"Yeah." She said flatly. "Roark tortured both Michelle and me, but he quickly realized that with the two of us together, we weren't going to crack. So, he separated us. Sai, something is really off about that guy. His mind seems fractured, like he's fighting to keep control of himself." She shuddered. "And Sai, I think you need to know; Michelle told me that she thinks Roark is her missing brother," She explained. "But, I digress. The last thing I remember was meeting Bram. His tome was a lot more than just offensive or defensive in nature. He used it to seep into the mind. He compelled me to give him my tome, but still, some part of me refused. After he realized his vampiric draw wasn't enough, he decided on the next best option." She shuttered again as she explained.

Without time to contemplate everything, Sai just focused on Bram. "So, he turned you?"

"Yeah, he told me if I wouldn't give in willingly, then there were other routes he could pursue. Next thing I knew, I was waking up in your arms." She seemed shaken by the retelling of this story.

"Amy." Sai placed one hand on her shoulder and stopped her. "I'm sorry it took me so long. I…"

She turned back to face him. "Stop; I'm the one who didn't listen to you about Oswald. I thought you were just jealous of him and… "

Sai interrupted her in return. "I was." He admitted. You both just seemed so enamored by him."

She gently placed her hand on his cheek and brushed a long black strand of hair away. "Well, that's not something you need to worry about anymore." Her eyes met his and seemed to linger there. "We have a lot to talk about. But now's not the time."

Sai nodded. "Of course."

She gave him a small smile and turned around once again. " Then let's go."With that, the two of them continued onward until they came to a fork in the road. "Which way now?" Amy contemplated aloud.

"Hmmm, wait." He turned to one side as something caught his attention. "That music, it's gotten louder. Can you tell which way it's coming from?" Sai turned from one side to another, trying to listen.

Amy cupped her hand around her ear before turning suddenly to the left passageway. "This way."

They continued on until the hall made a sharp ninety-degree turn. They wound around the hall, where several twists and turns made them lose their sense of direction. As they walked, the music grew louder and louder until they spotted an open door at the end of the hall. The doorway was brightly lit, and the music was clearly resonating from a large horned machine inside the room on the other side.

As they closed in on the room, they could see it was laid out like a huge amphitheater. Sai couldn't help but think that this room seemed extremely out of place this far below the surface. No sooner did they cross the threshold when a high stage came into view. Chained to the floor at the center of it lay their friend: Michelle.

"Michelle!" Amy shouted as she burst toward her. Sai caught her shoulder and stopped her in her tracks.

"Amy, wait. Look!" He pointed just to Michelle's left, where the masked man lay motionless.

"Roark," Amy murmured.

Origins

The two slowly approached and walked up the steps. As they got near, they noticed Michelle's chest rising and falling. She was still breathing. She was still alive.

"Keep an eye on him." Amy knelt down and checked Michelle's pulse. "She's alive, but what about him?"

"He doesn't seem to be breathing," Sai said as he stared at his motionless body.

Amy turned toward him. Slowly she reached for his wrist to check his pulse.

The music scratched to a halt as Roark grabbed her wrist and sat up. He looked directly at Sai. "Long time no see, little hero." His voice was just as elegant and menacing as it had been when they had first met back in Dione. He turned his attention to Amy. "And you brought the beautiful warrior along as well, I see. I thought Bram had turned you Red?"

"What did you do to Michelle?" Amy shouted as she tried to break free. Michelle seemed to just lie there motionless. They could see that her hands and feet were bound by rough chains attached to the floor, but she hadn't so much as made a sound since they entered. Amy summoned her sword and tried to bring it down with her free hand.

Roark released her, causing her to stumble backward. He stood slowly and straightened up. He wore a tight black armored tunic with black greaves to match.

"I haven't liberated her yet if that's what you're asking." As he stood, he pulled out the same red tome he had used in Dione. "In the middle of the journey of our life, I found myself within a dark woods where the straight way was lost. Awaken Inferno!" He opened the pages of the book and, from it, pulled his sword. Once again, the blade sparked to life, and a column of flame erupted from it.

Without hesitation, Amy summoned her shield and blocked it. Something, however, was different this time. As she absorbed the attack, Roark had moved somehow and was right on top of her with the blade raised, ready to strike. Sai moved without a thought and caught him in the chest with his pine sword. This attack forced him to backpedal for only a moment.

"A wooden sword?" The mocking nature of this comment was apparent in his tone. "What? Weren't worthy of a tome after all?" He straightened his back a bit as he spoke.

"Nope!" Sai ripped his tome from its holster and summoned Charlie to his side. "Awaken origins!" Charlie transformed into a fair-sized reptilian creature which stood on two legs adorned with razor-sharp claws. Beautiful feathers covered its long tail and short forearms. This was a transformation Sai had practiced in secret. It balanced the raw power and ferocity of the T-rex with the speed and dexterity of the titanis transformation.

"Deinonychus!" In a flash, the two went on the offensive. Charlie was a blur of claws and teeth while Sai attacked with his sword. "Amy, go get Michelle. We'll handle this!"

Without a word, Amy rushed past the whirling brawl and toward Michelle. Roark blocked every blow with expert precision. Out of the corner of his eye, he saw Amy move. Quickly, He stabbed his blade into the floor and ducked a blow from Sai's sword. With one swift kick up, he caught Sai in the gut and sent him reeling off the stage. This was followed up by a small explosion of flames which blew Charlie back and away from the fight.

Effortlessly he put himself right in Amy's path. "Going somewhere?"

Amy blocked the blazing blade with her shield and quickly lunged with her sword to counter. "I beat you once! I can do it again!" She shouted as he dodged her lunge. As he jumped back, she whirled around and slammed him in the chest with her shield. "First, you will come to the sirens who enchant all who come near them. Awaken Odysseia!" A beautiful melody sprang out from Amy's tome.

Roark could feel his senses beginning to fog. He staggered back off the edge of the stage only to run into Sai and Charlie charging in for another attack.

Origins

He tried to leap up and over them, but his body reacted slowly. Suddenly he was caught by the foot in Charlie's razor-sharp jaws. He came down hard with a thud as Charlie's claws and teeth repeatedly scraped against his armored clothing. If he had been wearing anything less protective, this would have been the end of it.

With this momentary reprieve, Amy jumped for Michelle. As Roark fought with Charlie and Sai, she made her way to her side.

"Michelle!" Amy cut through her bindings and cradled her in her arms. She shook her, and her eyes opened slowly. They seemed almost empty as a small hollow voice registered.

"Amy..."

Sai called Charlie off but had him place one foot on Roark's chest for insurance. "Don't move. This is over." He pointed his wooden sword down toward Roark's dominant wrist. He tapped the hilt, and the tip transformed into a downturned arch. Placing it over his wrist, it grew again and took root in the wooden beams below, pinning him solidly to the ground. Sai stepped over his beaten foe and headed toward the girls.

"You've seen the temporary fire, and the eternal fire; you have reached the place past which my powers cannot see. Stage two awakening, Purgatorio." Sai turned around just as a second snow-white katana appeared in Roark's other hand. He plunged it forward and sunk the shimmering blade into Charlie's chest. A deep roar erupted from his throat as he stumbled backward. The light within his eyes faded as he reverted back to a finch and collapsed to the floor.

All the blood drained from Sai's face as he took in what was happening. "Ch-Charlie..."

Roark snapped Sai's sword and stood. In each hand, he held a blade. Blood dripped down his arms from the open wounds he had suffered. His beaked mask had been torn, revealing the lower left side of his face. The drunkenness of the siren's song had melted away, and in its place stood something not quite human. He was a man no more. No, now he was a devil incarnate.

"You've been a thorn in my side for the last time. Now, I'll make you suffer!" With one swift motion, he charged at Sai, who was so in shock that he couldn't even try to defend himself. He didn't need to, however. Roark burst past him and was on top of the girls in an instant.

"No, stop!" Sai's scream echoed off the walls as Roark brought the deadly blowdown. Amy summoned her shield just in time. Shock registered on her face as the pale blade turned translucent for only an instant before materializing again on the other side of the shield. The blade ran Amy through and nicked Michelle. Just like with Charlie, the light in their eyes dissipated, and Amy collapsed onto Michelle. The white blade became incandescent for a moment before fading back to its original color. Roark turned back toward Sai with rage in his eyes.

"Let this lesson sink in. Let this teach you not to meddle in the affairs of a demon!"

Sai was visibly shaking. "Y-you monster..." He pulled his tome from its holster again.

An unprompted voice rang out, distorted and full of malice. It came not from Sai but from within the pages themselves. "A grain in the balance will determine which individual shall live and which shall die." Sai's tome glowed with an inky sort of darkness. Black viscous goo began to drip from the pages. It pooled around Sai's feet and began to climb up his legs. "I'll end you. I'll end you!" The darkness made its way down his arms, enveloping him completely.

"What is this?" Roark's sadistic smile could be seen beneath the tear in his mask.

Suddenly the tar-like fluid stopped and fell flat to the floor. As it did, something truly vicious took the place of the once carefree boy. His pant legs and sleeves had disintegrated up to his joints. His arms and legs were adorned by black double helix patterns formed from tiny lines of text that ran all the way up into his remaining clothes. His hair hung loose around his face, freed from its

Origins

tie. In his pupils, a single spinning blue double helix shone brightly. He cocked his head to the side and stared at Roark.

"A dark activation?" He looked Sai over as he stood savagely. "So, you truly were unworthy!"

Chapter 23: Kai

Sai blinked as he came to. Somehow he found himself lying on his back in what he could only describe as a dull grey void. This place had no walls, no ceiling, and no discernible features whatsoever. Slowly he sat up, and as he did, he noticed something odd. His body felt light, nearly weightless. He looked at his hands, but all seemed fine. He was in one piece, but how he had come to be in such a place and where the girls and Roark were, he had no idea.

"Uh oh. You're not supposed to be here yet." A soft sweet childlike voice broke the utter silence of this place.

Sai turned to face the voice and found a girl around four years old blinking her sky-blue eyes at him. She wore a yellow tee shirt and light blue denim overalls that stopped at her knees. On her feet, she wore purple shoes covered in stars which lit up when she moved. Her dirty blonde hair was held back in a messy ponytail, and under her arm, she held a beige stuffed animal, not unlike a rabbit.

"You didn't stop him yet. I can still sense him." She said in a confused tone.

"Who are you? Where am I?" Sai asked.

"Oh me? I'm Kai, and this is our meeting spot. I made it, so daddy didn't find out about you. Don't you remember?" She looked at him questioningly.

"No, do we know each other?"

"Of course we do. I made you." She giggled.

"Excuse me? You made me?" Sai gaped at her.

"Yeah, you're my S.A.I." She replied with an air of frustration.

"Yeah, that's my name. I'm Sai. But you made me?" He added.

"Not Sai, you silly." She laughed. "S.A.I. It's not a name. It's an acronym. It stands for Security Analytics and Infiltration. You're supposed to stop the bad guys."

"What are you saying? I don't understand?" Sai stammered.

"You're kind of like a program or an application." She explained. "My S.A.I."

"I'm not a program." Sai protested.

"You are. Why don't you know?" She seemed concerned. Suddenly she looked up and spoke loudly. "System?"

"Yes, Kairi?" A familiar melodic voice rang out from above.

"That's the voice from the mountain!" Sai shouted.

"Shhhh!" Kai shushed him. "System, please analyze the S.A.I. Program something's wrong."

"Right away." The voice replied. A blue ring appeared around Sai's body and seemed to scan every inch of him. "Error found. Code DC678," the voice announced. "Encoding error memory fragmentation detected."

"Oh no. Oh no. Oh no. Daddy is gonna be so disappointed with me." Kai paced around the lights on her shoes, keeping time with her steps. "He warned me this could happen, and I did it anyway."

"Hey, that code. It's the one from my note." Sai reached into his pocket, but for the life of him, he couldn't draw anything out from his inventory. "What? Where is everything?"

Kai stopped and looked at him. "You can't get anything from your inventory; your avatar body isn't here. Looks like only your consciousness made it. So where is your body now?"

Sai looked at her, shocked.

"System. Locate the S.A.I avatar."

A few beeps and boops rang out before the voice spoke again. " Avatar located. Location beneath Amalthea Forest. Would you like visual?"

"Let me see it," Kai commanded.

Suddenly the floor beneath them became transparent, and Sai could see his body standing off against Roark.

*****

Sai stepped forward slowly. As he did, the wooden beams running along the wall seemed to react to his very presence. They sprouted small branches with leaves and thorns. A beautiful floral aroma filled the air as white roses appeared at the ends of these branches. He knelt down and picked up the sword Roark had busted. In his hand, its damaged parts began to mend and regrow. The blade became a razor of rock-hard buloke wood, which Sai pointed toward Roark.

"You think that will be…."

Without warning, Sai's sword exploded into iron-wood splinters and flew at Roark with blinding speed and accuracy. He did all he could to avoid the attack, but several of the shards embedded themselves in his forearms, tore holes in his mask, and cut into his cheeks. Before he could recover, Sai was right in front of him, reaching for his chest. A hair's width separated them as Roark leaped backward and out of reach. Sai fell forward, and as his hand met the wood floor, a tree sprouted from the floorboards and crashed into the ceiling. It continued to grow until it began to creep through into the very soil above. The tree destroyed the stage, separated the two of them, and left Sai standing over the bodies of the girls. He stepped over their bodies and around the trunk of the giant tree.

"That's quite the power you've got there. But it won't be enough!" Roark lunged forward with his Purgatorio blade. With one swift move, Sai dodged it and reached for him again. Roark countered with the Inferno blade, which made contact with Sai's palm. The hit felt like hitting solid steel as it ricocheted back to reveal the iridescent rainbow sheen of nacre, mother of pearl, that coated Sai's palm. Sai placed his middle finger against his thumb and snapped only inches from Roark's chest. *Boom!* A bubble of air exploded against his chest plate, sending him flying backward at blinding speed. He slammed against the far wall with a huge seared hole in the chest of his robes. The plate mail beneath was warped and scorched.

"What the hell was that?" He groaned painfully as he got to his feet. He raised his Inferno blade to blast Sai, but he was gone. Suddenly, he appeared on all fours beside him, and in an instant, he rose and snapped his fingers, sending Roark flying yet again. Before he even landed, Sai blasted him again. He bounced from one blast to another in a flurry of explosions.

If I don't stop this, I'll... The thought barely had time to register before he was blasted into the floorboards. Sai landed and stood in a savage stance above him.

Roark groaned as Sai grabbed what remained of his collar, which began to react to his touch. The cotton fibers in the fabric seemed to morph and change beneath his fingers. With as quick a reaction as he could muster, Roark blasted himself backward with flames and tore the fabric from his tunic. Sai held what remained of the fabric, which morphed into a tangle of brambles in his hand. Roark brought himself to a low hover above the floor with jets of flame and caught his breath. Using his Inferno blade, he seared the part of his clothes Sai had touched. This seemed to stop the speed of the violent reaction.

"What have you become?" His armor hung exposed all over his body, and his mask hung loosely on his face. He rose higher into the air. *Just have to stay out of his reach.*

Sai cocked his head to the side before hunching over. A horrible ripping noise erupted from his tunic as dark black feathered wings sprouted from his shoulder blades. He rose into the air as bits of chainmail clinked against the floor as he ascended. The two floated on opposite sides of the room in a standoff.

*****

Sai and Kai watched from above as the battle intensified.

"What happened?" Kai asked. The concern in her voice was far more apparent this time.

"He killed my friends." Sai gripped the front of his tunic tightly.

"Your friends?" Kai looked at him, horrified. "You can't have friends; you're just a program. You're acting like you feel things toward them."

Origins

"I do. I care about them." Sai said defensively.

"You're not supposed to have emotions. This is bad." Kai added. "And why isn't your security code working? You touched him; it should be over."

"What do you mean it should be over?" Sai question.

"You had a program installed in your avatar. If you touch a corrupted individual, it should purify them, but now even your body is suffering a systematic corruption."

Sai's head was spinning with all this information.."I don't understand."

"System!" Kai shouted again. "Scan S.A.I. for the security protocol."

"Right away." The voice announced before performing the scan. "Security protocol fragmented, 50% of original code remains. Would you like me to scan for the other half,"

"Yes!" Kai commanded.

Another few beeps rang out. "Security protocol located 50% transferred to the secondary avatar. Avatar name: Michelle."

Kai looked over at Sai. "What did you do?"

"What did I do!? I hardly even know what's going on. Five minutes ago, I was down there thinking I was a human being. Now come to find out I'm just some bits of data?" He pointed toward the battle below.

"This is bad; we need time to figure this out." Kai was pacing again. "Daddy's gonna notice this for sure. But I have no choice." She stopped and shouted upward again. "System. Give me administrative control. Tome access, 'The Time Machine." Moments later, Zaman's tome appeared in Kai's hand. She placed her hand on it, and without a word, a shock wave erupted from it. The entire world below seemed to freeze in place.

"How did you…?" Sai was in awe.

"Stop. We don't have time to answer every question, but we need to talk. Tell me everything." Kai demanded in that squeaky little voice of hers.

210

Origins
Chapter 24: Reality

"... And then I woke up here," Sai explained as he tried to remember everything that had happened to him since the mountain.

"Okay, I think I understand. Guess it's time for me to explain then." Kai replied. "I know this will be a lot to take in, and I just want to say before I start, I'm sorry."

Sai nodded, ready to hear what she had to say.

"Okay, so I guess I need to start at the beginning. This world and everything in it exists in a virtual space. It's a little bit like a video game, but not really. It was created by a machine, and AI called The Dreamcatcher System, as well as myself." For the first time, the word dreamcatcher didn't seem muted and blurred to Sai.

"Dreamcatcher!" He shouted as his mind raced back to the circular object from Zaman's mantle.

Kai looked at him, confused.

"Sorry. Wait, you mean everyone down there is a program too?" Sai questioned. "And you made all of this?"

Kai shook her head slightly. "Not exactly, but I'll get to the people. Daddy created the machine and system; I was just the first person to integrate into it. But the world wasn't complete when I went in. My consciousness, my imagination, and my dreams were too much for the system to overcome, and because of that, my dreams formed this reality."

"Why would he put his four-year-old in something like this? And an unfinished version, no less." It made Sai angry just thinking about it.

"I don't know that he had a choice," Kai responded. "But that's not the point here. When I integrated into the system, it gave me access to all the knowledge banks and data this world provided."

"Oh, that explains how you're so well-spoken even at this age." The puzzle pieces seemed to be falling into place.

She sighed at him. "I know I look young, but that was just the age I was when I entered. I haven't aged in the

211

Origins

twelve years we've been here; no one has." She added. "But I digress. Being the first in also gave me administrative access to the whole system and the ship we're currently on."

"Ship?" Sai asked.

"Yes, a ship flying through space," Kai answered. "But, please slow down with your questions. I can't hold the world still forever."

"Sorry, please go ahead," Sai said.

"Well, I guess that brings us to the people you've met. Each person down there isn't a program. They're real, living, breathing human beings. Their bodies are in cryo-sleep aboard this ship. We're looking for a new home." She explained. "They're essentially dreaming. It's also why people who integrate into the system correctly do not dream; because they're already dreaming."

Sai just gave a quick nod trying not to interrupt again.

"Well, several days after we had taken off, I detected something moving inside the ship. Some life form was out of cryo-sleep and was freely roaming around. That life form turned out to be a seventeen-year-old boy. We didn't know it at take off, but we had a stowaway." She explained. "This wouldn't have been a problem, but this ship was not equipped to have unprotected inhabitants wandering the floor."

Sai grabbed his head as a small pain began to form behind his eye.

She looked at him hesitantly. "Over the next few days, I begged daddy to let me contact the robotic engineers aboard and have them bring the boy to a pod. But he knew the layout of the ship. He knew all one hundred fifty-three thousand cryo-pods were full, and we couldn't trade the life of one for another."

The pain grew more intense in Sai's mind as she spoke.

"I know it hurts, but bear with me. Slowly over the next few days, the boy grew weaker and weaker. He was being exposed to high levels of radiation as well as suffering from starvation without any food aboard. I knew even before he did that he would die."

Origins

Now the pain peaked, and Sai thought his head would split with the pressure.

"So, I did something awful. I had the engineer bots grab the boy without Daddy knowing. They took him to the storage hull and hooked him into an incomplete cryo-pod. It couldn't preserve his body, but it did have enough power to digitize his consciousness. I stored it away. That boy's consciousness is what makes up part of your data. His mind is why I think you're so much more human than I expected."

The pain ground to a halt with these words. Sai gasped and heaved, trying to catch his breath. "So, that boy was me?"

"Kind of. I just couldn't watch him die." She explained. "I took away that boy's choice in the matter, but something compelled me. I'm really sorry."

"So, what does that mean for me?" Sai asked bitterly.

"It means that you, unlike everyone else here, will never be able to leave The Dreamcatcher." She said solemnly.

Sai shook his head. His whole purpose felt like nothing more than a lie. Then something dawned on him. "So, the girls, Alister, and everyone else even. They could all return to their bodies one day?"

"Yeah, when we find a new home. Their consciousness data will be returned to their original bodies. The system is designed to keep the minds active while their physical bodies sleep. Although it's functioning incorrectly due to my influence, but there's nothing to be done about that at this point."

"So, what about those people Roark's killed?" Then another realization crashed over Sai. "Wait, that's what he means by being a liberator. He knows. He thinks by killing them in the dream; they will be forced to return to the real world."

Kai nodded hesitantly. "But, he's wrong. By killing them, he's purging the system of their consciousness data. There will be nothing to return to their bodies when we land, I'm afraid."

Origins

Sai's eyes widened. "So, that's why you froze time. You can't risk any more people dying."

Kai nodded. "Now you're getting it."

"But that still doesn't explain why I'm here." Sai contemplated again.

"I already told you. You're my S.A.I. Your programming has existed for as long as the system has." Kai went on. "When that man, Roark, appeared, I sensed it. He was a major threat to the system because, somehow, he was aware of what it really was. When he showed up, I created an avatar for you using the consciousness data of that boy we talked about earlier. You were simply supposed to go to Dione and stop him. One finger's touch would have been enough, but something happened. Somehow, you gave half the security code to that girl, Michelle."

Sai put his face in his hands and rubbed his eyes. "She was the first person I touched when I made it into the world. I must have given it to her then."

Kai smacked herself on the forehead. "Duh! That would explain why when she grabbed you during the trial; she overrode the firewall protocol. Which is set in the tomes to lock away avatars that have errors until they can be repaired and reintegrated."

This information explained what had happened to Zaman and even Sai. Somehow Zaman had been encoded at the wrong age; the tome corrected that by trapping and aging her until it matched the version of her from the real world. They both had errors in their consciousness data, and so the system tried to quarantine them and fix the issue. With Zaman, it worked. Her data was repaired, and her bad dreams subsided, but there was no way of fixing Sai. He didn't have a body to anchor to and was bound to have errors present because of it.

"So, that light that stopped the tome from consuming me, that was both halves of the security protocol interacting!" Sai exclaimed.

"Exactly, but her body isn't meant to hold that data, so it's causing her to be an anomaly in the system. The system isn't suppressing her dreams like it does everyone else's because it can't figure her out." Kai was

Origins

getting louder and louder with every light that seemed to flicker on. She danced around, giddy with excitement.

"So, that means if I go back, retrieve the security protocol from Michelle, and get ahold of Roark, I could end this!" Sai shouted.

Kai stopped moving, and the lights on her shoes blinked out. "Yeah, in theory, that could work. But, we have a problem." She pointed down at the still-frozen battle below. "Without your consciousness attached to the avatar, it's lost all control. It's damaging that body beyond repair."

"Well, send me back now. Maybe I can stop its rampage."

"I can't," Kai replied. "The body rejected you. Our only hope is the security protocol still present in your avatar. If it comes into contact with its other half, it should extinguish the tome's power."

"So what can we do?" Sai asked.

"We'll need to unfreeze time, and just pray that Michelle can make contact with you before too much more damage is done. That should drag you back to your body, and then you two together can stop Roark."

Chapter 25: Hero

  Roark grabbed the armor covering his chest and back. He unlatched the burnt, broken remains and let them fall to the floor below. Under his armor, he wore a thin black tunic which was now riddled with holes.
  "I don't know how you've come this far since Dione, but I'm ending this." The Inferno blade blazed intensely in his hand while the pale blade in the other seemed to flicker in and out of existence. He leaned forward and propelled himself toward Sai at blinding speed.
  In response, the still hovering Sai placed his legs against the nearby wall and bent his knees. They made three or four small clicks before the joint locked into place like the legs of a hopping insect. With a harsh pop, he released them and flew forward just as quickly as Roark.
  A jet of flame shot toward Sai from the Inferno blade, but he dodged it with a rolling spin to the side. Tucking his wings as he spun made him rotate even more violently. He came out of his spin as the two met at the tree in the middle of the room. Sai reached for Roark's chest just to have the second sword come ripping from the opposite side. Raising his arm, Sai dodged the blade and created another coating of nacre across his chest which deflected the strike. The rogue strike connected with the tree's trunk and slashed through it like butter. The entire tree top sheared clean through and began to slide off its base. Sai's hand barely skimmed the beak of the mask as the hilt of the other sword slammed into the top of his head and sent him plummeting to the ground.
  Sai landed just as the tree top came down on him. He raised his hands just in time and caught the heavy trunk before it could land on himself and the girls. Without a moment of hesitation, Roark landed in front of him and blasted him with a barrage of flames.
  "Oh? You are still in there somewhere! Still trying to protect them?!"

Origins

Sai only growled as the flames licked over his torso. Even the nacre coating couldn't protect him from the force of the blasts. Whatever trace of humanity was left in him was fading more and more with every transformation. He collapsed to his knees with the tree still above his head. Some part of him still wanted to save them and refused to allow him to drop the heavy load.

"This is over!" Roark blasted him again as Sai raised his black raven wings in a feeble bid to protect the girls from the all-consuming flames. Every bit of Sai's strength drained from his body as he sank lower to the floor. Every inch of his body was scorched and seared. His feathers fell in smoldering piles around him.

Roark raised the white blade over his head to deliver the final blow. "I'll show you the truth that I've known for so long! With this strike, I free you!" As the blade came down, something truly shocking happened.

A whale made of water exploded from below them and carried the tree top as well as Roark into the severely damaged ceiling. It left a gaping hole straight to the surface. Jumping in, a very human Oswald scooped up the girls in his arms. He carried them over and sat them near the entrance of the room.

Sai lay there heaving on the floor. Alister ran up and placed his hand on Sai for only a moment before ripping it away. "Ghaaa!" It felt like it was on fire. "What the... " He looked at his palm, which was scorched and covered in blisters. *Sai…* he thought.

Suddenly Sai sat up and looked at Alister before crouching, locking his legs into place once again, and blasting off. He flew toward the hole in the ceiling in search of Roark. He landed on top of the severed trunk and looked up.

"Alister!" Oswald's voice ranged out as he crouched next to Michelle. He made his way over to Oswald. He sat with his fingers on Michelle's neck. "They both have a pulse and are breathing, but they won't wake up. It's the same for the bird." He opened his other hand to reveal Charlie.

Origins

"At least they're still alive." Alister rubbed his injured arm.

"Was that Sai?"

"I think so, but I don't think he's in control. I only touched his arm for only a second, and this happened." He held out his hand where the injuries seemed to have expanded. Instead of just covering his palm, the blisters were now moving up his hand and wrist.

"Damn it." Without another word, he summoned a razor-sharp harpoon and removed the blade. He tightened a band of fabric around his forearm, and with one swift motion, he lobbed off the afflicted limb.

"Dear lord, why wouldn't you just use a potion to heal it?" Oswald looked at him in horror.

Alister used his teeth and pulled the cork from a potion in his other hand. He poured the liquid over the injured stump and drank down the rest. "Something tells me it wouldn't have worked. It was mutating. If I hadn't removed it, I'm almost certain it would have killed me."

"Killed you? With barely a touch?"

Alister nodded grimly. "I think It's killing him as well. His hands and legs looked to be in pretty bad shape. We need to stop him before it's too late."

Kneeling down, Sai placed his hand on the top of the severed trunk, and a new ironwood sword emerged. Sai grabbed the hilt and pulled it free just as Roark reappeared and descended back into the room. With another horrifying jump, Sai met with Roark about halfway up, and they clashed yet again.

Alister watched from below as he knelt near Amy. He wrapped up his arm as he spoke. "Any idea what's going on with them?" He gestured toward the girls and Charlie.

Oswald shook his head. "No, this is new to me. Roark has clearly done something to them, but I have no i... Wait!" Suddenly something dawned on him as he looked up at the battle overhead. "That sword! Roark was only able to use the flaming one before. Maybe that new one has something to do with it?"

"The white blade? It's new?"

"Yeah. I'm sure of it. He didn't have that before. He's done it. He anthologized his tome!"

"Then let's remove it from the equation, at least for now." Alister summoned another harpoon and cocked his arm back. "Just need to wait for an opening!" As Roark raised the pale blade above his head once again, Alister released all the tension he had built up at once. In the blink of an eye, the harpoon connected with the blade, snapping it at the hilt. As its blade shattered, a flash of light erupted from it. Three ethereal flares flew out of the hilt and seemed to home in on Amy, Michelle, and Charlie, respectively. As the lights sank into their chests, the three began to stir.

Furiously, Roark blasted Sai away with the Inferno blade before turning his attention to the party on the ground.

"What have you done!?" He raised the blade and prepared for another blast. Suddenly, an enormous eagle-like bird grabbed Roark's arm in its massive talons. It pecked away at him with its massive beak. In a panicked bid to break free, Roark fired the jets at his feet again. The two of them, locking in a heated struggle, blasted upward through the hole in the ceiling.

"Charlie?" Alister stumbled back as they disappeared into the darkness.

"Alister, focus up! We've got other issues!" He pointed past the remains of the tree, and standing in a settling cloud of dust and smoke was an even less human-looking Sai. He glared at them menacingly. Oswald got to his feet. Pulling out his tome, he began to speak before being stopped by Alister.

"Stop, don't forget we transferred your injuries to the other you and then administered Typhon to that body so you could go back to your human form. If you transform now, it's very likely you won't be conscious for the fight. Worst-case scenario, you don't survive the transformation whatsoever." Oswald stood down. "Stand back and protect the girls. I'll handle this." He summoned a harpoon and put his guard up.

Origins

Like a flash, Sai was charging toward them on all fours. His tattered wings were folded down and laid flat against his back as he bounded. As he approached, Alister readied himself for the first blow.

Suddenly, something darted from underneath Alister's guard and appeared in front of him. It was Michelle. With her arms spread wide, she caught the bloodthirsty monster in her embrace and clung to him tightly. Time seemed to stand still as Sai was stopped dead in his tracks.

"Pushing yourself too far to save someone else yet again, huh?" Sai seemed immobilized as she held him. "Sorry to put you through so much, but we're okay. You can rest now."

A wave of blinding light poured out from her and enveloped the two of them. As it faded, she dropped to her knees and held the broken and bloodied boy in her arms. The DNA-style markings had vanished, and his almost animalistic demeanor had melted away to reveal the carefree boy sleeping peacefully. She sat him down on the floor, where he lay motionless. As this occurred, Charlie, smoldering all the way down, plummeted from the hole in the ceiling and crashed across the room from them.

*****

"She did it!" Sai shouted as the body which existed with Kai began to glow with a faint golden light.

"She did. Time to go back, but Sai" She referred to him by his preferred name for the first time. "I can't guarantee you'll survive this. You can stay if you want. You've really done enough for this world. I may be able to find another way."

Sai shook his head. "No, even if it kills me, I want to protect the people I care about. Thank you for saving me all those years ago. Without you, I wouldn't have ever been able to experience this world. Or met all the people I have. Truly, thank you."

Kai nodded, and Sai's consciousness faded back to his avatar body.

*****

Origins

The group held their ground with their eyes fixed on the hole in the ceiling. They stood silently and waited for Roark to reappear.

"Where is he?" Amy questioned.

Alister shook his head. "There's no way Charlie was enough to finish him off."

"Wait, look!" Oswald pointed upward just as the dark figure tumbled downward and landed hard in the center of the decimated stage. It was Roark his clothing was torn to sheds. Pieces of all but decimated armor hung loosely all over his body. His mask was torn but seemed different in another way as well. The well-defined edge between his skin and the mask itself seemed blurred as if they had fused together.

He raised a shaky hand and pointed one finger at the group. Even beneath the mask's lens' the malice in his eyes was clearly visible. "Step aside and give me the boy."

"Not on your life!" Amy stepped in front of everyone else.

Flames built up around Roark's feet and crawled up his body. "Step aside!" He howled as he drew his flaming sword. The second snow-white blade appeared in the opposite hand, fully restored. The group readied themselves as Roark began to approach.

"If you want him, you're gonna have to go through us." Alister stepped forward, harpoon in hand.
Oswald looked at them both and nodded as he stepped up as well. "All of us!"

"Even you, Oswald? I thought you understood." Roark looked down before summoning his resolve. "Even after all I've told you, you still miss the forest for the trees! I'll kill you. I'll kill every last one of you!" His entire body erupted in hellfire.

"Michelle, your tome. It's gone, isn't it?" Alister glanced back at her.

She looked down mournfully as she sat with Sai.

"I thought so." He responded. "Amy, you and I will take the lead. Michelle, you, and Oswald will be our final line of defense. Stay near Sai. I don't want you getting into this unless you absolutely have to." With a nod, the group took their positions as Roark suddenly burst toward them.

The first blow landed on Amy's shield, and a huge burst of flame threatened to envelop her shield arm as she jumped backward. Without a moment's hesitation, Alister stepped into the fray. His harpoon was a blur as it sliced through the air, causing Roark to go on the defensive. The two exchanged blow after blow which created a dense misty fog that filled the air. The heat from the Inferno blade was only mitigated by the expert precision of Alister's water-based attacks.

CLANG! Suddenly the two were locked in a stalemate. Alister had managed to block both blades as they came down on him. Using all of his strength, he held off the attack.

"Why are you doing all of this?" Alister growled.

"I am a liberator! I simply wish to free every soul trapped in this world!" Roark pushed hard again the harpoon as he spoke.

"But, why use Oswald? And why are you after Michelle?" Alister's eyes darted over to Amy, who was silently making her way behind Roark.

"Deceiving Oswald was a necessary evil." He slammed the shaft of the harpoon yet again. This caused Alister to fall to one knee. His single good arm shook from the strain. " As for Michelle…"

With blinding speed, Amy came charging in from behind. With a giant leap upward, she grasped the hilt of her sword with both hands and came down with all her strength. Seconds from making contact, the pale blade disappeared from Roark's hand. He reached up suddenly and grabbed Amy by the throat. He held both attackers off with only one hand apiece. It was becoming abundantly clear that if Alister didn't do something fast, Amy would be done for.

"To the last I grapple with thee; from hell's heart I stab at the thee; for hate's sake, I spit my last breath at the! Awaken Moby Dick! " A thick coat of water began to form around and encompass Alister. It grew larger and larger as it crawled over the Inferno blade. The water took on the shape of a white whale as it continued to grow.

Roark tilted his head and gave a wicked half-revealed smile. Like a flash, the whale of water froze, encasing Alister and the Inferno blade in an instant.

"Ninth circle!" He released the blade and wrenched his hand free from the great statue of ice. Without another word, he turned toward Amy again and summoned the pale blade to his free hand. "Now for you."

"Roark!" Michelle's scream stopped him in his tracks. "Remember what you promised me? You said if I gave you my tome, you wouldn't hurt Amy!"
Looking toward Michelle, he spoke again. "Do you not think you forfeited that right when you ran to these interlopers."

She stood up and took a single step toward Roark. Oswald stepped forward and put his hand out in front of her. "Don't listen to him. He already broke that promise when he handed her over to Bram. She should be under his control now, but it looks like Sai must've stopped Bram before we arrived."

"You're right." Roark looked up at Amy, who was still thrashing in his grasp. He released her, and before she could even hit the floor, he brought the pale blade across her chest in a deadly slash. Instead of stealing her light, the blade left a deep gash across her abdomen. As she hit the floor, her shield rolled away from her coming to rest at Michelle's feet. Blood began to pour from the open wound. "I'm sorry, but she won't give up so easily when it comes to you. I can't abide her interference any longer." He grabbed her by her hair and, with his monstrous strength, flung her across the room.

"Amy!" Michelle cried. She tried to charge past Oswald, but he stopped her again.

"Wake him up. We're going to need his help." He gestured in Sai's direction.

Michelle stepped back. "What are you going to do?"

"Something I should have done when he first came to me." Oswald stepped up as he pulled a dagger from his inventory.

Origins

"You think you stand a chance against me in your current state?" Roark howled with laughter. "You think I can't tell that you can't wield your tome?"

"It was never 'my' tome to begin with. I'll show you the man I was before this, before you!" He charged forward and unleashed a flurry of strikes. Roark dodged furiously, but Oswald's speed was too much for the worn-down fighter. One after another, decisive blows began to connect all over Roark's arms.

Roark staggered back after deflecting a heavy strike with his blade. He stumbled backward and fell onto one knee. "You, you could've helped me free these people."

"Shut your mouth." Oswald stood over him, dagger at the ready. "You've used me to hurt so many people. This is the last time I hurt anyone!"

"Hurt these people? People are hurting everywhere in this world! Those oppressed by The Citadel! Those robbed of their memories, their family, their lives! You think that by stopping me, you're saving them?" Roark shook with anger.

Oswald raised his dagger. "Enough!"

"Arggg!" Roark ripped his blade upward and slashed up Oswald's chest. The light faded from his eyes, and he collapsed to the floor. As he fell, he used his last ounce of strength to grab Roark's mask. The fused portion of the mask tore away, leaving a large, bloodied gash across the left side of his face.

He stood and placed one hand over the wound. *That boy... His power must have caused a reaction in the mask.* He felt across his cheek, which was covered in blisters. *He got me when he touched the mask.*

Michelle could only watch as the battle-worn Roark grew closer. As she saw his face, her voice caught in her throat. His bright blue eyes shone beneath his jet-black hair. "Virgil." She muttered, her eyes full of tears.

"I told you never to call me that again!" He howled as he resummoned the Inferno blade. The whale of ice, which was rooted to the floor, shattered to dust. Alister was free but still immobilized by the sub-zero temperatures. Fire built up at Roark's feet, and he hovered there a foot off the floor. The flames sputtered as his body

Origins

betrayed him. "I'll burn you to ashes!" He screamed as he rocketed forward.

Michelle threw herself over Sai, but in his arms, she found something rough which felt like wood. In a split-second decision, she wrenched the object backward and planted its rubber foot into the floor. Without warning, she caught Roark in the chest with the handle of Sai's crutch and, using his momentum against him, changed his trajectory. He sailed upward and collided with the ceiling before bouncing off and slamming into the floor about twenty feet from them.

Michelle looked toward the crumpled mass in shock. She was only brought back to reality by the sound of Sai's voice.

"Michelle, you did it." He smiled up at her weakly. Looking down, she burst into tears. Sai's body was beaten and mangled, and even now, he knew the plan he had devised with Kai wasn't going to work.

"Sai. Thank the gods." She cried as she squeezed him. He groaned in pain, prompting her to release him. "I'm so sorry."

"Don't be." Sai wheezed. "But, this isn't over." As the words left his mouth, a terrible noise echoed out from across the room. "So, the little hero returns...." Roark rasped.

Michelle looked toward him, and her fear returned tenfold. His body blazed with flames that gave off heat that could even be felt at this distance.

"He keeps calling me that...." Sai laughed painfully. "He still doesn't get it."
Michelle looked down at him. "What are you talking about? Sai, you have to get up. You're the only one left who can stop him."

Sai smiled up at her genuinely. "I'm not the hero of this story, Michelle. You are."

"Me? No. I'm no hero. I have no tome. No power. I'm no one." Michelle sobbed.

"Stop," Sai commanded. "You have the power to end this. You have ever since we met in Dione." He held up a shaking hand, and an ethereal golden finch appeared

225

in his palm. "You are more than you will ever know, Michelle. You're the one who will protect everyone."

She stared at the finch for a moment before looking to Roark, who had found his way to his feet. He stood for only a moment before collapsing onto one knee. "If this must be the end for me, I will ensure the job is done." He spat. "Vexilla Regis prodeunt Inferni. Awake one final time, Inferno!" He wailed.

As he spoke, Michelle turned back toward Sai and scooped the small incandescent bird into her hands. Sai smiled up at her one last time as he faded into a shower of golden sparks. Grief-stricken and angry, Michelle pressed the bird to her chest, where it dissolved into her. Grabbing Amy's shield in one hand, she stood and faced Roark. Tears streamed down her face as she glared at him. He raised the Inferno blade to her as he finished the incantation. A massive build-up of ice and fire grew at the end, ready to explode as a devastating column of utter destruction.

Michelle clenched her free hand into a fist which began to glow with a blinding golden aura as she stepped forward. "You destroyed my village. You uprooted my life." Her voice rose as she picked up speed. "You took my brother from me!"

The blast released from Roark's blade and collided with the shield in Michelle's hand. Without Amy's influence over it, the shield didn't absorb the blow; instead, it refracted. The pillar of flame and ice splintered, sending multiple smaller beams shooting off to both sides of the room, causing one side to ignite as the other froze solid. Amy, Alister, and Oswald remained protected behind Michelle.

"And, now you've killed the one person I had left!" She screamed as she charged undeterred behind the shield. Without faltering, she slammed into the tip of the Inferno blade, shattering it into shards. With one more vault forward, she bashed the shield into Roark's chest, staggering him.

As his defense broke, Michelle emerged from behind the shield, and with fury in her eyes, she raised her power-infused fist and screamed. "Go back to hell!" She buried the blow in Roark's jaw, picking him up off the ground in the process.

    The Incandescent glow from her hand exploded into an all-encompassing sphere of light that blinded even her. The security protocol handed down from Sai activated, and like a flash, Roark was no more.

Chapter 26: Escape

  Oswald was the first to come to as Roark's defeat broke the incantation cast by the Purgatorio blade. He sat up and held his aching head. The room was destroyed. Half was still burning in unquenchable flames, while the other half was a waterfall of melting ice.
"What happened?" He said as he sat up and looked around. He could see Michelle standing alone with Amy's shield at her side.
  She turned toward him, and the look she gave him was nothing, if not empty. She had done the unthinkable she alone had stopped her brother. The man who destroyed Dione, who ultimately ended Sai's life, and who threatened the whole of existence. Without a word, she turned away from him again and collapsed to her knees. Oswald got to his feet and made his way over to Amy. She lay unconscious on the floor where Roark had tossed her. The pool of blood surrounding her made for a gruesome sight. Gently Oswald reached down and placed two fingers on her throat. Ever so faintly, he felt her pulse.
"She's alive." He announced, but Michelle didn't move. From his inventory, he drew a potion and poured it over the wound, which ran from her collarbone to her hip. The wound closed up almost immediately, and she took a deep breath. She hadn't quite regained consciousness, but he deemed her stable and so moved on to Alister.
  As he approached Alister, he found his old master in a puddle of frigid water. The ice that had surrounded him had melted as Roark fell, but the effects left behind stayed. Once again, Oswald placed his fingers to his throat and received a pulse. Alister's was far stronger than Amy's, and as the touch registered, he stirred.
  He groaned as he came to. Gripping Oswald's outstretched hand, he found his feet. "Is it done?" Oswald nodded. "I'm not sure how. But, it's over." He pointed to where Michelle sat like a stone.
  "Is everyone safe?" Alister asked while scanning the room.

Origins

"Everyone I've found, yes. But I've seen no signs of Sai." Oswald answered. "Amy should be coming around shortly. "She had an ultra potion in her inventory when I took her. I used it to heal her a few moments ago." As he said this, Amy began to stir.

"Sai." Alister clenched his fist, his head swimming with regret. It had happened again. Even with all of their training and preparation, he had lost another student. Together the two walked over to Amy, and Alister offered her his hand. As she reached up for it, she noticed Oswald standing next to him. "What on Earth is going on here?" She groaned in pain.

"fight's over. He's on our side now." Alister responded as he gestured to Oswald.

"Pfft." She scoffed as she got to her feet and rubbed her sore chest. The blade had cut deep, and even with the effects of the ultra potion, a clear scar was visible from the gap in her armor. "Your side, maybe. As for me, I'm not interested." Taking a moment to get her bearings, she stepped around both of them to see Michelle alone at the other end of the room. She took in the breadth of the scene before her with a sigh. "What the hell happened?"

Alister ignored her question. "Trust him or not, it looks like we'll need his help getting out of here." As Alister spoke, chunks of the burning ceiling collapsed to the left of Michelle, but she didn't budge.

"We need to leave now," Oswald added.

"I don't take orders from you." Amy snapped. "I need to check on Michelle and find Sai. You find a way out of here. We'll catch up."

Alister nodded. "Okay, but if you're not back with us in five minutes, I'll retrieve you myself. No one else is getting hurt on my watch."

"Got it." Amy brushed off the comment as she headed toward Michelle.

"Roark's personal room is just beyond the stage, well or where the stage used to be. He used to travel out from there. We should find something of use." Oswald added as he and Alister headed for a door off the side of the stage, leaving Michelle and Amy alone on the decimated battlefield.

229

Origins

As Amy approached, she couldn't hear a sound from her friend. "Michelle"? Amy said as she knelt down and placed a hand on her shoulder. "What happened?"

Michelle turned to her and shook her head. The shock and grief of all this had left her in a depressive void.

"Is he gone? Is it over?" Amy asked.

Michelle swallowed hard. "He is." She replied shakily.

"I'm so sorry. It must be unbearable."
Michelle shook her head in response. "No, Virgil has been gone a long time now. The creature I stopped was nothing more than a monster."

"And Sai?" Amy was almost afraid to hear the answer.

Michelle turned toward her again, and Amy's shield finally slipped from her arm. As it clattered to the floor, she fell into Amy's arms. "H-he's gone." She sobbed.

Amy wrapped her arms around her and held her tightly as the room burned around them. "What happened?" She asked gently.

"He gave me the last of his power. I watched him fade away. He's gone!" She cried again.

Amy patted her back as she held her. "Okay, all right. I understand." She said as she tried to console her.

"Michelle, I'm so sorry, but we can't stay here. We need to leave."

Michelle sobbed. "No, no, I can't." She sobbed. "Leave me here. I don't deserve..."

"Stop." Amy squeezed her as tightly as she could. "You did what you had to do. You used what Sai gave you and saved everyone. His sacrifice was not in vain." But still, Michelle refused to rise as more and more of the ceiling began to crumble and collapse. She pulled Michelle away from herself and looked her in the eyes.

Michelle stared back at her blankly. Her pupils were hollow and vague. She was clearly in shock. The breadth of all that had happened had dragged her so far beyond Amy's reach.

"Michelle, Please," Amy begged, but she still didn't budge.

Origins

"I have no one left," Michelle muttered. "Leave me here. I'm the reason all of this happened. I'm the reason Sai is gone. I'm the reason you got hur…."

Without warning, Amy planted a hard kiss on Michelle's soft lips, which shut her up in an instant. Her blank eyes widened before falling slowly as she gave into the surprisingly warm sensation bubbling up from her core.

Amy pulled away from her, and Michelle opened her eyes once again, and she blushed profusely. "I'm not no one, and don't you dare forget it!"

"You?" Michelle stammered.

"Yes, me!" Amy shouted. "And I will not lose anyone else today!" She demanded with tears in her eyes. And recalling the words Sai had used against her so many weeks ago by the pond in Iapetus, she spoke softly, "Now get up, or I can drag your unconscious body out behind me."

Michelle nodded breathlessly. "I… I, okay."

Amy grabbed her hand and pulled her up. Together they headed for the stage door. More and more of the room fell behind them, closing off the original exit. Only inches from the door, a sound caught Michelle's attention. "Wait." She said as she stopped in her tracks.

"Michelle, we have to go!" Amy commanded.

"No, Amy, do you hear that?" She said as she tugged Amy in the opposite direction.

"What are you…?" But Amy stopped mid-sentence as a faint sound registered from off somewhere to their left. "Is that chirping?"

"It sounds like…" Michelle replied as she knelt down next to a nearby rubble pile and began to dig.

"Charlie!" She shouted joyfully.

"Wait, it can't be," Amy replied. "You said."

"I know, and I did. I watched him fade, but I have no doubt this is Charlie!" She shouted as she turned with her hands cupped together. The small brownish finch chirped weakly in her palms as she held it up for Amy to see. His feathers were scorched, and he looked very weak.

"Wait, you don't think?" Amy added.

Origins

"Sai could still be alive!" Michelle shouted teary-eyed.

*****

On the other side of the door, the girls entered a long hallway that led to a single room where they could hear both Oswald and Alister riffling through Roark's abandoned belongings.

"All of this? How can this be real?" Alister said as Michelle and Amy entered the room.

"Yeah, this is the research Roark had compiled on what he referred to as 'The Dreamcatcher,'" Oswald replied. The word had become less and less blurred as they were exposed to it more.

"We need to go through all of this," Alister added.

"Ahem!" Amy cleared her throat. "That entire room is coming down. Do we have a plan?"

"There's no apparent exit from here," Oswald interjected. "Was the other room passible?"

Amy shook her head. "The entrance got blocked off before we came through."

"And the fire is spreading, but we found Charlie!" Michelle added.

"Good to hear," Alister replied. "But no Sai?"

Michelle just looked down at her feet. Amy placed a hand on her shoulder. "No, not here, at least."

"Can you use your tome to put out the flames?" Amy asked Alister.

He shook his head. "I don't have the stamina to conjure water strong enough for that. Are either of you aware if Sai used the warp crystal I gave him? It would get us back to The Citadel, which isn't ideal, but better than being buried alive down here."

"Sai used the crystal to send all the kidnap victims back before we came down here. But, ultimately, that doesn't matter. Sai isn't here, so no crystal, regardless." Amy replied.

"That's how we'd planned it, so I figured it would be a long shot." Alister continued. "That also means there's nothing stopping The Citadel from tracking where we are at this point using that crystal."

Origins

"I'm telling you, Roark used to travel to and from this room," Oswald said impatiently.

"Then make yourself useful and tell us how!" Amy snapped.

"I don't know," Oswald said flatly. "But, it wasn't with warp crystals. No, there's no way that would've been manageable for how frequently he did it."

Suddenly a loud crash echoed down the hall as the rest of the main room behind them collapsed. A wall of ash and soot piled into the room, making it impossible to see. Amy held tight to Michelle's hand, and they found the nearest wall.

"Is everyone okay?" Alister shouted.

"We're all right!" Amy replied.

"Me too," Oswald added.

"Feel around for anything on the bookshelves; pull everything down! It's possible one of those shelves is hiding a passageway!" Alister commanded.

Without any argument, they all began ripping books off of every self they could find. One after another, pages scattered across the floor, but nothing else happened. And then, as if by magic, something incredible occurred. As Oswald grabbed for the final book on his shelf, a loud clang echoed through the room, and a sudden gush of fresh salty air poured in, pushing back on the dense noxious cloud.

"This way!" Oswald shouted.
Amy and Michelle headed for his voice, trailed closely by Alister. As they stepped through the large opening, they could smell the odd salty scent of the ocean. Without a thought, they tumbled out onto an immaculate beach through the entrance of a small cave. As they did, the room behind them caved in, and the warp gate collapsed with an electronic crackle. They all coughed and heaved as they stumbled onto the beach. The sun peeked over the horizon and painted the white sand in brilliant pinks and reds.

"We're alive." Michelle gasped.

"And nowhere near where we were by the looks of it," Alister added. With a quick swipe through the air, he opened his inventory and selected a map. A huge map of the entire continent labeled 'Galaxias Kyklos' appeared. A faint red dot showing their location blinked on the far left of the window. It seemingly showed them standing in the middle of the ocean. On one of many small islands which dotted the vast sea. They were now nowhere near the main continent.

"We're on one of the uncolonized barrier islands," Oswald added. "Makes sense, really. Roark probably wanted somewhere unmonitored by The Citadel, just in case."

"Of course," Alister added. "Eighty-Four's power can't see all the way out here. Seems to be a rare bit of luck on our part."

"So we're safe?" Michelle questioned as Charlie squirmed in her cupped hands.

"I think we are." Amy slapped her on the back with a closed eye smile.

"We'll have a look around. Regain our strength and head for one of the inhabited islands soon. We're going to need a doctor." Alister said as he stood and slapped the sand off his pants. "But for now, I think we could all use a bit of rest."

Epilogue

The dome of the citadel gleamed against the brilliant blue sky as Umbra shoved Zaman and Alicia off of the platform at the center of the square. People buzzed back and forth from place to place as they went about their day.

"Some things never change, huh?" Zaman stopped for only a moment to take in the scene before being pushed once again.

"Keep walking." Umbra's attitude had been one of frustration since she watched Sai and Alister vanish before her eyes. In normal circumstances, she would have stayed behind to track the warp path that they had taken, but her new prisoner took priority in this case.

As they walked through the large courtyard, people paid them no mind. To the citizens of the citadel, they were but another set of criminals being escorted to Cylus to be judged. They made their way to the doors of the grand library, which seemed oddly lifeless for this time of day.

Entering through the large front doors, they found the library completely devoid of people. The books were all neatly arranged in their given sections. Even the staff that tended to these many tomes seemed to be nowhere in sight.

"There are so many of them," Alicia remarked as she looked upon the shelves adorned with hundreds, if not thousands, of volumes.

"These are copies of all of the tomes collected over the years. Every time one is fully awakened, a copy of it and all of its contents is created. It's then placed here in the grand library. Cylus says they're housed here out of transparency for the public. In all actuality…" Zaman was cut off by Umbra, shoving her forward once more.

"Enough talk." The group stopped at the base of the staircase leading up to the second story. "You seem to know a lot about this place. Cylus is waiting for you just up those stairs. Go up and around the horseshoe to the door at the far end. You will go next." She said to Alicia.

Origins

With her hands still bound in front of her, Zaman began to ascend the staircase. She strode confidently up each step with such grace that it barely made a sound. For someone who had only just pushed herself to the limit with her tome, she still seemed incapable of moving without grace.

She reached the final step and turned onto the U-shaped walkway that ran along the wall. As she turned to vanish out of sight, Alicia's stomach turned. *I hope you know what you're doing.*

With a silent smile, she strode confidently down the walkway until she reached the door at the end of the room. She stood silently before the large wooden door, which swung open unprompted.

"You realize what the punishment for aiding enemies of The Citadel is? You will be given the trial." Cylus sat in a large swiveling chair, staring out the bay window behind his desk. He didn't even give her the courtesy of turning to face her.

"To think I used to believe you were all seeing." She mocked. "And, yet, you don't even know who's standing in this very room."

Cylus turned in his chair and faced the recusant voice. "Oh? Do you believe you are of some importance to me?" His gaze was dull and empty; his once vibrant irises were now clouded milky versions of themselves.

Zaman's voice was somber and flat. " So, it's like that, is it?"

Cyrus's eyes widened as a memory washed over him like a great flood. " Wait, that voice. It can not be, Isabel? How is this possible?"

Zaman gave a slight laugh in response. "Haven't been called that in quite some time, and that's a good question, old man. I thought perhaps you could tell me." Without a word, her bindings fell to the floor, and she pulled out her concealed tome, freezing time at once. "Let's talk."

Tome Reference Guide

Origins (Specialty type): Sai's tome, which is based on Charles Darwin's *On the Origin of Species*. The tome grants its user the ability to modify living things on the biological level. While it is possible for Sai to affect any living object, the tome's power is most often used to transform his partner, a small finch named Charlie, into many different biological forms. Note: Full breadth of abilities unknown.

Odysseia (Specialty type): Amy's tome based on Homer's *The Odyssey*. When used, Odysseia can summon an impenetrable shield and an unstoppable sword. Note: Full breadth of abilities unknown.

Fables (Defensive type): Michelle's tome based on Aesop's *Aesop Fables for Children*. This tome has a variety of uses ranging from incapacitation of enemies to summoning creatures to aid the user.

Inferno (Offensive type): Roark's tome based on Dante Alighieri's *Inferno*. When used, this tome can summon a flaming katana capable of producing all-consuming hellfire from its hilt. Note: Full breadth of abilities unknown.

Moby Dick (Offensive type): Alister's tome based on Herman Melville's *Moby Dick*. This tome has many abilities all of which are offensive. These abilities range from summoning many harpoons to summoning an enormous white whale made of water. It can also conjure a nearly unending amount of salt water from its pages. Note: Full breadth of abilities unknown.

'84 (Specialty Type): Cylus' tome based on George Orwell's *1984*. This tome allows Cylus to monitor and observe anything and anyone he wishes. Although using this power can take its toll on the user. Note: Full breadth of abilities unknown.

Origins

Dorian Gray: (Specialty type): User data unknown. Based on Oscar Wilde's *The Picture of Dorian Gray*. Note: Full breadth of abilities unknown.

Observations (Offensive Type): Umbra's tome based on Benjamin Franklin's *Experiments and Observations on Electricity.* This tome gives its user control over powerful electrical attacks. It can also summon a kite and key combination which the wielder can use to fly. Note: Full breadth of abilities unknown.

Time Machine (Specialty type): User data unknown. Based on H.G. Wells *The Time Machine*. This tome allows for the creation and use of concentrated temporal fields. Note: Full breadth of abilities unknown.

Dracula (Specialty Type): User data unknown. Based on Bram Stoker's *Dracula*. This tome grants the user the abilities of a vampire. They can turn victims into thralls, drink blood, and possess superhuman strength amongst other things. Note: Fill breadth of abilities unknow.